D1460916

About the author

Susan Parry began writing when her twin daughters were small, and she was working full time as a university professor at Imperial College. She now devotes her time to consultancy work, including forensic studies and archaeological investigations that form the basis for her writing. Her husband, Mark, is retired so they are now able to spend more time together in the family home in Swaledale, where the views from her house provide inspiration. Together they have walked many of the areas described in the books, accompanied by their Airedale terrier. Her grown up daughters, Elspeth and Alice both have careers in crime – on the right side of the law. Visit her website at www.SusanParry.co.uk.

By Susan Parry

CRAVEN SCAR

SUSAN PARRY

Viridian Publishing

First published in the United Kingdom in 2010 by
Viridian Publishing

This edition published in the United Kingdom in 2016 by Viridian
Publishing

Viridian Publishing
PO Box 594
Dorking
Surrey
RH4 9HU

www.viridian-publishing.co.uk
e-mail: enquiries@viridian-publishing.co.uk

ISBN 978-0-9544891-8-2

For Kym

Chapter 1

'Are you with the bride or the groom?'

'Neither, I'm afraid,' Mills turned to the man sitting beside her. It was the first time he had spoken. 'I'm with the best man.'

He was playing nervously with his napkin and looking down at the table. 'Ah.'

The elderly woman sitting next to him, who was dressed entirely in purple, continued the monologue concerning her health. But every now and then, Mills was aware of him staring at her.

She ate in silence. The old gentleman to her right was very deaf and her earlier efforts to converse were abandoned at the soup stage.

'Do you work for the police as well then?' The shy man was looking at her expectantly.

'No, not exactly...'

'A pity, I thought you might. But your boyfriend, he must be a friend of the groom. He's in the police, then?'

He's probably younger than he looks, Mills thought. It was the baldness and the fact his suit was too big for him.

'Not exactly. He's a forensic archaeologist.' Mills took another gulp of the sweet wine and tried to relax. The waiters had cleared the main course and were serving dessert. Once again she was left to consume her crème caramel self-consciously while her fellow guests conversed animatedly on the opposite side of the large circular table. The lady in purple silk stood unsteadily, announcing to the table that she was off to powder her nose. Immediately the man turned to her.

'When I heard that the groom was in the police I thought he might be able to help me but I suppose it's not the right time, not here. But your friend could help.'

'What is it you want him for?'

'You don't know?' He drew his hand across his forehead. 'My wife disappeared.' He stopped, as if to judge the effect his statement had made.

'Disappeared?'

'Gone without trace.' Again he paused, waiting for her response.

'How awful.'

'You would think so – I thought so. But no-one cared. The police didn't want to know and even my family have told me to forget her. Move on, they say.'

Mills sipped her wine while she considered how to react. The man fumbled in his wallet, pulling out a photograph.

'This is Georgie on holiday in Tenerife. It was taken three years ago but she hasn't changed much.'

The girl was sitting at a restaurant table in the sunshine, with the sea behind her. The most striking thing about her was the thick wavy red hair which was blowing around her shoulders.

'She's very pretty.' Mills said politely.

'Yes, she is.' He took the photo back, staring at it before replacing it carefully in his wallet.

'She was a teacher, she taught the little ones. She didn't start out doing that. She went to art college but then, when we met, she said she wanted to teach. She said it would be good for the holidays; we could have loads of kids and she could carry on working.'

Mills looked round to see if anyone was watching them. The man's voice was wavering; it would be embarrassing if he made a scene.

'Then, one day, she disappeared. I was away with work and I didn't get home until late, about seven. She wasn't there. There wasn't a note. Nothing.'

Mills prayed that the toasts would begin. Over on the top table Phil was in animated conversation with one of the bridesmaids. She would have to say something to the man, the silence was unbearable.

'So what did the police do?'

'Nothing. They said she'd left of her own accord and I should accept the fact.'

'Surely not.' Mills felt indignant on his behalf. 'If she didn't leave a note or anything, surely they would be concerned.'

'There was a postcard.'

'A postcard?'

'It arrived a few days later. By that time I was going out of my mind. It said she was starting life with someone else... that I should look after myself!'

'Oh.' Mills looked across at the top table. Surely they would have the speeches now.

'Even my parents said it was best to forget her.'

'Well... they might be right.'

He thumped his fist on the table causing some of the guests to look at them. He leaned in closer to her, lowering his voice. 'She didn't take any clothes, none of her papers like her passport and birth certificate. All her photos, everything left just as it was. She'd need shoes and make up, wouldn't she?'

Not if she was starting a new life, thought Mills. Someone who'd been to art college might find this man a bit stifling, rather intense. Perhaps she *had* found a new love and just went for it.

'She has never contacted her mother or sister. Not a birthday or Christmas card. Nothing. She wouldn't do that, she couldn't. It would break her heart.'

'I'm sorry...'

He leaned back in his chair, breathing out slowly. 'No, *I'm* sorry. What must you think?' He reached into his jacket and pulled out his wallet again. This time he produced a business card.

'... I would like to have a word with your friend before I go. He might be able to give me some advice. I need to find the right person to approach. You see...'

He was interrupted by the sound of a glass being tapped to attract the attention of the guests. Someone introduced the father of the bride and suddenly the room was silent. Mills moved her chair round to get a better view, turning her back on her neighbour. She hardly heard what the bride's father and the groom said. While the other guests were laughing at the jokes, she was watching Phil's face as he waited for his turn. He'd had his hair cut especially for the occasion and it made him look more mature... in control. He may look calm but she knew he was very nervous and wished she was up there to prompt if necessary. But she needn't have worried. His carefully prepared speech went well and as he asked the guests to join him in raising their glasses to toast the happy couple, he gave her a cheerful wink.

As soon as the formalities were over the shy man pushed back his chair and stood up.

'It was very nice to meet you,' he said, offering his hand.

She rose to shake it but realised that he was passing her his business card.

'It's got my phone number on. I'd really appreciate it if you could give it to your friend.'

'But what shall I say you want him to do?' She was scanning the room full of people moving from table to table but there was no sign of Phil.

'I need to know what's happened to my wife.'

He was a sad figure, sweating with the heat of the room and apparently almost in tears. She stopped herself from backing away and stood fiddling with the card.

To her relief, there was a woman in a large straw hat approaching them. She smiled at Mills while she gently tapped the man on the shoulder.

'Tim, we've got to leave. Your father wants to go now, dear.'

His shoulders drooped. 'Just a bit longer.'

'He wants to get moving before the rush.' She turned to join the crowd shuffling slowly towards the door.

'Are you OK, Mills?' Phil was standing behind her.

She turned to him with a smile. 'Yes, I'm fine. Liked the speech, by the way.'

She could feel Tim waiting, ready to take up his story and she willed Phil to give her an excuse to leave. Her attention was diverted by a tall willowy girl in a vivid green dress who was making her way towards them.

'Hi Phil. Where have you been hiding yourself?'

Before he replied Mills felt someone brush her arm.

'I'd better go but please ask your friend to help. I can't go on like this much longer. Remember her name. It's Georgina, Georgina O'Neill.' He walked away awkwardly, joining his mother just as she was disappearing through the door.

Mills looked at the card he had given her. His name was Tim O'Neill. It seemed he was a "Claims Manager" for an insurance company. Mills suspected that the job sounded more important than it was.

The girl in green was laughing loudly, hanging on Phil's arm for support as she struggled to keep her glass of sparkling wine from spilling. She calmed down when Mills joined them.

'Hi, I'm Claudia. Phil and I go back a long way, don't we?' She looked to him for confirmation and he grinned awkwardly.

'Hello. I'm Mills. I've only known Phil for a year or so.'

He shot her a nervous look. 'Claudia and I were at Wetherby together,' he explained.

'Yes.' Claudia beamed. 'I'm into forensics too. Of course I've been set up on my own for some time now. I have my own company.'

'How interesting.' Mills tried to sound pleasant but she knew it wasn't fooling Phil.

'DNA mainly but we cover other services. You must come over and see the set up.' She was looking directly at Phil as she flicked her sleek blonde hair behind her shoulders. The drink nearly went flying again.

'Whoa!' Phil's hand went out to steady her arm.

'What am I like?' she giggled.

A booming voice interrupted them. 'Phil! We need you for more photographs. It's stopped raining now.'

Obviously relieved, Phil rushed off, leaving Mills alone with Claudia. They followed Phil, who joined the bride and groom as they left the hotel for some final shots by the River Wharfe, accompanied by the bridesmaids. They tagged along behind the group and watched the antics of the photographer until Claudia finally broke the silence.

'So what do *you* do?' She had an irritatingly posh accent.

'I'm an archaeologist.'

'Really? How interesting.' She was staring over the wall at the group below. 'Where do you work?'

'At the university mainly. I'm standing in for a colleague at the moment.'

The woman was not interested in what she was saying. She was too busy watching the group below them. 'Do you know the groom?' Mills guessed she would be likely to know Phil's friend if they went back a long way as she had implied.

'Yes, a crowd of us were at college together for a while. That's where Phil and I met originally. Before Wetherby.'

Mills guessed she meant the big laboratory which was run by the government's forensic science service. She tried half-heartedly to continue their conversation but it was hard work and Mills was relieved when Claudia, joined by more college friends, returned to the hotel, leaving Mills alone on the bridge.

'Thanks for coming up here.' Mills was hanging onto Phil's arm as they walked in step along the track that crossed the lower part of the quarry. There was no way they would be getting inside; the gates were padlocked and severe signs warned against the danger of entering such a hazardous environment.

'No problem. I needed some fresh air after last night.'

'Too much to drink?' She tugged his arm.

'Just a bit. Still, it was an excellent night. I think we gave them a good send off. Shame about the football, though. If we'd beaten the USA it would have been a perfect day.'

'Yes.' Mills could agree that they had had a good send off but not that the night had been excellent. She had hoped Claudia was not staying all evening but she was part of the group of Phil's college friends and could not be avoided. Mills didn't understand why the woman irritated her so much, apart from her being slim, blonde and the fact she could dance in stiletto heels. Mills remained in the floral dress she had worn for the ceremony but Claudia had changed into a tight fitting black number that showed off her tan and the fact that she obviously worked out.

'You did enjoy it, didn't you?' Phil looked concerned. 'I saw you were stuck on a table between the old guy and someone with the bald patch.'

'That was Tim.' She had been rehearsing how to approach this. 'He had a very interesting story.'

'Really?'

'His wife disappeared last year.'

'I'm not surprised. She probably hadn't bargained for his early baldness!'

'No. She really disappeared. I mean, there was a postcard...'

'What did it say? Sorry darling, I can't bear the baldness?' Phil was guffawing.

She had known he wouldn't take it seriously. She wasn't sure she could herself. But there was something about the man with his haggard expression and his obvious love for his wife that had touched her.

They climbed the steps that led through a gate onto open pasture. The view across the quarry revealed the extent of the workings. In some respects it was an eyesore and yet, like much of the industrial landscape in the Dales, it was an important part of the economic history of the area.

Mills had wanted to look at the Threshfield site ever since she had seen the report from the National Park. Plans for the quarry once it was no longer used identified some of the finds in the surrounding area, including evidence of lime kilns that were quite early. She hadn't known what to expect but it was larger than she had imagined and with no access to the site she could only peer from the gate at the massive walls that had been hewn away. She spent a long time taking photographs before finally sitting on a small bench and surveying the caravan site in the distance. Static homes, some quite palatial with extensions and conservatories were neatly arranged below them. In the background, across the river, was Grass Wood, according the map.

'So. Is the quarry *very* old?' Phil asked.

'Only a hundred years or so.'

'Oh.'

'But there was coal mining on Threshfield Moor from the seventeenth century which must have supplied the smelting mills in Grassington.'

'They used coal in the lime works?'

'Yes, but it seems it wasn't much good. So they brought it in from outside on the railway line. Apparently the station was down near the bridge before you get into Grassington.'

'And why are you so interested in these industrial processes, all of a sudden?'

'It's a thought I had when I saw the plans for the quarry on the web. There could be the opportunity to have part of it for a museum or heritage site or something to show how lime was worked in the past.

There are a number of early field kilns in the area and I want to spend some time researching them.'

'Have you got funding to do that?'

'No but I thought if I do a bit of work between my lecturing at the university, I might raise enough interest to get support from the quarry project or the National Park or ....'

Phil was yawning. 'Sorry, couldn't help it. It's not you. I'm just tired.'

'Four hours sleep doesn't help.'

'I didn't want to miss my breakfast. I don't get put up at "The Red Lion" every day.'

'Are you still serious about having lunch as well?'

'Absolutely.'

'We'd better get back there then or it will be too late... But I will definitely want to come back again soon.'

The afternoon went too quickly for Mills. They hardly had time to wander along the Wharfe after lunch before it was time to leave Burnsall and head back.

'Do you have to go back tonight?' asked Phil, as he unlocked his motorbike. 'Can't you stay at the cottage tonight?'

'Afraid not. Nina's working on and off this weekend and I promised I'd be back for Rosie.'

'Yes. Right. I'm sorry.'

The countryside flashed by as Phil manoeuvred the bike past motorists who also wanted to linger in the early summer evening. Mills found herself wondering whether the need to help Nina out, now she had the baby, was simply her excuse for not moving in with Phil. It was convenient living so close to the university although if she had her own car... They braked suddenly then swerved to avoid a sheep before rattling over a cattle grid. A car would mean she would be more independent even if she did move to Arkengarthdale to be with Phil. Then there was Earl. Would the dog accept her entry into his household?

As usual Phil didn't stay long. As soon as he'd gone, Mills asked Nige where Rosie was.

'She's asleep upstairs,' he replied without looking up from the newspaper.

'Has she been there long?'

'What time is it now?'

'Ten past six.'

'I think it was after her lunch.'

Mills ran upstairs to find the child lying happily in her cot playing with a furry toy.

'It's lucky that you're such an angel, Rosie. Although your Mum won't get much rest this evening if you've been asleep all afternoon.'

She changed her and put her dungarees back on.

'Let's see if we can tear your Dad away from the crossword.'

Mills dumped Rosie on Nige's lap and went to put the kettle on. By the time she had made the tea, Rosie had managed to get her father's attention by jumping up and down on his stomach.

Mills related the details of the wedding, despite Nige's obvious lack of interest. She avoided talking about the quarry because he usually became more agitated where work was concerned. Finally he broke his silence.

'Nina said she'd be home by six.'

'Only half-past. She won't be long.'

When Nina arrived home at seven, Mills followed her into the kitchen.

'He was worried,' said Mills.

'I told him I would be later tonight. Is Rosie OK?'

'She's fine. Had a good sleep this afternoon.'

Nina nodded knowingly. 'She gets plenty of sleep that's for sure. I wish he'd take her to the park occasionally.'

'How's work?' asked Mills.

'Oh you know, same old same old. Hazel gets all the good jobs. I do the rest. I thought it would change when I started back full time. Have you heard anything from the university about your extension?'

The subject was important to them all. The university had offered Mills a contract which covered Nige's lectures when he was in hospital and while he remained unwell.

'No.'

Soon there would be no more guaranteed sick pay for Nige so a decision would have to be made about his future at the university.

'I've heard nothing from the university either,' said Nina, opening the refrigerator and placing a cooked chicken on the work surface. 'I don't know what we would have done if I hadn't got back into work full-time.'

'I think you've done fantastically, Nina.'

'I wouldn't have done it without you. If I hadn't got out of that wheelchair and back on my feet before Rosie came along, I don't think I could have managed.'

'It just goes to show what you can do when you put your mind to it.' Mills was scrubbing at the potatoes.

'Exactly. So what do I have to do for Nige? He needs serious help, otherwise he'll vegetate here forever. The doctors say that physically he's as right as rain.'

'Presumably it's psychological help he needs, to overcome the trauma of the attack.'

'I told you he's been offered therapy sessions but refuses to go.' She stopped carving the chicken and turned to Mills. 'By the way, when I rang your department about Nige's pay they told me that Jake was back in the country. I hope you don't mind but I asked them to tell him to get in touch.'

'No problem. I meant to tell you myself.' Mills had heard rumours that he was returning from the States, possibly to replace Nige on a permanent basis. He had been a good friend to Nige long before she had met him. Her relationship with Jake was over a year ago; her feelings shouldn't prevent him visiting Nige.

There was a howl from the other room and they rushed in to find Rosie red in the face, struggling in her father's arms. Nige handed the child to Nina.

'She wanted to say hello when you came in,' he said accusingly.

'Hello darling. How's my Rosie Wosie?'

The baby's skin was lighter than Nina's but she had the same dark hair and eyes. She was as beautiful as her mother. Even Nige could not hide a smile at the sight of his wife and daughter happily reunited.

After supper they sat down with their diaries as usual to plan the week. Generally Nina could keep to normal office hours but occasionally police work dictated a change of plan. Unfortunately it was unlikely to be predictable so Mills expected to be quite flexible. Nige looked after Rosie most of the time but she had always been there to help when it became too much for him, particularly in the early days when she was a small baby.

'What about you, Nige? Doing anything this week?' Nina asked this routinely despite the fact that she always received the same negative response.

'I've got someone coming over on Tuesday,' he replied.

'Oh, who's that?' Nina looked pleased.

Nige glanced at Mills and then back to Nina. 'I'll tell you later.'

'If it's Jake there's no need to worry on my account,' said Mills, trying to sound indifferent.

'Is it?' asked Nina.

'Yes, as it happens. He starts back tomorrow. They've given him a temporary lecturer post until... until things are sorted out.' He had become quite animated and for a second Mills had a glimpse of the old carefree Nige again.

'Well, young lady,' said Nina, picking up her daughter, 'I think it's time for bed.'

Mills often helped Nina bathe Rosie. It was a time to relax and chat about their day. Nina would unload her anxieties about work and her family.

She was squeezing water from a sponge while her daughter beat the surface of the water with her tiny hands. 'I should talk to Jake; explain about what Nige has been through. Warn him that he's not his old self.'

'D'you want me to tell him? After all, it was someone from the department that attacked him.' Mills absently flicked bubbles at Rosie, who tried to catch them clumsily.

'Would you really do that?' Nina seemed surprised.

'Why not?' Mills shrugged. What was the problem? She was happy with Phil, and Jake probably had someone by now. 'We're going to have to get on if we're sharing lecture courses anyway.'

'But he treated you so badly, Millie. I know he was offered the job in the States but you didn't want to go and...'

'I would have done the same, Nina. And so would you, I bet.'

'Maybe.' She lifted Rosie onto the towel across her knees and began to dry her gently. 'So tell me about the wedding? Did the speech go well? What was the bride wearing?'

'I think it was white and long.'

'I could have told you that! You need to pay attention; your father's fiancée might need some help choosing her outfit.'

'Don't, please! I am sure that Fiona will have plenty of ideas. Probably something very short with a plunging neckline.'

'And what about you? Will you have to wear a frilly bridesmaid dress?'

'I told you, I'm a maid of honour and she wants me in pink or purple.' Mills flicked water at Nina. 'Anyway it's ages away yet and she'll have forgotten by then.'

'I think it's lovely, finding love so late in life.'

'Dad might be getting on but *she's* not even forty.'

'I still think it's romantic. I'll want to see lots of photos remember.'

Mills ran her fingers through the warm water and recalled the events of the weekend. She decided not to tell Nina about Claudia with her long blonde hair and posh voice in case she sounded jealous. But then there was Tim and the sad tale of his missing wife. The last of the soapy water disappeared down the plughole with a loud gurgle and Rosie laughed.

'Nina, can I ask you something? It's about a missing person called Georgina O'Neill.'

Chapter 2

It wasn't how Mills had planned it, meeting Jake after so long. Thankfully she'd had her hair done for the wedding but it needed washing again. And she was wearing the top with the frog on the front because it was the only thing left that didn't need ironing.

Of course *he* looked great with his California tan and sun-bleached hair.

'You look as if you've been on a year's holiday.'

'Don't you believe it.' His teeth gleamed white against his brown face.

They were standing awkwardly in the office she'd been using since she joined the department again. Mills noticed a briefcase on Nige's desk.

'Are you in *this* office?'

'Is that all right? They said to use Nige's desk until...'

'Until what?'

'Until they decide what to do.' He stood looking at the desk, uncomfortably. 'How is Nige?' He didn't look at her.

'You know what happened to him?'

'Yes. I heard he'd nearly died of exposure.'

'He was in hospital for weeks and it's affected his heart.'

'Is that why he's not back yet?'

'No. He's not himself. Doesn't like going out. Almost like agoraphobia. But he won't get help.'

'Can I see him?' He was looking at her now, smiling.

'Of course. Nina really wants you to go. She thinks he'll cheer up when he sees you again.'

'Great. Hey, d'you want a coffee? I was just going...'

'No, I'm fine.' Mills picked up a folder from her desk. She tried hard to keep her tone light. 'I'm off to the library.'

'I'll see Nige then.' Jake called as she left.

'Yes.' Mills walked quickly to the lift. It was stupid. She'd known she would be seeing him eventually. But the meeting was more emotional for her than she had anticipated. After all, she was happy with Phil and it was her decision not to go to the States with Jake when he asked her.

The library was quiet except for a few undergraduates who hadn't finished their exams. It was stuffy and all the empty tables were by the windows in the direct sun. There was no way she was going back to the office so she threw her folder down, opening it at the section on sow kilns. Her decision to research lime kilns was part of her plan to find work that would keep her in the Dales when she was no longer required at the university. Now Jake was back, he would be the most likely person to replace Nige if he didn't go back to work. Jake had worked on the technical side of archaeological investigation; he knew all about radar and other ways of seeing what was hidden beneath the soil. She'd struggled to teach Nige's courses and knew it was not sustainable.

Across the car park, on the grassy slope beyond, students who had finished their exams were lying in the sun or playing football. It seemed a long time since she and Jake had been sitting down there. They had both grown up in the last year or two. She wondered if there was a girlfriend back in the States. Perhaps she had also taken the difficult decision to get on with her career.

Mills opened her laptop to make notes on why lime was important in the seventeenth and eighteenth century. She knew it was good for the garden because she remembered her grandfather sprinkling it round his onions when she lived in Purley. Apparently farmers needed it on a large scale and so hundreds of kilns were built in fields across the Dales. They were the typical sort of kiln she could recognise, with a chimney and an arch at the base. What fascinated her was the fact that there were earlier kilns which were completely different. In the seventeenth century they used a round earth structure about two metres diameter with a narrow funnel and a central bowl. The limestone and fuel was stacked in alternate layers, covered in turf and left to burn slowly like charcoal. What really excited Mills was the report that said *there were no excavations of these sow kilns in the Dales*. What if she was able to locate such a kiln near Threshfield and ...

'Hi, I thought I'd find you here.' Jake took the chair opposite, staring at her over the top of the laptop. 'I've just spoken to Nige. You were right; he's definitely not himself. I said I'd go over tonight. He told me you were staying there. We could go together.'

'OK.' She knew she sounded evasive.

'About five?'

'Yes. OK.'

'I ought to take the baby something, shouldn't I? You couldn't help me find something suitable?'

'Rosie, she's called Rosie. Sorry, I'm a bit busy really.'

He looked disappointed. 'Right then, I'll see you in the office about five?' He smiled as he stood up. 'It's great to see you again, Millie.'

How strange to hear him call her Millie, a name that was so rarely used now. Even Nina and Nige called her Mills when they remembered.

She watched him make his way through the bookshelves then returned to her research. As she looked further back it was obvious that farming hadn't been the first reason for using lime. It was used in mortar which became increasingly important for building houses once they were bigger than a single storey cottage. There were definitely kilns in Arncliffe in the early seventeenth century and as she flicked through her notes she found there had been an important monastic house at Kilnsey. Perhaps lime had been used to build it. The afternoon passed quickly as she pieced together the information she needed to develop her proposal to the National Park and all too soon it was time to return to Nige's office.

'I've hired a car for a couple of weeks until I can find a flat round here,' Jake announced proudly.

They walked in silence to the far end of the car park, where a silver Mondeo was sitting in the hot sun.

'Don't worry, it's got air conditioning. It'll soon cool down.'

The seat belt buckle was almost too hot to touch. Mills sat uncomfortably with her bag and folders piled on her knees.

'You can put those in the back.'

'I'm fine.'

There was a queue of cars at the gate waiting to turn right into the traffic. Jake tapped the steering wheel for a while and then turned on the radio. It was the local news.

'It seems weird to think I was sitting on the highway heading for the beach just a few days ago.'

'I expect it's disappointing coming back here.'

'Yes... and no. It was great to spend time in the States but I hadn't seen Mum and Dad for ages.'

'I bet Toby was pleased to see you.'

'Yes, although they did come out last summer and we took him to Disneyland. But he's grown up so much. He'll be eight in a few months. Mum says he's already talking about going to university when he's old enough.'

'Following in big brother's footsteps?'

'Something like that.'

A small gap appeared in the stream of cars as a bus came along and he changed gear. The car shot out into the road and Mills grabbed the sides of her seat.

'Sorry, I'm used to an automatic,' he remarked with a laugh as they almost immediately screeched to a halt at traffic lights. They crawled along the high street until finally they were out on the other side of town.

'Don't be surprised if Nige is rather... taciturn, Jake.'

'Taciturn?'

'Well, quiet, unresponsive. I don't know... difficult to talk to. Just don't expect him to be his old self. Not like when you shared a flat together.'

'It's all right. I have spoken to him remember. He sounded pretty weird to me. As if he's lost the plot, you know? But he did seem interested in what I've been working on in the States. I've got some stuff on my laptop if he's interested.'

'Just don't expect much, that's all.'

They had to park at the end of the road and walk back to the tiny brick house in the row of identical properties. The red front door alone distinguished it from its neighbours. Last year the house had looked neat and tidy with hanging baskets and tubs of flowers but now the paintwork looked tired and rubbish had blown into the tiny bare front garden.

Inside, Nige was in his usual position in front of the television watching "Deal or No Deal". The room was hot and airless. Rosie was sitting in her playpen and reached her arms above her head as soon as they came in.

'Why don't you two go and sit in the yard?' Mills asked, picking the baby up. She checked she was dry and handed her to her father. 'Nige, take her outside. It'll be shady out there. I'll get some cold drinks.'

'Got any beer?' Nige took Rosie carefully, smoothing down her dress and stroking her hair.

'No,' lied Mills, 'I'll bring some squash out.'

She stood at the window and let the cold tap run while she watched Jake move the bench back into the shade. Nina liked to sit in the sunshine when she had the chance but Nige hadn't been out there all summer. He stood motionless with Rosie in his arms until Jake sat down. Mills made a jug of squash and prepared a feeding cup for Rosie. She left them sitting side by side staring into space, the tray perched between them and returned to the kitchen to observe.

'I've got some news, Mills.' There was a breeze through the house as the front door opened and closed, announcing Nina's arrival. 'Jake's coming over.'

Mills pointed through the window.

'Oh my goodness, he's already here. And I wanted to tell you about Georgina O'Neill.'

It took a moment for the name to register. 'Really? You've found out something? Look, they're fine out there.'

'They're just sitting looking into space.'

'They'll be fine. Come and sit down. I want to hear about this.'

Nina sank down onto the sofa and kicked her sandals off. 'Well, I had a look at the records, missing person and all that. Not that there was much really. Not much at all.' She pulled an envelope from her bag and turned it over. 'I made some notes.'

Mills stood waiting.

'She was formally reported missing on the sixteenth of June 2007 by her husband. She hadn't come home the day before and he had made informal enquiries but the official registration was on the next day. That was it, she hadn't come home.'

'So what happened then?'

'Nothing, except the usual checks at hospitals. There were some enquiries at the school on the Monday... her car was left there after the end of school on the Friday. But on the Tuesday the husband received a postcard from her and that was the end of it.'

'Did you see the postcard?'

'No, it wasn't retained; no point. It seems to have been a clear case of the wife leaving for greener fields. What's he like?'

'Ordinary. Bit shy.'

'Well, the photograph in the file is quite stunning. *She* looks like a model. I was really surprised to read she was a teacher; even an art teacher. Very tall and slim with this amazing red, no auburn...'

'Hair. Yes, he showed me a photo. She was quite striking.'

'Is, Mills. Is.'

'But she didn't take any clothes. Nothing.'

'It happens. The husband is clearly finding it difficult to accept she has left him. It's been three years. He's got to come to terms with it.'

'She hasn't contacted anyone. Not even her mother or sister.'

'Some people prefer to make a clean break. Perhaps she's gone abroad.'

'She didn't take her passport.'

'There are ways, Mills. Passports can be replaced if they are missing. If she's married her name will have changed.'

'She can't have married; it would be illegal... wouldn't it?'

'Don't get involved, Millie. I can't... Look, I'd better go and see Jake. And Rosie should have had her tea by now.'

Nina moved swiftly into the back yard to avoid any further discussion. It was her friend's inquisitiveness that had got her husband into trouble before. She stood and watched Nige, the concrete warm beneath her bare feet. He was sitting motionless while Jake held Rosie on his knee awkwardly. He looked relieved to see her and quickly handed the excited baby to her.

'She's beautiful, Nina! I said to Nige, how can he produce such a lovely baby? Obviously her looks take after your side of the family.'

'Hello, it's lovely to have you back.' She gave him a peck on the cheek. 'I hope Nige has been entertaining you?' She gave her husband an exasperated look as she joggled Rosie up and down in her arms. 'Come and give me a hand, will you Jake?' He jumped up and followed her into the house obediently.

'Mills, would you mind changing Rosie? I just want to have a quick word with Jake.'

Once they were alone she asked him how he found his friend.

'He seems rather distant. What's really wrong with him?'

'Nothing... physically.' It felt like a betrayal, talking like this behind his back. 'He's recovered, except for a weakening in his heart. But his mind hasn't caught up somehow. I think being attacked in that way, by someone he knew and left to die in the snow... it's destroyed his faith in the world somehow. I know it sounds silly.' She took a deep breath to stop herself from crying. Straightening up she took another breath before saying what she had been waiting to say. 'Jake, please help us. You were his best friend before this happened. He missed you when you went away. You must help him.'

There were footsteps above them. Mills must be waiting up there with Rosie, giving them space to talk.

'That's if you have the time,' she added.

He came across and put his arm round her shoulders. 'Of course I have time for Nige,' he said. 'But you'll have to help me. I don't know how to get through to him.'

'It will take time, Jake. You will need patience.'

'And how's Millie?' he asked. 'She seems different as well.'

'It's been a long time Jake. She's been working hard for her qualifications. She deserves to be doing something better than part-time lecturing to help us out.'

'It's difficult to find good jobs in archaeology now.'

'It's not that. She's been doing it for us. I wouldn't have been able to work if she hadn't been around. With Nige at home, even with the sick pay we couldn't have managed. She has given up everything for us. I'm sure she would be living with Phil by now if she could.'

'Phil?'

'Phil... her boyfriend. Didn't she say?'

'No. She hasn't really said very much so far. I expect she would have mentioned it. We share Nige's office now.'

Nina looked out into the yard. Nige appeared to be asleep on the bench. Soon the university would decide whether he would be returning to his post. It was complicated. He was still within his probationary period as a permanent lecturer. They were careful, very careful. It would be very difficult to remove someone with tenure. Having Jake in the wings would make their decision easier. His friend could cause the end of her husband's career. Did either of them know that? She hoped not.

'Would you like to stay for supper?' she asked. Something to say. A change of topic. She knew the invitation did not sound sincere.

'It's OK. Mum and Dad are expecting me back. I'm staying there until I get something sorted out.'

'If you're sure?'

'I'll just say goodbye to Nige.'

Upstairs Mills waited until she heard Jake leaving.

'Tell Millie I'll see her tomorrow,' Jake called as Nina saw him out.

Mills, my name is Mills. I'm not a teenager anymore, she thought.

'Millie!' Nina was standing at the bottom of the stairs. 'Ah, you're there.'

Phil was cooking fish when the phone rang. He glanced at the clock and the lurcher looked up at him.

'It's all right, Earl. It'll be Mills.' He grabbed the receiver. 'Hi there. How are you?'

'Phil?' The voice was wrong. 'It's Claudia. Have I called at a bad time?'

'Er, I'm just cooking my tea.' He knew he sounded detached.

'Sorry. It won't take long. I just wanted to catch up work-wise. After we met up again at the wedding I was thinking we should talk. Obviously you have a good job but the changes going on must be affecting you as much as everyone else.'

It was true there had been talk about the unit moving but any rumours about closing them down had been quashed some time ago.

'I don't think there's any danger of me losing my job, Claudia.'

'No? I'm surprised.' There was a pause. 'Anyway, it's good to know everything is going well for you. Don't forget, if you need any forensic testing send it to Bishop Laboratories. I always need extra work. It's a war out there now everything is privatised.'

'Yes I will.' Not that he ever needed any testing done. It wasn't his job to send samples off for forensics. That was someone else's responsibility.

'I'll let you get back to your tea, then.'

'Claudia, how did you get my number?'

'Just a bit of detective work. A friend of a friend, you might say. Must dash. Speak to you soon.'

The call was unsettling. He poured himself a beer and sat down. He'd been surprised and, yes, shocked, when Claudia had appeared at the wedding. But she didn't seem concerned, she was a cool one. When she'd asked him for his phone number he'd given her his business card. She was certainly pushy. He sat for a while then picked the receiver up again and rang Mills. It went to voicemail so he left a brief message and went back to his half-cooked haddock.

He ate his meal in front of the television while Earl gazed longingly at the plate. He was scraping a good portion of his fish into the dog's dish when his phone rang again and this time he answered more circumspectly.

'What's the matter, Phil? Are you busy?'

'No, it's fine. I thought you might be someone else.'

'Who?'

'Just someone from work. How's things, Mills? What've you been up to?'

'Nothing really. Just work.'

Phil waited for her to continue but there was silence. 'What are you working on?'

'Just the lime kilns. I told you about it on Sunday.'

Phil detected irritation in her voice. 'Yes, of course. So how is it going?'

'Oh, you know...'

It was obviously not a good time to talk. 'Mills, you sound a bit... are you all right? Would you like me to come over later in the week? We could go out, do something.'

'No, it's fine. I've got work to do. I'll be over at the weekend as usual.'

'Don't make it sound such a chore.'

'It isn't, honestly. I just... it's hot.' There was silence and then she came back with a cheerier tone. 'I expect it's cool and fresh in Arkengarthdale.'

'Don't you believe it. The cottage is full of flies and it's so hot I've had to let the Rayburn out so it's salads for the next few days.'

'That's cool. We'll eat healthily for a change. No more pizzas and curries.'

Once Mills was more forthcoming they chatted for over an hour before Phil admitted he had a report that had to be finished by the morning. He didn't tell her but he had a new and challenging project over near Whitby which would test all his skills as a forensic archaeologist. The details were sketchy and so far he only knew that a body had been found buried on the shore close to Runswick Bay. He was going over tomorrow to see it *in situ* before it was removed for post mortem.

John had already been warned that Earl would need bread and board for a few days. Fortunately his neighbour appeared pleased to have the dog now he was living on his own; he seemed to enjoy the company. When Mills moves in, Phil thought, they would be able to juggle looking after Earl themselves. It was a prospect that he anticipated with pleasure while at the same time it gave him a strange feeling in his guts. He was thirty-two and he had been living on his own for eight years. It was time for a commitment again... now that he had recovered from his past devastating relationship. It had taken that long for the pain to fade and he cursed Claudia's arrival for reminding him of it. He opened another beer and started on the report.

Next morning was a perfect day for visiting the coast and Phil enjoyed the trip despite having the sun in his eyes most of the way. He threw off his leather jacket and knelt down on the sand in his T-shirt and leather trousers as a gentle breeze blew off the sea. The local force had constructed a roomy white tent over the spot and taped off the beach; not that it was a busy part of the coastline. It took a bit of effort to get to the sand from the road and it was a puzzle how the body had been brought down for burial.

'D'you see how they'd put a rug on top of it?' the young constable offered.

'Yes. Did *you* uncover it?'

'No, sir. It were found by a fisherman who digs here for bait. He were hereabouts last night and saw a bit of the fabric. When he dug around it he saw the body.'

'Must've given him a fright.'

'Oh, aye. He were still shaking when we arrived. He thought he'd found treasure at first, see. He soon changed his mind when he saw the body.'

'Are we above the tide here?'

'Yes, sir.'

'That would explain why it's not deteriorated. It's been preserved in the dry sand. The rug probably helped as well.'

He stared at the exposed feet and part of one leg. It would take some time to uncover the entire body. It was fortunate that the shallow grave was shaded by the tent arrangement but even so it would be hot work.

'Are you allowed to open this up a bit? No-one will see if we open the flap on the sea side.'

The constable lifted the sheeting up and a cool breeze filled the space as Phil started work on the legs. He had already determined that he would reveal the face last. However hardened he had become, he didn't want to spend too long in the dead woman's gaze. For he could tell from the bones of the feet and toes, this was not a man's body.

Chapter 3

'It really is time we asked Jake to stay for supper,' Nina announced as she was leaving for work.

'When?' asked Mills, preparing to make up a plausible excuse.

'When we are all here.' Nina's response was pointed, although she was smiling sympathetically. 'It won't be that bad. Can you ask him when would be best for him? You know when you'll be here.'

'I'll be going to Arkengarthdale on Friday,' Mills warned.

'So make it Thursday.'

It was bad enough that Jake insisted on giving Mills a lift into work every day. 'It's no trouble,' he had said. 'I'm virtually passing the door on the way. It means I can pop in and see Nige on my way home to Bainbridge in the evenings.' She couldn't refuse him the chance to build a bond with his friend but, as she had complained to Nina, it meant she had to exchange pleasantries when most of the time she was managing to avoid him, despite the fact they were sharing an office. 'And why is that?' her friend had asked. But Mills couldn't find an answer.

'I've been thinking about Georgina O'Neill,' Mills began.

'Georgina who? Oh, the missing wife.'

'Yes. I was thinking I might get in touch with Tim O'Neill and ask which school she worked at.'

'And why would you want to do that?'

'Because someone must know if she had a secret lover. Her friends might know where she went.'

'Millie...'

'But if we could show that she was happy and nothing had happened to her...'

'It's not a good idea. Leave well alone, Millie. That's official advice. Now hurry up. Jake's waiting outside.'

'Nina wants you to come to supper on Thursday.' She got it over with as soon as she was in the car.

'That's cool.' There was a pause. 'There's a suggestion I want to make to Nige and I need to discuss it with Nina first.'

'What is it?'

'Ah, you'll have to wait and see.' He smiled, looking very pleased with himself.

Mills resolved to say nothing and he switched on the radio. They were sitting in stationary traffic.

'Nina told me you're with someone now?' His face was expressionless as he studied the car in front.

'Yes.' Mills was surprised by the question.

'What does he do?'

'He's a forensic archaeologist.'

'Really?' He sounded genuinely impressed.

'He works for the police,' she added unnecessarily.

'Is he from round here?'

'No, he lives in Arkengarthdale.' Mills couldn't hide her irritation.

'Cool.'

Neither spoke again until they reached the university car park.

'Want a coffee before the day starts?' Jake offered.

'No thanks, I'm going to the library.' She pulled her rucksack from the back seat and left without looking back. She didn't know why she was being so off-hand.

The library was always empty first thing in the morning while the students were making their way in by bus and train or were still in their halls of residence. Mills liked it best when the tables were empty and it was quiet except for the hum of the photocopier. She had decided to prepare a report that would contain all the necessary background information about the history of lime kilns in the Dales. It would provide support for her proposal to investigate kilns in Wharfedale with the purpose of using the findings for a special exhibition or museum on the site of the reclaimed quarry. She soon discovered that a lot of work had already been done by the Yorkshire Dales Landscape Research Trust and she would certainly need to contact them, as well as the National Park, about working with the university.

She was re-writing her introduction to include this new angle when an e-mail appeared from Phil. *Still in Whitby. I could drop in on the way back on Thursday – about six. We could go out for chips!*

She clicked on "return". What was she going to say? *Sorry, busy...* she erased it and started again. *Nina has friends round...* No, that wouldn't work. *I have to help Nina with meal for friends. Can't do Thursday. Will be over as usual on Friday.* She pressed "send" and immediately regretted it. She closed her e-mail and tried to concentrate on the report. The library was filling up with the rustling of paper, murmurings and outright chattering. Mills found it increasingly difficult to concentrate until finally she pushed her papers into her rucksack and left, shoving her chair under the table with a loud scraping sound that was particularly satisfying.

Outside it was warm and sunny, the oppressive humidity of the past few days having been replaced by a wonderfully refreshing breeze. The office was empty so she used the opportunity to call the number on Tim O'Neill's business card. In the corridor she could hear Jake's voice, chatting to one of Nige's students.

'Yes, he's getting better,' she heard him say.

'So he'll be coming back soon?' the student was asking.

'Not yet. It might be some time. But if you want to have a chat about your work, come and see me. I'm sure I can help.'

'Oh thanks, that would be great. It's been difficult, you know...'

'Of course, any time.'

Mills quickly replaced the receiver and pretended to be writing as Jake came into the office. He seemed surprised to see her but said nothing while he tidied his desk. He sat back in his chair and looked across at Mills.

'I don't suppose you fancy lunch?'

'Bit busy,' she said without looking up.

'Yes, I'm finding it quite hectic after the US.'

'Particularly when you have to look after Nige's students!' She was surprised by the intensity of her remark.

'They're missing him and getting a bit lost. I don't mind giving them a hand, until I have my own to look after.'

'And then what?'

'I hope he'll be able to look after them himself.'

'Really? Do you really?' She had to get out. She grabbed her things and left.

Behind her she could hear him calling, 'Are you all right Millie? Millie!'

She turned out of the main building and walked quickly along to the park. It was lunch time and students were sitting in groups on the lawn. There was an empty bench under a large ornamental tree and she sat with her eyes closed waiting for the rage to subside.

How she longed to be alone. Somewhere isolated and remote. If she had her own car she would go now to lose herself for a while in the countryside. She took Tim O'Neill's card from her pocket. Maybe that's what Georgina had wanted; to get away from all the pressure of family and colleagues. This time she let the phone ring until a voice answered.

'Tim? Tim O'Neill?'

'Speaking.'

'It's Mills Sanderson here. We spoke at the wedding... about Georgina?'

'Yes?' His response was cautious.

'I thought... I mean... I wondered if it would be helpful to speak to her colleagues at the school.'

'Right.' His voice was non-committal and Mills guessed he was not alone in the office.

'Could you give me the address?'

'Er... Yes, certainly. Can I send you the information?'

'Yes, of course. I understand. Can you text it to me.'

'Yes, that would be most satisfactory.'

While she waited, Mills considered how she might make a trip to visit the school without telling Nina or Phil, who would obviously disapprove. A few minutes later, when the message came through, Mills was surprised to see that St Bride's Middle School had a Leeds address and post code. She could go tomorrow afternoon and be back before anyone noticed she was gone.

Phil was awake early as usual. School was not over but there were plenty of couples with young children and babies and the walls were thin. By seven he was alone in the restaurant, pouring his juice and ripping open the cereal packet, as he waited for the full English that was adequate, if slightly disappointing.

It was a short drive from Whitby to the bay where at last he would supervise the removal of the body before returning home. A uniformed constable was sitting in one of the cars parked above the crime scene, drinking from a thermos cup.

'Just finishing?' asked Phil politely.

'Aye. The boss is down below. He's waiting for a photographer before they remove the body.'

The dry sand shifted under his feet as Phil made his way to the tent. He ducked under the cordon before introducing himself to the Chief Inspector.

'So what have you found?' The burly man was sweating in a dark suit.

'A Caucasian woman between thirty and fifty who suffered with a long term back problem. I guess she's had children...'

'I meant how did she die?'

'Nothing obvious. Nothing affecting the bones, no fractures or penetrations. There's not much skin left, unfortunately.'

'How long has she been there, then?'

'Difficult to tell. I would guess maybe twenty years. The dry sand can preserve bodies.'

'So it could be longer?'

'I'm not sure. The rug might help. My colleague will look at the pattern and fibre and make some judgement. It would help if we knew of anyone fitting the description...'

'You must be kidding. Twenty years ago?'

'DNA might help.'

'No records back then.'

Phil talked the DCI through his report, explaining how he came to his conclusions. A constable appeared with lidded paper cups bearing the logo of a coffee shop in town.

'Thanks, Tyrell. We ordered the cappuccino for you,' he said handing it over to Phil.

It was three hours later before they came to remove the body. The rug was bagged separately and Phil had a quick look at the bottom of the hole where the body had been lying. There were no blood stains, just a faint darkening of the sand that was to be expected as the tissue aged. The SOCO team would take over and check the scene thoroughly again, possibly digging a wider area in case anything had been missed. Finally the hole would be filled and left without a mark to distinguish it from any other part of the beach. It would be the focus of curiosity for visitors now that the local papers had picked up the story but only for a week or two. Soon the body on the beach would be history. Another missing person who wasn't found until everyone had forgotten her.

The journey to Leeds was straightforward but once Mills reached the city she wasted time finding a street map to locate the school. Eventually she was on the bus, hoping the driver remembered to tell her when she reached her destination. Perhaps she would have guessed anyway from the line of cars and gaggle of mothers at the gate. She had to fight her way into the playground and through the front door against a stream of small children in brightly coloured dresses of green, purple and yellow. There was not a boy to be seen.

'Can I help you?' The woman looked cool and elegant. Mills pulled away the hair that stuck to her forehead and wiped the sweat from her upper lip.

'Are you the headmistress?' she asked awkwardly.

'No, she's at a meeting today. I'm the school administrator. Can I help you?'

'I'm here about Georgina O'Neill. I wanted to speak to her colleagues...'

'Georgina O'Neill?' She said the name slowly as if trying to recollect its significance. 'Is she a pupil at this school? I don't recognise the name.'

'Sorry, no, she was a teacher. About three years ago?'

'Oh. I've been here eighteen months so I wasn't here then I'm afraid.'

'But there must be teachers who remember her?'

'Possibly. Would you sign the visitor's book and wait here. I'll go and ask in the staff room. Some of them have gone home already and others have after school activities but a couple of them stay to mark homework before they go.'

She disappeared along the corridor and returned with a youngish woman dressed for tennis.

'Hello. I'm Penny Meadows. I understand you're enquiring after Georgie. I'm afraid she doesn't teach here any longer.'

The administrator went inside her office, shutting the door behind her.

'I know,' said Mills, 'but I wanted to speak to someone who knew her.'

'Will I do?'

'Of course. Can you tell me what she was like?'

'There's nothing much to say really. She was very pretty of course and pleasant to everyone. She was lovely with the kids. They adored her. They really missed her when she... Look, are you a reporter?'

'No. I'm from the university. I'm studying people who disappear.' It was what she had planned to say if anyone asked.

The woman looked out at the playground which was quiet now the children had gone. 'It was an odd business, very odd.'

'They think she went off with someone.'

'Yes, I believe so.' She was still looking through the window.

'Do you think she was having an affair?'

She turned to face Mills. 'No. I don't. Not that she necessarily would have told me, we weren't that close... but you think you would guess, wouldn't you?'

'Did she have any special interests where she might have met someone? Hobbies?'

'No. She came to school and went home again, that's all I knew. Of course I met her husband when we had any social functions. He seemed nice. No, there was certainly nothing to suggest she was having an affair, as you put it.'

'Is there anyone else who might know?'

She thought for a moment. 'No. Funnily enough I'm really the only one left who was friendly with her. One or two oldies still about but they tend to keep themselves to themselves.'

'What about the headmistress?'

'She only came to the school last year. Made a big difference it has.'

Mills thanked her and headed for the playground. It was deserted now and the road was clear of cars. She walked slowly towards the gate regretting her impulse to visit the school at all. Now Tim would be expecting a call which would only disappoint him.

'Hello! What do you want?'

She turned to see a stocky man in jeans and a white vest marching towards her brandishing a brush.

'The school's closed. What are you looking for?'

'I'm sorry. I was just visiting the headmistress.'

'She ain't 'ere.'

'Yes, I spoke to your administrator.'

'Oh, right. That's fair enough.' He stood looking at her, smiling.

'I was speaking to Penny?' She hoped she'd remembered her name correctly.

'Miss Meadows? She's all right.' His accent was from the South. It was unusual to meet a cockney up here.

'She seemed very nice.'

'They're all OK in their own way, I guess. Too many women bossing you about but what d'you expect from a girls' school, eh?' He laughed and began sweeping the ground in front of him.

'I was asking about Georgina O'Neill,' Mills tried.

'You a friend of 'er's?'

'No. I was just asking about her, you know, because of her...'

'She went. That's what 'appened. She went without a word. She was a lovely girl and it broke 'er 'usband's 'eart.'

'Why do you think she went?'

'They say she 'ad a lover.'

'Did she?'

He stopped brushing to consider the question. 'Maybe.'

'Why do you say that? Did you see her with anyone?'

'Not exactly *with* anyone.' He was looking at the ground.

'But you saw something?'

'I saw 'er get in a car after work sometimes,' he said quietly.

'Really?'

He was leaning on his broom now, looking pensive.

'A few times in all. I reckon maybe three times. This posh car pulls up, she jumps in and off they go. I reckoned that must've been 'ow it was the last time. Up 'e comes in 'is Jaguar, or whatever, picks 'er up and off they go together, forever. That's why 'er car was left 'ere.'

'Did you tell the police?'

'Police? There were no police to talk to. She sends a postcard. It were obvious what 'ad happened. Weren't no police involved.'

A door swung open. 'Archie! Can you get on with the dining hall now please? Now!' It was the school administrator.

He almost jumped to attention. 'Got to go. She who must be obeyed, eh?' He smiled and waved, disappearing indoors with his broom, leaving Mills to ponder what she had heard as she sat on the bus back to the station. Now she knew there was someone else involved she could make some enquiries, see if she could track Georgina down and finally end the mystery of her sudden disappearance. Until then she was not going to tell anyone what she was doing.

'I've been trying to call you,' said Jake when Mills walked into the office.

She looked at her watch. 'It's only six. I've been in the library,' she lied. 'Plenty of time.'

'I thought I should tell you about my idea,' Jake began as they left the campus. 'So you can see that I'm only trying to help.'

It was the first time Jake had spoken to Mills since her outburst on the previous day.

'Go on.'

'I spoke to the Dean on Monday... about what's to happen to Nige. I was worried that there seemed to be an assumption that I would take over some of his work on a permanent basis.'

'Some of it? Don't you mean all of it?'

'No, hang on a minute. I made a suggestion to him, the Dean I mean. He was keen to get any new arrangement in place for the start of next term.'

'You mean he wants to get rid of Nige by then.'

'Possibly but that's not the point.' He held up his hand. 'Please listen. I've suggested to him that Nige starts back half time.'

'What? He won't cope. He'll mess it up and then they'll sack him.'

'I know, but wait. I can help him, Millie.'

'Mills. How can you help? He'll fail.'

'Not if I'm there. I can support him. Help him with it. Do it if necessary. Anything, as long as he seems to be getting better. They can't sack him if he's improving, can they?'

'You'll never get Nige back half time.'

'We can if we all work on him. It'll take teamwork, Millie. Nina, you and me. We need him to feel he can do it. I'm going to start by taking him to the field site where his students are working. A day out will do him good.'

'Well good luck with that. He hardly leaves the house these days.'

'That's why I need to talk to Nina.'

Mills went out to sit in the yard with Nige while Jake broached the idea with Nina. She could see them through the kitchen window, deep in conversation. Rosie was lying on a rug while her father dangled a small knitted toy above her head. He seemed more relaxed and she hoped it meant Jake was helping relieve his depression. Nina was waving from the kitchen. It was time to eat.

Nothing was said about the plans over supper but Jake dominated the conversation with arrangements to visit sites and suggestions for new projects which could only mean that Nina had agreed with his plan. Nige appeared to take an interest in Jake's ideas although he was quiet throughout the meal. When it was time to leave, Jake hugged Nina and winked at Mills.

'Nige, I'm driving down to Driffield tomorrow, just to have a look at what's been happening while I've been away. I could do with some company.'

Nige looked up. 'What about Rosie?'

'No problem,' said Nina. 'I'm back at lunch-time and...'

'I can be here in the morning,' offered Mills.

'Aren't you going to see Phil?' Nige asked.

'No, it's fine for the morning. I'll go in the afternoon as usual.' Mills could feel her cheeks reddening.

'Are you off to Arkengarthdale tomorrow?' asked Jake with a grin. 'I can give you a lift. It's not really out of my way to Bainbridge. I'll take you when we get back from Driffield.'

'No,' objected Mills.

Nige looked from Jake to Mills. 'But you usually leave early on a Friday. I can't go if it makes you late.'

Everyone was looking at her.

Mills sighed. 'If it means you'll go to Driffield, I'll get a lift with Jake. Happy?'

The journey back from Whitby gave Phil a chance to unwind. The bike was performing well and he was going against the traffic most of the way. Earl was waiting to greet him and John insisted on sharing a beer before Phil could unlock the cottage, throwing open the windows to let the flies out and the cool evening air in. He heated his dinner in the microwave and filled Earl's bowl before settling down in front of the television news until he was woken by the phone ringing. Jumping up, his plate clattering to the floor, he tripped over the dog in his rush to answer it, thinking it was Mills.

'Phil? It's Claudia. Sorry to ring so late but you were out earlier. Did you not get my message?'

'Message?'

'The body you've been working on? A funny coincidence. We've been asked to work on the case. I thought we could have a chat about it.'

'Yes?'

'Look, did I wake you? You sound...'

'No, go ahead.'

'We've been asked to do some tests. Toxicology, DNA, the usual.'

'Fine. Good.'

'You'll need to come over to Harrogate to discuss the results, obviously.' Did she sound irritated?

'Er, right.'

'Shall I let you know when we've got the data?' Her voice was sharp, yes almost sharp.

'That would be fine.'

'It would be so nice to see you again, Phil. We should keep in touch now we've caught up.'

Phil replaced the receiver slowly. Why had she re-appeared when he was beginning a new period in his life? Just as the memories were finally fading and he was beginning to bury the whole ghastly episode. Surely she could see that it would be better to avoid each other and carry on with their lives? It was almost as if she wanted to revive the past.

Chapter 4

Nige had left, reluctantly, with Jake, and Nina was at work. As soon as she was alone, Mills picked up her mobile. Tim O'Neill had been disappointed when she told him she'd learned nothing at the school and she thought it best not to mention the Jaguar. He didn't have details of any special friends of his wife but her mother or sister might be aware of a potential confidante, so Mills asked for their phone numbers. If her school-teacher friend knew nothing about another man perhaps she had confided in them. Mills thought the mother was likely to be home during the day but there was not even an answer machine at the other end. Without any optimism she tried the sister's number, which was answered almost immediately.

'Yes?' The voice was tense. A radio or television was playing in the background.

'April?'

'Yes.'

'I'm Mills Sanderson. Tim gave me your number.'

'Tim? Tim O'Neill? Is this about Georgie?'

Mills gave her standard explanation about researching missing people. April appeared to accept it without question.

'I wondered if your sister had mentioned meeting anyone... anyone special before she disappeared.'

'You mean a man?'

'Well, yes. The postcard suggested she had left her husband for someone else...'

'Is that what you think?' She sounded annoyed.

'Isn't that what happened?'

'Who knows? I'm sorry. It's just that it was so unlike her to just take off like that.'

'It was certainly unexpected.'

'It wasn't just that it was out of the blue. It was the fact she hasn't contacted us. Mum was devastated. To tell the truth she's never got over it.'

'So there was no hint, nothing to suggest it was going to happen?'

'Nothing.'

'And are there any close friends of Georgina's that I should talk to?'

There was a pause. 'A girl at the school, if she's still there. I think she was called Penny but I wouldn't know how to get hold of her.'

'Was Penny her best friend?'

'She's the only one I heard her talk about.'

Mills thanked her and said she might want to speak to her again. If Penny Meadows was Georgina's best friend, she clearly had no special confidante that Mills could talk to... unless Penny was not telling her everything she knew.

Rosie was trying to climb out of her playpen and Mills resolved to spend the morning entertaining her young charge, rather than attempting to get any work done. However, only twenty minutes later an unrecognised number rang her phone.

'Hello. I don't know your name but you rang my daughter a little while ago.'

'You must be Georgina's mother.'

'Yes, that's right. April said you'd been speaking to Tim O'Neill. Have you heard something? What's happened? I must know.'

'I'm sorry, Mrs... I don't have any news. I spoke to Tim and he gave me your number. I'm doing some research.' She was embarrassed by her deception, made worse because she had raised the woman's hopes.

'What's he been telling you? That she left him for another man? It's lies, all of it.'

'I don't think he believes it either, Mrs...'

'Dawn.'

'He wants to know the truth.'

'What does he know about truth? I won't listen to him. I've told him not to call.'

Mills wanted the conversation to end. She was lost for words, wishing she'd not interfered.

'If you want to hear the truth about Georgie you can come and talk to *me*, not him.'

Mills grabbed a scrap of paper and scribbled down the Hebden address.

'I could drop in on Sunday, if you like.' Mills reckoned Phil could take her down there.

'Yes. Yes, that would be convenient. Just call me when you are coming.' The dialling tone indicated that Dawn had put the phone down.

Mills played absent-mindedly with Rosie in the yard while she considered her next move. She was excited by the prospect of meeting Georgina's mother but had no idea what she intended to say to her. Should she tell Tim of her plan? What about April? By the time she was spooning out Rosie's lunch, she had resolved to ask Nina's advice, particularly about the Jaguar.

'You want me to do what?'

Rosie was having her nap when Nina got back. Her friend was relaxing in a deckchair when Mills broached the subject. Now she was sitting upright glaring across at her.

'I just thought if I found out what colour it was, you might be able to get a short-list of owners in the area. It's quite an unusual car, isn't it?'

'It doesn't matter how unusual it is or what colour it is, I can't make those kinds of requests without reason, you know that. I've told you before.'

'But it's for a good reason. Georgina's mother is sure there's something fishy about her disappearance and...'

'So you want me to put my job on the line? Eh?' Her tone was cold.

'Well...'

'Do you realise how close I was to giving it all up? How keen they were for me to take a desk job? How hard I have to work just to keep up?' She seemed close to tears. 'I have to be careful, Millie. I can't afford to take a step out of line, not with Nige losing his job.'

Mills, unable to think of anything to say that would come out right, got up and knelt down beside Nina.

'I'm sorry.'

'I know. Let's wake up sleeping beauty.' She looked at her watch, 'Goodness. It's time for you to get some work done before the boys are back.'

Mills went obediently up to her room and sat down in front of her laptop. She had been giving Nige's lectures on identifying sites of interest for the last term but now she had to prepare the next one so that Nige could start to take the class again. This meant writing down everything in detail so he could use her notes himself.

The afternoon passed quickly, interrupted only by Nina bringing her a mug of tea. It was hot and stuffy in the tiny box room and there was no breeze even though the windows were wide open and the curtains held back as far as possible. An irritating fly buzzed at the ceiling. Mills spent much of the time looking out of the window at the yard below where Nina was reading to Rosie. Eventually, unable to concentrate, she began packing her things for the weekend. If Phil was taking her down to Hebden, she thought, they could look in at the Threshfield site for evidence of lime kilns. She put a map and notebook in her bag, together with a pair of shorts and a clean sleeveless top. The forecast was for a hot sunny spell.

It was gone five when Jake arrived back with Nige. She could hear excited voices below.

'Mills, listen to them,' Nina said when she reached the top of the stairs. 'I've not seen Nige so happy for ages.'

'A good day then?'

'Apparently. Nige is still going on about it. Come and see.'

She sat listening as Nige and Jake described their visit to Driffield. Nina sat on the arm of the sofa, beaming at her husband. Mills indicated to Jake to follow her into the kitchen.

'It went all right then?' she asked softly.

'Yes, after a while. He sat in complete silence on the trip down but I made him help me with some measurements and he sort of dropped into it. By the time we went for lunch...'

'In the pub, no doubt?'

'Right. By the time we came out he was really quite chatty.'

'I've been getting the lecture ready for him.'

'Great. I'll suggest it to him on Monday. Are you ready to get going? The time's getting on.'

Mills was not looking forward to the ride to Arkengarthdale but it was the only way to get there now. 'I'll fetch my stuff.'

They left Nina smiling protectively at her husband and daughter playing on the mat. The traffic was always bad on a Friday night and tonight was slower than ever. Jake had the radio playing which allowed Mills to ponder on the weekend ahead. First she had to explain her lift away and then persuade Phil to drive her to Hebden to meet Georgina's mother. She knew he would disapprove as much as Nina did and it irritated her knowing that Jake would probably jump at the chance to help her. He leant forward to switch off the news and they drove without speaking for a while.

'So what are you up to this weekend?' she asked, as the silence became uncomfortable.

'Not much. Dad wants a hand around the farm but nothing too onerous. I thought I'd just chill out.'

'I expect Toby's glad to have you around.'

'Yes. But I don't expect to be lodging with them for long. I'd like somewhere of my own, nearer town.'

When they reached Richmond, Mills directed him onto the Reeth road and then into Arkengarthdale. She said Jake could drop her at the end of the lane but he insisted on taking her up to the cottage. Earl was wandering about outside and came across to investigate the strange car. She thanked Jake, quickly jumped out, grabbing her bags off the back seat. She heard the front door open and ran to greet Phil before he came into the road. Thankfully the car had turned and was making its way back along the track before he had finished kissing her.

'Didn't you invite your friend in?' he asked.

'No. No need.' She was fussing noisily over Earl. 'So how was your week? Have you finished with the body at Whitby yet?'

'Yeah, pretty much.'

He carried her bag into the hallway and went into the kitchen. Mills prepared a salad while Phil carved thick slices of cold meat.

'I hope you don't mind staying here,' he said as he took a bottle from the refrigerator and turned the screw top. 'It's so hot I thought we'd eat in the garden... and England's playing Algeria.'

What he called the garden was a patch of grass outside the back door, divided from pasture by a wire fence to keep the sheep out. They sat in the shade of the apple tree, flapping flies away from their food. Phil was unusually quiet. Mills wanted to tell him about the trip Nige had taken but it would have meant mentioning Jake. So they ate in silence until the midges became too much and they went inside to watch the World Cup.

It was a humid night and Mills spent a long time getting to sleep. When she did, she dreamt of the red-headed girl who had disappeared without trace.

Phil had been into Reeth for a paper and bread rolls by the time she was awake. They had a late breakfast in the garden, catching up with the week's news until mid-day. It was time to broach the subject of a trip into Wharfedale tomorrow, Mills thought.

'So why do you need to visit this woman?' Phil was still reading the sports section.

'She... she's part of my research,' she lied.

'How come?' He turned a page.

'Well... she knows about the lime kilns at Threshfield.'

'Ah.'

'I thought we could have another look at the area... and then I'll drop in to see her. Just for a few minutes. You don't need to come in.'

Having decided to barbecue later in the afternoon, Phil went into Barnard Castle to do his weekly shop. Mills, wanting to ring Georgina's mother, excused herself on the pretext that she was going to catch up on her sleep. In fact she did doze for a while in the hot sun until the sound of the telephone indoors disturbed her. She was tempted to leave it but then jumped up, thinking it might be Phil. She stubbed her toe on the kitchen step and hopped towards the phone as it switched to the answer machine. She was about to pick up when she heard a woman's voice. *Hello Phil, it's Claudia. About next week, I thought we could have lunch. There's a nice Italian nearby. Give me a call and we can arrange which day is best for you. Looking forward to meeting up again. Bye.*

Mills hobbled to the sofa. She could see Claudia's blonde hair swishing round her face as she danced with Phil at the wedding. Just the one dance, she had begged, as Phil initially refused. Was he really under such duress or was it an act for her benefit? The red light blinked at her as she dialled the number Tim O'Neill had given her and made arrangements with his mother-in-law to drop in the following day.

'I think the phone went when I was asleep,' she called to Phil when he came into the garden. Mills watched him return to the kitchen to unpack the groceries. Eventually she heard the female voice repeating the message on the answer machine.

'Was there a message?' Mills asked as he sat down beside her.

'Just someone from work,' he said, picking up the sports section he had discarded earlier.

April was looking through Georgina's wedding photographs. She had always been the pretty younger sister but on that day she had been radiant. That's what they called the bride wasn't it? Radiant. Tim looked smug beside her. Not the world's best catch, he looked slightly ridiculous in his morning suit. Mind you, her own Dave hadn't looked much better on their wedding day, grinning like a Cheshire cat. You could tell he'd had a bit too much to drink even then.

'April?' Her mother had sounded anxious when she rang that morning.

'What's wrong, Mum?'

'I've had a phone call about your sister. She wants to talk to me.'

It was the researcher. Tim must have given her Mum's number, the idiot.

'Mum, there's no need to worry. It's just someone doing a research project. Don't talk to her. You don't have to!'

'But I have done. She's coming round tomorrow afternoon. She might be able to help. I told her I'd see her.'

'Oh Mum. Ring her. Tell her not to come. Say you've changed your mind.'

'Why?'

'Don't worry, I'll call her and tell her not to come. I'll ring you back, Mum.'

She used her phone to look back at calls received and found a mobile number she didn't recognise. She tried several times over the next few hours but there was no response. Once Dave was back with the kids she explained what had happened.

'I told you no good would come of it. This busybody will just stir it all up again. If she wanted to be found she would have contacted you or your mother herself. Let it be. Leave her alone to get on with her life.'

April said nothing. She agreed with Dave that Georgina probably had gone off with someone. She couldn't have stuck living with Tim for very long herself. But she knew that Georgie would have contacted them if she could; she wouldn't have let Mum worry for long unless something or someone was stopping her from doing so. Had she met someone so manipulative that he prevented her from letting her family know she was safe? Perhaps but wasn't that better than believing she was dead, which was what Mum thought.

When she told Dave she was going over to Mum's the next day, he said he had planned to mow the lawn while the weather was good. He could have done it then, instead of watching football all day but it suited her to go without him. The boys, on the other hand, liked visiting their grandmother so she agreed they would go after they came back from cricket practice and they'd had their roast lunch, provided Dave promised to deal with the washing up.

Her sons arrived home next day red in the face, their hair stiff with sweat. She ordered them into the shower with a shampoo bottle, leaving Dave to supervise while she dished up. All their mealtimes were over before they'd hardly begun and today was no exception. Despite the Sunday traffic they were soon through Pateley Bridge and driving along the open road past Stump Cross Caverns to Hebden. The boys were bundled into the garden to play with the old border collie that had been Mum's faithful companion since Dad died.

'Are you all right, Mum? I mean about this woman coming.'

'Yes dear. I looked out some photos of your sister and I found the cutting from the Craven Herald.'

April took the strip of newsprint and smoothed it out. Tim had persuaded a friend to get something in the paper about Georgie's disappearance, even though by the time it was printed he'd received the postcard and all local interest had gone. Her mother was in the kitchen making tea when a motorbike stopped outside the house. The passenger removed his helmet to reveal a short bob of bright red hair. To April's surprise she realised it was a girl. Standing at the window, she watched her remove the leather trousers and jacket and hand them to the driver before striding up the path. As April opened the front door, she heard the sound of the bike's engine and saw a dark shadow move swiftly past the gate.

'Hi, I'm Mills.'

'Yes, Mum's expecting you.'

She led the girl into the sitting room, indicating a seat on the sofa. She was slim, thin not gangly and looked about twenty. Mum came running in, fussing over the cushions, excusing herself to fetch the tea, *and* her special homemade biscuits, April noted.

'I hope you don't mind me coming to talk to you. I'm doing some research on missing people and when I met your son-in-law he suggested I spoke to you.' Her tone was self-assured, despite her apparent youth.

'Why would he do that?' April asked. 'Did he expect you to find her?'

'Not at all...'

'You must forgive my daughter,' said Dawn. 'She... we are both still very upset about her disappearance. I have become more adjusted to the situation as time has gone on. I do not have any hope of seeing her again but April...'

'I can speak for myself, Mum.' She sounded irritated but Mills watched her pat her mother's hand. 'My mother knows what I think... that she's still living somewhere with another man.'

'She would have let us know if she was,' argued Dawn. 'I've spoken to a medium... several times. I'm convinced she's dead, God bless her.' She pulled a tissue from her sleeve to blow her nose, almost surreptitiously.

'Tim thinks she's still alive, Mum.'

'He knows more than he's letting on,' Dawn muttered.

Mills looked at April for a hint but she shook her head silently.

'I looked out some photos,' Dawn continued. She passed them to Mills one by one, describing where and when it was taken. '...and this one was when she was in the Girl Guides,' she said finally.

Then Dawn poured tea, offering round her biscuits. 'Ooh. I must take some squash out to the boys,' she remarked, jumping up.

When she had disappeared into the kitchen, April turned to Mills, staring at her intently. 'Why are you really here? What do you do, truthfully? Are you some sort of journalist? Only I don't want this plastered all over...'

'No, honestly. Your brother-in-law asked me if I could help. He seemed really upset when I met him. He thought I was with the police and I'm not but I do know some people and I said I'd try to help.'

'Well don't tell Mum. She thinks he's behind it all.'

'Really?'

'Something the medium said about her meeting a violent end at the hand of someone she knew. And something about a scar. Mum was convinced at the time, even thought about telling the police until I dissuaded her. Everyone has scars don't they?'

Two small boys came running in and bounced on the chair beside their mother, making it impossible to continue the conversation. Dawn followed, carrying two glasses of squash.

'They wanted to come inside. It's too hot out there.'

'Look, I'd better be going,' offered Mills, standing up. 'Thank you for the tea.'

Dawn sorted through the photos, handing over the most recent one, taken at her daughter's wedding. April followed Mills into the hall, standing with her hand on the handle of the front door without opening it.

'Mum may think she's dead but I don't believe it. I think she wants to contact us but whoever she's with won't let her. If I can help, I will. It's the least I can do.' She gave Mills her mobile number, telling her not to ring the house phone again. 'It's Dave. He thinks Georgie is safe and well, living in Barbados or somewhere equally ridiculous. Can you see a red-head wanting to live in the Caribbean? Just let me know if I can help.' She smiled as she finally opened the door.

Mills felt only relief as she left the house and walked slowly down the lane to the corner where she was to meet Phil. Why hadn't she realised what an impact her questions would have on the family? This wasn't some research project, a bit of entertainment;

here was a mother, a sister, desperate to know what had happened to a beautiful young woman. She hurriedly pushed the photograph into her back pocket as she turned the corner where Phil was waiting.

'Good meeting?' he asked, as she pulled on the leathers and helmet.

'Yes. Very helpful.' She swung onto the back of the bike, tapping his shoulder to indicate she was ready to leave.

As they drove through the lanes she could smell the freshness of the early hay meadows, feel the sun on her back. There were plenty of cars around Burnsall but Phil was able to overtake them so it was not long before they were back at Threshfield, passing the limestone quarry. She'd found the grid references for two sites of possible early kilns but she'd only brought the ordnance survey map with her.

'You mean you don't have the GPS system with you?' Phil asked scornfully. He was marching ahead as she struggled across the rough ground trying to work out where they were exactly.

'I'm sorry. I forgot. This is hopeless.'

'It is rather a waste of time if you don't know where we're going.'

'I know where we're going,' she replied, 'I just don't know where we are.'

He stopped to let Mills catch up, taking the map, turning it round and peering out across the countryside. 'Let me have a look.'

'I suppose you know better than me?' she asked, irritated by his patronising tone.

He paused. 'No, I've no idea where we are.' He sat down, laughing.

'It's not funny.'

'It is. You should have asked your friend in Hebden to join us. She would have known how to find them.'

'Yes, I suppose so.' Let him think she was visiting a member of the local heritage group. It was a white lie, she told herself, just to avoid him getting cross with her for interfering. As it was, the afternoon had been a waste of time all round.

They found shade against a dry stone wall and watched a curlew circle slowly above the dale. There was no other sound except for an occasional shriek from the caravan site where families with young children were enjoying the last few hours of the weekend. Soon they would all be packing up to return to their city lives until the summer holidays began in earnest. Mills thought about the coming week when Nige would be taking his class again under her guidance and Jake was going to take him out on a field visit. Then she remembered the message on Phil's phone.

'Was it funny seeing your college friends last week, after such a long time?' she asked casually.

'It was OK. Not really fussed about it though. Things move on.'

'Not even Claudia. She seemed very nice.'

'Especially not Claudia.' He was looking straight ahead so she couldn't read his expression.

'Oh, I thought she was a special friend of yours.' She wanted her voice to be light and teasing but it came out sounding rather spiteful.

'No, she wasn't. I didn't know her very well at all, actually.'

'So you won't be seeing her again?'

'No.'

Chapter 5

The usual discussion broke out again as Mills gathered her belongings at the end of the weekend. Phil asked her, once more, when she would be moving in and she repeated that she needed a car before she could live in the Dales while she was working at the university.

'So how long will that be?' he asked.

'I don't know. Until Nige is back at work I suppose.' It wasn't true because if Jake did his job they probably could manage without her before that. But what would she do then? She resolved to chase the application she'd made to the National Park as soon as she got back.

'Perhaps we should do something about getting you a car then.'

She kissed him. 'I can't afford it, I told you. And it's nearly seven so we'd better get a move on!'

Mills normally felt depressed as she watched the sheep behind the stone walls become fewer until they were eventually left behind on a Monday morning. But today there was a lot to think about: the lecture with Nige, not to mention Phil's lunch date with Claudia during the week. The fact that he hadn't mentioned it... virtually denied it... proved he had a guilty conscience.

When Phil dropped her off at the university gates, she simply arranged to phone during the week and keep in touch by e-mail.

'Good morning!' Jake was already at Nige's desk, drinking coffee, and a lidded paper cup had been placed centrally on the table she occupied.

'Cappuccino, just how you like it,' he announced.

'Thank you.'

'Good weekend?'

'Yes, thanks.'

'How did you get back?'

'Phil brought me.'

'That's cool.'

'Not really. He thinks I should get a car.'

'I told you I could have picked you up. You only have to ask.'

'No, honestly it's fine. Can we discuss this lecture that Nige is doing, please? I've written him some notes but it would be best if you could go through it with him before Wednesday.'

'Great. No problem.' He took the papers and leafed through them while Mills settled down to catch up with her e-mails.

'This is great. I'll talk to him about it tonight.' Jake said after a while. 'Actually, I was thinking about the car thing. The hire car goes back next Monday. I was going to borrow Mum's until I got sorted. What about we look out for a car to share? How environmentally friendly is that? Car-share, eh?'

'No, it wouldn't work, Jake.'

'Why not? You could have it at the weekends. I can borrow Mum's then. She only needs it in the week to take Toby to school.'

'No. It's a kind offer but I just think it's a really bad idea.' She turned back to the e-mail she was compiling to the National Park office, reminding them of her request to carry out a project on the lime kilns in Wharfedale.

When her mobile rang later that morning she assumed it was a response to her message but was surprised to hear April Webb's voice.

'I've been thinking about what you said, about Tim asking for your help. It can only mean he believes she's still alive, doesn't it? I'm sure she is, so we should be trying to find her, shouldn't we?'

'Yes, of course.' Mills was cautious.

'So what do you want me to do?'

She was caught off guard. She was without any plan. 'I'm not sure. I asked about her friends but no-one seems to have been close except this Penny at the school. Was there no-one else? Someone with a Jaguar?'

'A Jaguar?'

'Yes, a Jaguar car.' Mills was clutching at straws and she knew it.

'A Jaguar.' There was a pause. 'I'll have a think, ask around. A Jaguar, you say?'

'Yes... and anyone you can think of, any clubs, classes, anywhere she may have met someone.'

'I was thinking. Tim had a postcard, didn't he? From her, after she left. I haven't seen it, have you?'

'No. But it's important. I should ask him about it.'

As soon as she had finished speaking to April, she took out Tim's business card, stared at it for a while and then replaced it in her bag. It was no good; she just couldn't face talking to him, not yet. Instead she looked up the number of the school in Leeds and, when the secretary answered, asked if she could speak to Archie. She needed to know the colour of that car.

The Forensic Archaeology Unit was fairly relaxed but Phil was looking for promotion and he knew that, in addition to his record in helping solve crimes, factors like time-keeping were also important. He was always late on Monday mornings and to make it worse, the fibres and textiles expert, Brenda, was hanging around, waiting to ask him about the rug, which was due to arrive that morning. After that he worked on his report until lunch-time without a break. There was no cafeteria in the building, just a small kitchen with a kettle and microwave. At mid-day it was busy with women heating left-over suppers or lads making pot noodles, so he waited before venturing down the corridor to make himself a coffee.

'Phew what a disgusting smell of curry.' Brenda came in, propping open the door with the fire extinguisher.

'That'll just spread it down the corridor,' Phil remarked.

'Won't worry me, it should only get as far as finance.' She stood waiting for him to finish with the kettle.

'Did the rug arrive?' he asked.

'Yes. Interesting. It looks like an old Persian design but that doesn't mean anything these days. I'll examine the fibres this afternoon. Once we've got the mixture it will be easier to date.'

'Not that it will tell us when the victim was buried with it.'

'No, that's true. But it might indicate the type of household she came from. Is there any more medical information about her? What about DNA?'

'That's been farmed out to a private laboratory.'

'Really? Do you know where?' Brenda asked.

'Bishops. It's near Harrogate.'

'Never heard of it.'

'It's new.'

'What about clothing, for hair and fibres?'

'Same thing.'

'So we won't get to see any of that?'

'Apparently not. We are supposed to be forensic *archaeologists* remember.'

He picked up his mug, following the odour of curry down the corridor to his desk. His report on the body at Runswick Bay required only the addition of some information regarding further tests for identification. He already knew that the woman had had a child, that her back problem was probably due to damage to a knee at an early age and she'd had cosmetic dental work carried out. Her age was estimated to be around thirty. In his view, the body had been buried for about ten years. Although DNA now played a significant part in identification of victims, he felt that any chance that it would help in this case was slim unless there was any material on the body from the murderer. Normally he would be chasing the laboratory for the results of the DNA and fibre analyses but that would mean ringing Claudia.

'It is a valuable old Persian carpet.' Brenda stood triumphantly over Phil as he stopped typing.

'Unusual?'

'Fairly. It also has a number on it which means we might be able to identify the shop where it was purchased. I've asked the office to do a bit of ringing round for me.'

'Well done.'

Once she had left, Phil sat reading his report, complete apart from the finishing touches. If Brenda could track down who bought the carpet, this poor young woman might not remain an unknown corpse found on the beach after all.

There was something different about Nige. Mills noticed it when she went into the house. He was out in the yard with Rosie as usual but the picture was different. When she took a closer look, Rosie was dressed in flowery dungarees, with a ribbon in her hair. Someone had taken care getting her ready. Nige had changed out of the red T-shirt that had been his uniform for several weeks and was sporting a short-sleeved shirt and a pair of chinos had replaced the beige shorts. Also his hair was brushed, his stubble gone but it was the smiles on both their faces that made the transformation complete.

'Hi, Millie.' He was waving his daughter's arm at her. 'Ooops, no, say hello to Auntie *Mills*, Rosie.'

'Pleeease, don't call me auntie. It sounds ancient!' She stepped into the cool air. 'You're looking pleased with yourself, Nige.'

'I had a call from the department this morning. They asked if I felt up to coming in for an assessment. Just a chat, to see how I feel about starting back.'

'That's good news.' She hoped that her interpretation was correct.

'Yes. I'm going in on Friday to see Occupational Health.'

'Has Jake asked you about coming in on Wednesday for the remote sensing lecture?'

'He did mention it, yes.'

'And what do you think?'

'Don't know, really.' A cloud seemed to move across his face, obliterating the smile.

'Perhaps see what Jake says this evening.' She picked Rosie up to give her a kiss before going inside to start the evening meal.

Nina was on late shift so it was just the three of them sitting down to supper. Jake had been chatting with Nige in the yard since he arrived and now he appeared more positive about the impending lecture.

'I'd feel better if Jake was going to be with me,' he confided.

'Sorry, mate. I've got the second years for practicals in the afternoon. Millie will be able help you though.'

'*Mills*, Jake. She likes to be called *Mills* now, don't forget,' he whispered.

'Don't mind me, boys. I'm not here. Look, if you're not sure, Nige...'

'No. No, I'll be all right. I just need someone to be there. You'll do fine. Really.'

'Thanks, Nige.' She took his hand and dropped it again, immediately feeling foolish. She carried the dishes into the kitchen, busying herself with the washing-up until she heard Jake leaving.

'He'll be all right on Wednesday,' Jake said. 'He's done the whole talk perfectly, don't worry.'

After Jake had gone, Nige insisted on running through the lecture again. He was clearly worried about it but she reassured him, even though some parts were a bit difficult to follow. She blamed herself for that; it was not a subject that she was very familiar with so her notes were a bit dodgy in places.

Nina returned from work exhausted, eating the reheated meal ravenously and then slumping on the sofa to be regaled with Nige's news. As soon as he carried Rosie up to bed, Nina begged Mills to explain what his assessment might mean but she assured her there was nothing to worry about, explaining how he was to deliver the lecture on Wednesday with her help.

'You and Jake have been real friends to us, Millie. I don't know how I can ever repay you.'

'There is something you could do for me, Nina.'

'Oh no, what are you thinking?' She pulled a face indicating mock horror.

'Just about the Jaguar parked outside the school before Georgina went missing. I've found out the colour. It was dark green. It would really be helpful if you could have a quick look to see if there are many around Leeds.'

'How do you know it was green?'

'I rang the school. It was seen several times. Always the same... parked outside the school.'

'I'll see what I can do.'

Mills excused herself, taking her computer upstairs to see if there was any response from the National Park or the local archaeology group at Threshfield. She could hear Nige singing to his daughter, then quiet. A board creaked as he tiptoed past the door and down the stairs.

'She's fast asleep.' Nige whispered, sitting down beside his wife on the sofa.

'She looked pretty today. Did Millie dress her?'

'No. I did. I thought it was time we both tidied ourselves up a bit. Jake's right.'

'Right about what,' Nina asked, yawning.

'Everything, really,' he replied enigmatically.

'You're right, you know.' Mills was staring out of the window while Jake typed rapidly on his keyboard.

'About what?'

'It's impossible to do anything without transport.'

The site she wanted to work on was in the middle of nowhere and she needed to speak to archaeologists who seemed to be dotted across the Dales, including the Park Authorities, the Craven District Council and individuals living in tiny villages miles apart.

'I'd lend you the hire car but I don't think the insurance would cover you.'

'It doesn't matter.' She stared at the computer screen. *Dear Dr Sanderson, We wish to discuss your communication in more detail. Please telephone to arrange an appointment.* It was signed by an officer of the National Park. Another message from a local heritage group: *How interesting that you wish to find out more about our lime kilns. Call me and we'll meet up for a chat.*

'Why don't you sign up for the minibus? The test isn't difficult. Then you can borrow it whenever you need to, provided it's for work.'

Jake was right. The test was just to show she could manage without driving into anything. She went out with one of the technicians in the newest vehicle so the gears changed easily and the brakes worked. He seemed satisfied with her performance, adding her to a list of authorised drivers, simply asking to see her licence before handing over a card with insurance details on it.

'Can I take it anytime?' she asked.

'Just book it through me when you want it,' he replied, walking off.

'Thursday?'

'Just write it in the book if it's free,' he called back.

She rushed to the office, stopping only to book the minibus. She planned to spend the afternoon arranging a day full of visits to initiate her plan to be independent of the university by the time Nige was ready to return to work full-time.

There was a woman standing in the corridor who looked familiar but Mills couldn't place her. She was dressed in a flowery skirt and wearing flip-flops.

Mills passed her with a smile but stopped when the woman called her by name.

'Dr Sanderson... I'm sorry to bother you but I was coming into town and I looked you up on the internet. You said you were from the university and I recognised your photograph.'

'April!'

'I hope you don't mind.'

Mills led her into the empty office, pushing the door gently until it shut behind her.

'I hope you don't mind, Dr Sanderson, but I went to see Tim yesterday after you left Mum's.' She reached for something in her straw shopping bag and handed Mills a postcard. 'It's the card my sister sent after she went missing.'

The handwriting was large and neat. She turned it over to reveal a picture, a black and white drawing. It was a view of a hillside. On the back was a brief message: *I'd like to start fresh with the help of my guardian angel. I'm moving to a new address. "Look after yourself." XXXX.* There was no signature

Mills looked closely at the postmark but it was a blur.

'The picture, does it mean anything to you?'

'No. My sister went to art school; she loved paintings and collected prints. Although it does look familiar.'

'At least it's a UK stamp,' Mills pointed out. 'May I keep this?'

'Of course, and my brother-in-law said that you are welcome to call or visit him if you want to ask any questions. He understands how difficult it is but he really appreciates you trying. He said he's happy to pay whatever you charge.'

Mills felt her face reddening. 'Oh, I wasn't expecting to be paid,' she muttered, 'I'm not a professional.' To cover her embarrassment she asked April if her mother knew she had come to see her.

'No.'

'I hope I didn't upset her on Sunday.'

'She's all right. She's convinced Georgie is dead. Nothing will dissuade her from it.'

'Did Tim say anything when you collected the postcard?'

'He just wants to know she's all right. He wants her to be happy, that's all.' She stood up with a smile that fooled neither of them. 'We just want to know she's not *unhappy*, that's all.'

Mills pushed her chair back but the woman waved at her to remain where she was. 'I can find my way out, don't worry. Please ring me if you want anything, anything at all.'

Mills sat for a while turning over the postcard, studying the writing, staring at the picture, trying to make sense of it. The message was clear enough but the way it was expressed seemed a bit weird. She would never call anyone her guardian angel. She certainly sounded besotted with this new man of hers. Placing the card in her desk drawer, Mills resolved to get on with her own life for the rest of the day. She had appointments to make if she was taking the minibus to the Dales on Thursday.

Phil was caught off guard when the call finally came. He was feeling particularly bright, having finished his application for a level D position in the unit.

'Good morning, how may I be of assistance?' he asked, putting on a southern accent and grinning across at Brenda.

'Could I speak to Phil, please?' There was no mistaking Claudia's voice; the southern drawl that almost masked her northern origins.

'Speaking.'

'Phil, darling, the results will be ready for you if you come over for lunch tomorrow.'

'OK.'

'I'll explain how to get here...'

'Claudia, I can find my way there.'

'But you need to know the route to get to the lab, it's...'

'No, I'll find it, don't you worry.'

'Phil, sweetheart...'

'I'll see you tomorrow, bye!'

Brenda looked up as he put the phone down quickly. 'Was that Claudia Bishop?'

'Yes.'

'Are you two big buddies? She seems to know you very well indeed.'

'We were at college together.'

'That all?'

'Yes, Brenda. That was all. I've got to pick up the DNA results tomorrow.'

'Can't she fax them?'

'Apparently not. By the way, any more news on the rug?'

'Not really. The design is quite unique but we've had no success tracing where it was purchased – if it was bought over here.'

'Any fibres or hairs?'

'Claudia's lab hasn't found anything useful yet. She likes to take her time that one. Has she been running the business long?'

'I really don't know. She was working in Wetherby until the re-organisation. Presumably thought she'd make a go of working privately now.'

'So how long ago when you were at college with her?'

'I really can't remember, Brenda.' He switched off his laptop and packed it into his rucksack. 'I'm going to work at home for the rest of the day.'

There was something distinctly disturbing about Claudia which made it difficult for Phil to settle after their conversation. As soon as he was home, he called Earl and set off upstream towards Whaw. No-one was likely to be out walking on a Tuesday afternoon; only the birds in the woodland were there to disturb him as he sat watching the beck move slowly across the stones. There had been little rain so the water was low – so low that Earl had to lie right down in it to drink.

'Come out of there you daft thing!' he called, immediately regretting it as the large dog stood beside him shaking his wet hair.

They stayed beside the beck for an hour or so, in the dappled shade of the wood. Enough time for Phil to recall the events that had faded into something part-imagined, which had almost evaporated since he graduated. But as soon as he saw Claudia at the wedding he knew it would have to be faced. His fear was that by agreeing to have lunch with her, it would all flare up again.

He worked until late, stopping only to prepare cheese on toast. Earl emptied his dinner bowl in less than a minute but Phil ate slowly, concentrating on a publication he had found on Persian carpets. When the phone rang, it was Mills. For the third time he let the machine click in, listened to her asking him to ring back and continued his work.

'It's not important Phil. I just wanted you to know that I'm coming over on Thursday. I'm going to be driving so you'd better watch out if you're on the road. Seriously, I could come and see you later in the day. If you want me to, give me a call.'

She switched off her mobile and threw it on the bed. He'd probably been called out to an incident, a body, something important. They had no arrangement that she would call, why should he tell her if he was going out? In fact he was free to do whatever he wanted and was probably out with a mate. She wandered downstairs where Nina was watching television.

'What's the matter?' Nina continued to stare at the screen.

'Nothing.'

They watched in silence for several minutes.

'I asked for a search on the green Jaguar, by the way.' She still didn't look away from the screen.

'Really?'

'Yes. Three cars in the school's catchment area.'

'Seriously?'

'I can't give you details, you understand?'

'Why not?'

'Why not? Because it's police information. That's why not.'

'Do any of the owners have children at the school?'

'Millie!'

'I only asked.'

Nina turned to face her. 'If I thought there had been a crime committed, I would help. But there's no reason to believe there has been, is there? Sorry Millie but I can't do any more.'

'I've got the postcard. Her sister gave it to me.'

'And?'

'I thought it seemed a bit weird. I can get it.'

She fetched it from her room for Nina, who hesitated before examining it for some time.

'Is it her writing?'

'Her sister and husband think it is.'

'And did it seem strange in any way to them.'

'They didn't say so.'

'In that case I guess she's happily established in her new home with her "guardian angel".'

'Odd that she put kisses, don't you think?'

'Sign of a guilty conscience, I imagine.'

Chapter 6

The address for Bishop Laboratories was an industrial estate outside Harrogate. The site was a maze of identical buildings distinguished only by letters of the alphabet. Bishops was Unit M, the entrance sandwiched between a carpet supplier and a printer. Phil left his bike in the visitor's parking bay, and pressed the buzzer. When the door opened he was at the bottom of a flight of stairs leading to a door marked "Reception".

'Delivery?' asked the woman seated behind a desk in the office.

He removed his helmet. 'No, I've come to see Claudia Bishop. She's expecting me.'

The woman walked across to an inner door and leant in. 'Your visitor is here.'

Phil waited two or three minutes before Claudia appeared. She was wearing a low cut summer dress, her lips were a vibrant shade of orange, as her hair swung loosely around her shoulders it seemed to glimmer in the sun. A musky perfume quickly filled the tiny room.

'Hello, darling. I've booked the "Trattoria" for half-past.' She checked the clock. 'So we'd better get going.'

She brushed past him and down the stairs without waiting for an answer. Phil followed reluctantly. He had meant to decline the invitation, to suggest a sandwich, although he was unsure where they might find food on the industrial complex.

'What are you driving?' she asked when they emerged into the hot sun.

'I came on the bike,' he indicated, unnecessarily since he was dressed in leathers and was carrying a crash helmet.

'Look, take those off and leave them upstairs, I'll fetch the Mercedes.'

A few minutes later they were sweeping along narrow country lanes with the roof down. Claudia was driving fast and Phil clung to the passenger seat as the stone walls flew by beside him. The "Trattoria" was in an old country pub, a small restaurant with chequered tablecloths and candles in wine bottles. When, as the only customers, they were invited to select a table, Claudia chose the most secluded corner, declaring it was her favourite.

'So,' she began, after they had ordered from the specials board, 'it's so nice to catch up at last.' She paused, as if expecting Phil to say something.

'Yes.'

She had already drunk half the wine in her glass and Phil was wondering whether she planned to have another before driving him back to the laboratory.

'We never really got to know each other very well when we were at uni, did we?' She was twirling the glass round in her hands.

'No, not really.' There was a reason for that. He hadn't liked what he had seen. Manipulative was the word most used about her.

'You know, I was devastated about what happened. I so admired how you coped with it all.'

'Thank you.'

'It's nice to see that you obviously have moved on. You've done really well.'

They were interrupted by their starters arriving, much to Phil's relief.

'And *you* seem to have done well for yourself, setting up on your own,' he said.

'Oh yes. You have no idea how much I wanted to get out of Wetherby.'

'What? A big forensics lab like that?'

'Yes but I wanted to be my own boss, Phil. I could see the writing on the wall.' She was attacking her prawns vigorously.

Phil ate his salad slowly while she listed the many complaints about her old laboratory. She did not get on with her colleagues, calling them overcautious, too methodical and having no sense of adventure. Attributes Phil had always considered important in police work. The young waiter removed their plates, returning with the main courses. Claudia cut her steak, revealing the raw interior.

'Lovely,' she said, 'just how I like it. How's your fish?'

'Cooked thoroughly,' Phil replied. 'Just how I like it.'

Claudia drained her glass but before Phil could decide whether to look for the waiter, she had called him over herself.

'Another beer, Phil?'

He shook his head. 'No, I'm driving,' he said pointedly.

She ignored his remark, ordering another of the same, a large glass of chardonnay.

She became more vocal as the meal progressed, gesticulating and naming colleagues back at Wetherby that had irritated her or had got in the way of her promotion prospects.

'Anyway, you've got your company now. You're your own boss.' Phil hoped to steer the conversation round to work, allowing him to leave as soon as the meal was over.

'Oh yes. And it's extremely successful, I'll have you know. In fact... well I might as well say it... I was thinking you might want to consider joining me.'

He looked at her, about to speak when she waved a hand at him.

'No, listen. I've been thinking about it. I don't mean to work *for* me, no, no, no. I mean to work *with* me. Join me as a partner in the business.'

Completely nonplussed by the suggestion, Phil was speechless. He finished the last mouthful of fish in silence while Claudia waited expectantly.

'It's a nice offer...'

'You could have equal share of the running of the company. We'd even change the name to Bishop and Freedman. What d'you think?'

'You've certainly thought it all out.'

'Oh I've spent some time thinking about it and I'm sure it's the right thing to do. I looked up your CV when I was at Wetherby and you've got just the right experience for the sort of work I want us to specialise in: identification of bodies after large incidents, explosions, terrorist attacks. We could build up a reputation, not just in this country but abroad. I know you've been in Eastern Europe...'

'Steady on. I am flattered but I don't plan to make any moves at present. Thank you but... no thank you.'

The smile disappeared. 'I think you should at least do me the courtesy of considering the offer. Financially it will be a significantly better option than where you are at present.'

Phil was acutely aware that his personal details would have been accessible through the Forensic

Science Service documentation but he couldn't see how she would know the salary in his current post.

'Shall we get back to the lab?' he asked. 'I'd like to discuss the DNA tests before it gets too late.'

She seemed to compose herself, the orange lips drew back into a smile. 'Of course, Phil. I'll just get them to put the bill on my account.'

They drove back in silence, while Phil speculated over the reason why Claudia would want him to join her business. Was he being overly suspicious of her intentions? Perhaps he was the only professional she felt able to approach. Maybe her company was in financial difficulties and she needed a gullible fool to bail her out. Anyway, the subject was not raised again during the scientific discussion. It transpired that the laboratory had carried out the DNA test, but the results were not ready yet. Fibres found on the body matched the rug it was wrapped in but Bishop Laboratories could not identify its origin.

'Brenda's trying to locate where the rug might have been sold in this country,' Phil offered.

'One of my technicians suggested we might be able to establish where it came from by the dyes used. He thinks chemical dyes were banned in Iran until the early twentieth century so it might help narrow down the date of manufacture.'

Brenda could probably tell by just looking at it but Phil was happy to humour her. 'Might be worth a try. You'll have to ask whoever's in charge of the investigation.'

'I already have.'

She filled two paper cups from the cooler in the corner of her airless office. A small fan on the desk did little, except move the humid air around the room. Phil stood up, drank the water and left the office.

'Keep in touch, Phil. We mustn't leave it so long next time.'

He closed the door firmly behind him.

On the way home he considered dropping in to the university. Mills would be surprised, but perhaps she wouldn't be there, and, if she was, he'd have to explain why he was passing. As the junction flashed by, he decided it was best to go straight back to work and not to mention his lunch date to Mills, for a number of reasons.

'Do you realise how many different types of Persian rugs there are?' Brenda was standing with her hands on her hips. Her face was screwed up as she lifted her dark curly fringe to wipe sweat from her forehead with a tissue. Phil noted that the shorts and vest combination did nothing to flatter her ample figure.

'Quite a few?'

'There must be at least a hundred.'

'Doesn't that make it easier?'

'No. It doesn't, Phil. Particularly since I am still trying to identify which it is. The fact it has had a putrefying body wrapped up in it hasn't helped.'

Phil explained that Claudia had asked to look at the dyes in the fibres.

'I don't think she needs to do that. I know natural dyestuffs were used. I just need time to go through the pictures on the web. If I could be left to get on with it?' There was no mistaking the hint, so Phil packed up his papers. It was nearly five and there was nothing to keep him there.

The lecture theatre was full. Mills held the door open and waited for Nige to go in first. The clapping began slowly as the students in the back rows noticed his arrival. Soon the room reverberated with the sound of stamping feet and cheering. He relaxed visibly at the welcome, taking the steps two at a time down to the podium at the front of the class. Mills slipped into a seat at the end of the back row and left him to introduce the lecture himself. As she told Jake later, there was so much goodwill in the room, he could have recited the shipping forecast and the students would have sat enthralled.

'So how do we go about locating a buried site?' he began.

Much of what followed was now familiar to Mills, although her understanding of the technology was superficial. She had given a couple of classes in the subject now and could describe how aerial reconnaissance, thermal imaging, resistance, magnetometry and ground probing radar are used to locate buildings, graves and even bodies. These days it was common to investigate archaeological sites without disturbing them and Nige drew on numerous examples of the use of these techniques, describing them with such enthusiasm that no-one could fail to be excited by their power. Mills wondered whether she could make use of them to discover hidden lime kilns in the Dales and made a note to ask Nige about them later.

She had started a new page in her notebook, entitled "How to locate a buried site". How to locate a missing person, that's what I need a lecture on, she thought. She began to make a list. Talk to relatives and friends – she'd already done that. Check with bank accounts etc – the police had done that before and it was a dead-end. Search familiar places and old haunts – she must find out where she went on holiday, did she have any distant relatives? She scribbled out the first two items on her list, underlined the last one and looked at her watch. Only another few minutes before Nige would have to stop.

'So it's important to look at all aspects of the site. Technology is fine but you must see what's in front of you, the geology, the vegetation, depressions, even shadows can expose differences due to a buried object. You have to be a bit of a detective to put all the pieces together. After all, you must have a suspicion that something might be there, otherwise it's unlikely you would find it by a random search.' He closed his presentation. 'Well, that's all for today. Thanks for your attention.'

There were calls of "thank *you*!" and spontaneous applause. Several students gathered round him as he collected his notes together and Mills watched with pleasure as he chatted, almost back to his old self.

'I think you enjoyed that,' Mills said as they made their way downstairs to the office.

'You know, it was all right. In fact, it was better than all right. It was great.'

Jake was waiting for them and Mills gave him a "thumbs up" behind Nige's back.

'Hurry up,' he shouted, 'I've been waiting to celebrate with these doughnuts.'

'Sounds good to me,' said Nige, 'I've worked up quite an appetite. Have they got raspberry jam in?'

He was obviously buoyed up by the success of his performance, continuing to chatter while they drank their tea, giving Mills the opportunity to ask him about using his surveying tools to look for lime kilns. Soon he was pulling books from the shelves and publications from his filing cabinet until Mills was surrounded by a pile of paper.

'Well, thanks, Nige. I'll have a look through these and get back to you next year!' she joked.

'Don't worry, I can help.' He looked across at Jake. 'You'll give us a hand won't you?'

Mills smiled, thanking them both, knowing she would not want Jake to be helping her with her work in Wharfedale.

The rest of the afternoon was spent roaming the department for Nige to say hello to colleagues he had not seen since the accident. The fact that he had been left for dead by someone from the department, albeit a visitor from the States, meant that everyone knew what had happened but it didn't stop them asking him for the details. Eventually they arrived in the departmental office, where it was someone's birthday so cake was offered. The world cup match between England and Slovenia was on the plasma screen outside in the main entrance hall and they sat watching to the final whistle. Nige was obviously exhausted when Mills suggested they went home.

'Nigel Featherstone, you look shattered!' Nina was waiting for them. 'Go outside and sit down, I've put the deckchairs out.'

He obediently followed Jake into the yard, allowing Nina to quiz Mills about her husband's day.

'So it really was all right?' She watched Mills anxiously.

'Yes, he was brilliant, honestly. They loved him.'

She gave an involuntary sigh of relief. 'I didn't think... I was so... I've been in a state all day,' she admitted.

'Sorry. I should have called. We were a bit carried away with it all. He's been round the whole department seeing everyone.'

Nina looked into the yard. 'It must have done him good, Mills. You go out, I'll bring some squash.'

Jake and Nige were supporting Rosie as she made a few hesitant steps. They let her back down onto the rug as Mills joined them.

'Carry on – I can see you're all enjoying yourselves.'

Rosie put up her arms to be picked up again and Mills lifted her onto her lap. Her little arms were brown and warm, her hair smelt of lemons.

'Nige was saying he wants to go into the department more often now. Isn't that great?' Jake was looking at her and nodding encouragingly.

'Yes, super,' she replied. It was but it meant that he would be around less to look after Rosie in future. Did that mean she would have to step in? If so, any chance of moving to Arkengarthdale would go out the window.

The party atmosphere continued over supper. They toasted Nige with the wine Jake had provided and it was late by the time Mills was helping Nina put Rosie to bed.

'It's good to see him being so positive again,' Nina said, as she dried her daughter. She gently pulled a white cotton nightdress over Rosie's head and combed her hair before carrying her into the tiny bedroom. Mills followed, with the pink rabbit that would stay in the cot overnight.

'He'll be wanting to go back properly soon,' Mills ventured.

'Not full-time, not yet,' said Nina. She pulled the curtains. 'I'll stay and read her a story. I know you must want to call Phil, it's getting late.'

Mills went to her room to check her phone; there were no messages. When Phil didn't answer straight away she was tempted to give up but eventually she heard the familiar voice.

'Hi, sorry, I was in the garden with Earl. It's almost his bedtime you know.'

'Sorry, we were busy celebrating Nige's first day back at uni. Anyway, you could have called.'

'Hey, I got your message. You said you were driving tomorrow. Have you got transport? Does that mean you can come over here?'

She knew what he meant. He thought she had rushed out and bought a car so she could move in. She deliberately ignored him.

'I'm using the minibus from the department. I won't be able to come up to Arkengarthdale. I'll be down in Wharfedale mainly.'

'Oh.'

Did he sound genuinely disappointed or was he relieved because he was going to see that woman? The phone message from Claudia had said lunch *this week*.

'Have you been busy, Phil?'

'No, just work really. Look, can you have the minibus for the weekend or is it just in the week?'

'I can only use it for work.'

'Oh... It doesn't matter. I can fetch you. Perhaps we should have a look at some garages this weekend.'

'Yes, all right.'

After the call she looked at her bank account online knowing she couldn't afford a car on her savings. Anyway, she wasn't sure she wanted to stretch herself so that she could more easily see a man who was having secret assignations with an old flame. So she did what she always did in those circumstances and concentrated on her work, spending half the night researching lime kilns until she fell into an exhausted sleep.

Rosie had a routine that began early in the morning, ensuring that everyone was up and about by seven. Nina was feeding her daughter with porridge while Mills rushed about preparing for her trip to the Dales. Nige, still on a high from the previous day's success, was showing interest in the reasons for her expedition.

'Remember if you need any help with surveying, Jake and I can give you a hand.'

Nina looked up and gave Mills a smile before gently pushing another spoonful towards Rosie.

'Thanks, Nige, I'll bear it in mind.'

She had hoped for sunshine but the clouds persisted as she collected the minibus and completed the log book. Although she had had the test run in it, she drove gingerly off the campus, leaving plenty of room before pulling out into the traffic. The engine was noisy, there was a constant rattling from the back, but it went well, even on the hills as she drew nearer to Bainbridge.

On the way she rehearsed her speech, listing the reasons why she felt it would be a good idea for the National Park to support her work in the Dales. She was a trained archaeologist with experience in a number of fields, including lead mining. Admittedly she had no direct experience of lime kilns but she was researching them and the university was behind her.

The visit got off to a bad start when she arrived twenty minutes late. She hadn't realised that the offices had moved and it took her a while to find them. And that was just the start. The rest of the visit did not go as well as she had hoped. They offered her coffee and listened politely while she explained her plans to survey the area near Threshfield Quarry for lime kilns. But then they pointed out to her that an extensive survey had been carried out, part funded by the National Lottery and if she was serious about working on lime kilns, she really needed to talk to the Ingleton Archaeological Group about it. Naturally she had seen the reports of that work but she had to admit that she hadn't spoken to the authors. Of course they acknowledged that the university interest was significant but since she had not located any funding... Their patience and their expression of understanding made it worse. Irritated that she had let herself down by being so naive, she left the meeting, resolving to contact the Ingleton Archaeological Group immediately.

Her enthusiasm was curtailed as soon as she was back in the minibus; she had no mobile signal to connect her laptop. It was only when she reached Hawes that she was able to look up the details for the group and send an e-mail requesting a meeting. The town was busy with visitors so she left the car park, heading towards Wharfedale until she found a quiet spot by the side of the road, where she sat with the window open, a mild breeze scented with heather blowing on her face as she munched a sandwich. Occasionally a vehicle would go by and once a single cyclist passed her, disappearing over the top and out of sight while she struggled to open a bottle of water. The clouds were thinning so now there was more blue than white, she started the engine, moving noisily back onto the road towards Threshfield. If she was to convince the funding authorities, she needed to familiarise herself properly with the area.

The map showed the lane petering out onto the moorland so she went past the quarry, gingerly pressing the minibus forward along the narrow lane, moving down a gear as the road began to climb onto the moor. Uncertain how far she would be able to take the vehicle, she pressed on until a notice declared that the public road was at an end but already she had attained quite a height. She surveyed the pasture as she pulled on her boots, packing the rucksack with camera, sample bags and trowel, just in case. There was a breeze but the sun was so hot she left her jacket in favour of a second bottle of water before carefully locking the minibus. She planned to spend the afternoon exploring until at least four o'clock.

The ordnance survey map showed evidence of coal pits on Boss Moor, which would provide a reason for lime kilns to be situated in the area. Mills had read that coal was mined from Roman times and lime kilns needed fuel so it was obvious they went together. It meant taking the track down to Bordley, a tarmac road leading to a small hamlet with just a couple of farms. Once she was on the road she felt the familiar sense of freedom, there was no-one to tell her what to do, she was her own boss now. She had noticed that Gordale Scar was not far away, Mastiles Lane, Malham Cove, they were familiar names to be investigated. So, when she reached the group of farm buildings, the working dogs barking at her from their runs, she made a decision based on curiosity rather than purpose and set off in a completely different direction away from Boss Moor.

It was easy walking up on the tops, across pastures that presumably had been farmed for centuries. Mills knew the history of Mastiles Lane, the drovers' road leading from Malham, linking the Grange at Kilnsey with the estates of Fountains Abbey in the Lake District. But she had assumed it was in a desolate area, not surrounded by farmland. She thought she might follow the wide green lane all the way down to Kilnsey but was distracted by the uneven nature of the fields and went off to investigate. The almost symmetrical depressions could be indications of the shallow open coal pits that were worked by the Romans. She photographed them and sketched the distribution of the circular dips in the pasture. What she was really looking for was the sign of an early lime kiln. There had been a time when farmers made their own lime for the fields but the trouble with sow kilns was that they didn't stick out like the ones with chimneys so it would mean a thorough survey of the area. She admitted that help from Nige with his geophysical instruments would be essential if she was going to find out what lay beneath the grass, although she really wouldn't want Jake involved too.

She took a swig of water and looked out across the fields. She needed something to keep her here in this beautiful countryside a bit longer. The thought of having to return to Manchester, leaving this and Phil behind and, worse, saying goodbye to Nina and Rosie... and Nige... and Jake? They were all friends she would miss and, hopefully, they would miss her. And Phil? Would he miss her too? She checked her mobile and to her surprise found a signal. She went to call him but stopped, distracted by another name: O'Neill. On an impulse she made the call. He seemed taken aback but pleased to talk about Georgina, inviting her to his home in Skipton after work. Mills quickly sent a text to Nina, letting her know she would be back late. Phil would have to wait.

In the next field were more of the same shallow circles. Her attention was drawn to four stones that appeared to mark one of the circular depressions. Unlike the rest, this one had a spur to one side. She moved over to examine the stones, searching the grass for signs of stone in the circle itself. The sow kiln design would have had a channel running off one side to allow air to be drawn into the kiln. Was this an indication that it might not be a coal pit but something more interesting? She knew she had to be cautious but her heart was thumping as she took out her camera and took shot after shot to show someone more expert than her.

The rest of the afternoon was spent making careful measurements of the circles, including the mysterious one that had been picked out and marked by stones. She seemed to have the dale to herself, seeing no-one all afternoon. She had been so absorbed in her work that she was surprised to find it was already nearly four o'clock. Reluctantly she packed up and returned to the minibus, opening all the windows in an attempt to cool it down and remove the smell of diesel before she drove to Skipton to ask Tim O'Neill about the green Jaguar.

Chapter 7

Phil was concentrating hard while Brenda attempted to explain the intricacies of Persian rugs.

'So you can tell exactly where it comes from by the number of knots?' he asked, to show her that he had been listening. Brenda was a formidable colleague with endless enthusiasm for her subject, which was "fibres": wool fibres, nylon fibres, carpet, rugs, curtains and clothing, which meant she was indispensible since many bodies they dealt with were clothed and often wrapped in bedding or floor covering of some sort.

She ignored his question. 'Unfortunately Heriz rugs are quite common in that they are popular among collectors, so it makes our job more difficult.'

'And how do you know it's from Heriz?'

'Because of the medallion design, and the colour, which is typical of the area.'

'Nice work.'

'No, Phil, it's not. It's like finding a piece of furniture from IKEA, or better still, Heal's. It could have been owned by anyone.'

'Can it tell us *anything*, Brenda?'

'Like...?'

'Well, such as...' he paused as he searched for an example, 'such as... if... it was in a dirty environment, in town, or was it in the country? There must be different sorts of dust?'

'Correct, they're looking through a bag of vacuum dust as we speak that might be promising. It already looks like there was a dog.'

'And what about the rug itself? Is there anything particular about the wool?'

'Interesting you ask that. The wool is particularly strong – something to do with the diet the sheep have. I read somewhere that it's high in copper.'

'Perhaps that should be analysed?'

'Indeed. You were lunching with Miss Bishop yesterday, weren't you? How about asking her.'

'How did you know that?' Phil felt he looked guilty, even though there was no reason to be.

'Oh, I have my spies at Bishop Laboratories you know. I hear about these things.'

'Well, she hadn't got any results yet. She'll ring them through when she has.'

'So you're not going back again *this* week?'

'Certainly not. The woman gives me the creeps.'

'I'll agree with you there but maybe you should ask her if she could analyse the wool for us.'

Phil had several missed calls from Claudia but it was only a matter of time before he would have to speak to her, if only to get confirmation of the DNA results. He turned back to his computer with the excuse he had a report to write but opened his e-mails to see if Mills had sent a message. He had an idea that *she* might be able to help with analysis. Nothing from her but three messages from Bishop Laboratories in his inbox. He opened them reluctantly in turn. The first was to let him know the results were on their way. The second contained the results sheet as an attachment. He opened it eagerly, although it was not really his business. There were no matches and nothing remarkable either. He forwarded it to his colleague who was dealing with the identification of the body. The third message was a personal one from Claudia. It was asking him to reconsider his decision, which was made rather hastily. She was sure she could change his mind. Perhaps he'd like dinner at the weekend? He was tempted to report this to Brenda, who was seated just a few metres away, but she would probably tease him and, worse, tell the rest of the team. He deleted the last message, closed down his computer and picked up his rucksack.

'I'm working at home if anyone asks.'

Half-way down the corridor he stopped. Brenda was in the doorway calling him back.

'Hang on a minute. I've got a message for you on my e-mail.'

Without thinking he returned to the office, where Brenda was back at her desk.

'It's from your pal Claudia. She says she wants to pick up the wool from the rug tonight. Are you expecting her?'

'No.'

'It would be useful to get the analysis moving.'

'I might be out.'

'Never mind, I'll pack them in a jiffy bag for you. You can leave them on the doorstep if you're scared to let her in.' She was clearly enjoying his discomfiture.

'Don't worry, I'll take them in the polythene.'

He signed the evidence form and stuffed the bag in his rucksack with a resigned shrug.

Tim O'Neill lived in a neat row of terraced houses on the outskirts of Skipton. He had told her to park the minibus on a spare piece of ground at the end of the road and she could see why as she walked back to his house. The Victorian terrace had no garages, so parking space was at a premium. There were no Jaguars, green or otherwise, in the line of closely packed vehicles along the road, she noted. The paintwork on number thirty-five was smart, the curtains neat and the tiny front garden beautifully kept, with small ornamental trees in pots forming a guard of honour as she approached the front door.

She didn't recognise Tim without his ill-fitting clothes, which had been replaced by jeans and a short-sleeved shirt, giving him a casual look that suited him better. He appeared relaxed as he invited her in and motioned for her to take a seat in the tidy sitting room. There was a tray of tea on the table with a plate of biscuits neatly, almost too neatly, arranged on a floral plate.

'You got the postcard?' he asked, as he poured her a cup of weak tea.

'Yes thank you.' She wished she could say something helpful – he was looking at her so expectantly.

'April said you'd been talking to her. Does that mean you've got something?'

'I'm sorry, I shouldn't have said I could do anything. I'm not really in a position...'

'But your friend. He can help?'

'No, I'm sorry. The case is closed as far as the police are concerned.' There was a long silence. 'Do you know anyone with a Jaguar?' she asked casually. 'The car, that is.'

'No,' he answered slowly. 'Why d'you ask?'

'Just something someone said.' He looked puzzled and Mills was concerned he would ask more about it so she continued quickly, 'Georgina's car was left at the school?'

'Yes. It was there for several weeks before I could bring myself to pick it up. Had a job getting it going and the AA had to relay it back for me in the end.'

'What was wrong with it?'

'I don't know. I didn't bother to find out. I haven't used it. It was Georgie's not mine. It's in the garage I rent, in the next road.'

Mills drank the tepid tea.

'I thought it would be useful to find out more about Georgina's interests,' she said, unsure what he expected her say.

'What do you mean?'

'Like hobbies and things,' she suggested, accepting a biscuit.

He looked down at his cup. 'We didn't have much time for hobbies. Mostly we were doing up the house.'

Mills looked around. It was obvious that a great deal of care had been taken in the choice of wallpaper, the fireplace, the furniture.

'It was a wreck when we moved in. She... Georgie... she loved planning everything, she made the curtains and she did the upholstery herself.' He jumped up. 'Come and see!'

Mills followed him round as he proudly showed her the rest of the house. It was immaculate, beautifully furnished with period pieces they had found at sales and restored. She could tell how much they both must have loved the house. She couldn't help noticing the make up in the bathroom, a woman's dressing gown hanging on the back of the bedroom door.

'I haven't done anything much since she...' he trailed off 'Lost heart somehow. But I make sure I keep it how she expected it, you know, just in case...'

They were standing in a small bedroom which had been decorated as a nursery. Mills couldn't bring herself to ask the question but returned downstairs in silence.

'I spoke to April... and her mother... but they couldn't suggest anyone else so I thought you might give me a list of names of friends and acquaintances.' He didn't answer. 'People who might know of any connections... you know, people...' She didn't want to say what she really meant – men friends.

'I'm sorry, I can't help. We were both working so hard. Any free time we were doing the house up. We didn't have money to spend on going out. Her only friends were at the school.'

'But the postcard, it was of a pen and ink drawing. Did she visit galleries or exhibitions? Perhaps...'

'No, not round here. As I said, we didn't go out. We'd watch telly or do the crossword if it was raining. She liked to do the cryptic one on a Saturday.' He looked across at her, 'I suppose you think we had a boring existence, but it wasn't like that. We enjoyed it.'

Mills finished her tea, and then picked up her bag, saying she should go. As they stood in the hall she recognised a small pen and ink drawing in a narrow wooden frame

'This is the same as the postcard!' she exclaimed.

'Yes, that's Georgie's. She loved to sketch up on the tops, whatever the weather.'

'So where is it a view of?'

'Simon's Seat. It's on Barden Fell. We'd go walking most weekends.' He looked pensive.

Mills studied it. Not a bird or sheep in sight, just the hills and the sky. 'So how did it come to be on a postcard?'

'She got it printed. On the internet, just a few.'

So it definitely came from her, thought Mills. 'I'm sorry I haven't been much help.' She wanted to take his hand to reassure him. Tell him she would find the truth but she could hear Nina admonishing her.

'No. I shouldn't have bothered you. April said it was silly of me and she's right, of course.'

Unable to add anything to reassure him, Mills went to leave but stopped to stare once more at the drawing of Simon's Seat. 'Do you think the postcard was significant?' Mills asked.

'Depends what you mean by *significant*. It changed my life for ever but if you mean the choice of card... I don't think so.'

She left him standing on the doorstep of the immaculate house. Turning to close the iron gate behind her, she gave a small wave before leaving. He smiled wanly and made an almost imperceptible movement with his hand.

'Fiona rang,' Nina announced as Mills arrived back later that evening.

'What, Dad's Fiona?'

'Yes, *you* know... your future stepmother!'

Mills pulled a face. 'I'll call her later.'

'No you won't, you'll call her now. She wants to talk about the dress.'

'Her wedding dress?'

'No your maid of honour dress.'

Reluctantly Mills went upstairs, shutting her bedroom door carefully behind her before making the call.

Fiona came straight to the point. 'You've got to come down for a fitting. It's been ready for ages but mine will be delivered next week so we can go together.'

'Where?'

'London of course. Can you be here next weekend?'

'Whatever. I can come down Friday and go back Saturday.'

'I thought we could make a day of it, perhaps do a show and your father will want us all to get together on Sunday.'

'Why?'

'It'll be fun. We never go out as a family. And if you wanted to bring a special friend...'

'No, it's fine. Just me.' Had she responded too quickly? Why didn't she want Phil to come?

'Good, that's settled then. I'll tell your father to be around the entire time.'

Good luck with that, thought Mills, it'll be a first.

Downstairs Nina wanted to hear all about the dress.

'I don't know whether it's got sleeves or not,' Mills replied, 'all I know is that it's purple.'

'Does she know you have red hair?'

'Of course she does.'

'And does she know about the sunburn?'

Mills felt her face, which was still glowing from her day outside and pulled up the sleeve of her T-shirt to survey the point where her arm changed dramatically from red to white.

'You'll have to stay indoors between now and July!' Nina said with a laugh.

Mills didn't reply but went outside to find Nige. She needed his advice over the circles on Malham Moor. He and Jake were discussing the fact that England would be meeting Germany in the next round of the World Cup.

'Sorry to interrupt, Nige. Would your resistivity measuring device tell the difference between a coal pit and a lime kiln?'

They both burst out laughing.

'What?' she asked.

'Sorry,' said Nige, 'it's just the sudden change of subject.' He considered for a moment. 'Probably, if the kiln is lined with stone. Radar will give an idea of any structure under there. Why? Are you thinking of doing a survey?'

'I don't know. I think I may be onto something but there's no money for the work. When I spoke to the National Park they said the last project had lottery funding.'

'Not much chance of that then. And it will take ages to get a research grant from elsewhere.'

'I know. I just needed something to justify an initial survey.'

'Happy to help. I'm not doing anything at the moment as you know.'

She stayed a while to tell them about the site until Jake had to go. Back upstairs she was soon distracted by the thought of Tim O'Neill sitting alone in his perfect house. She found the postcard and studied it closely. There was no indication that the drawing was by Georgina, no name or title on the back but when she examined the drawing in detail she could see a tiny G.O'N in the bottom right hand corner. She looked over the rest of the page, screwing up her eyes to stare at a tiny blob she had dismissed as a spot of dirt previously. Soon she was running downstairs calling for a magnifying glass.

'What do you see if you look at that under the glass?' she demanded of Nina, who was sitting with Rosie on her lap.

Her friend studied the postcard, moving the glass towards her face and then away again. 'Can you take this little madam for a minute, Millie? She keeps moving and I can't focus properly.' She continued to stare at the card. 'By the way, Jake said to let him know if you want a lift to Phil's tomorrow.'

Mills sat with Rosie, unable to contain her impatience. 'What do you see?' she asked.

'Did you hear what I said about Jake?'

'Yes, yes, but can you see it?'

'Is it a sheep?' Nina asked. 'Or a cow, perhaps?'

'So you think it's something?'

'Yes, a sheep probably.' She put the magnifying glass down, smiling. 'Do I get a prize?'

Mills snatched the card back and stared at it again. 'You know, I'm sure that wasn't on the original. It's as if it's been added later using a very fine pencil.'

'There's one way to find out.'

'How?'

'Try rubbing it out.'

'But that will remove it and it could be evidence!'

'Evidence? I thought we agreed that the case was closed? What are you doing Millie?'

'I'm just trying to help.' She took the card and carried it upstairs, wondering why Georgina would want to add a tiny sheep to her picture of Simon's Seat. The sound of an e-mail arriving on her computer distracted her temporarily. The Ingleton Archaeological Group had sent links to reports of work on a sow kiln near Kilnsey. It was the excavation funded by the lottery grant that the National Park had described and for a while she forgot all about Georgina O'Neill.

Phil usually rang Mills on a Thursday evening to confirm their plans for the weekend. They would discuss the possibilities enthusiastically, such as whether to take Earl out on the moor or travel further afield to a part of the Dales that Mills hadn't explored before. Tonight she sounded distant; the conversation seemed disjointed, as if she was distracted by something.

'Are you OK?' he asked.

'Fine, really. I was just thinking about work. I'll tell you all about it when I see you.'

'Righto. I'll come over about five.'

'There's no need,' she said, 'I can get a lift. It's not a problem.'

When Phil put the phone down he stroked Earl, absentmindedly. He'd seen the warning signs before and was worried that Mills was losing her interest in him. He glanced around him, deciding that the cottage was suddenly looking untidy and rather grubby. Dragging himself out of the chair, he spent the next two hours clearing every surface of newspapers, files and dirty crockery. The phone rang just as he was putting the finishing touches to the kitchen. He looked round with a satisfied nod before answering it.

'Hello Phil darling.' He'd forgotten about Claudia. 'I just thought I'd ring to make sure that you are in.'

'Unfortunately I'm going out. Perhaps...'

'Don't worry. I'm just down the road. I'll be there in a minute.'

He was about to ask how she would find the cottage but she was already gone. He put the phone down with a sigh, reaching into his rucksack to find the evidence bag.

Phil had decided that he would try to be as amiable as possible, forcing a smile as he opened the door. Claudia almost fell into the room, clutching at him so they were in an embrace before he could avoid it. Her perfume was overwhelming and he noticed that Earl, who had begun to move towards their visitor, rapidly retreated back into the kitchen. Phil offered her a chair while he fetched the wool sample,

'Aren't you going to offer me a drink? I have travelled all the way from Ripon, you know.'

'Sorry, would you like a coffee? Or tea?'

'D'you have a scotch, darling? It's been a long drive. These narrow lanes are hard work.'

He fetched her a whisky.

'Aren't you joining me, Phil? Now you're making me feel naughty. Go on, you must have one too.'

He reluctantly poured a small glass for himself.

'That's better. Cheers.' She looked around her. 'This is so sweet. And so remote.'

'How did you know where to find me?'

'Oh, I have my ways,' she said with a triumphant laugh. 'I told you I'm a bit of a detective.' She leant back, looking relaxed. She seemed to enjoy teasing him. 'So have you thought any more about my offer? I'm serious about wanting to make you a partner, honestly.' She was fiddling with the buttons of her blouse; it was silky, orange and sleeveless; her arms were slim and tanned. 'I know it seems a bit out of the blue but I've kept an eye on your career, did you know that? I knew you'd do well after leaving Wetherby.'

'I thought you specialised in biological and chemical analysis in your laboratory. I wouldn't think my background would fit into your business plan.' It was a strategy designed to finish the discussion but it was a mistake.

'No, Phil, that's exactly where you're wrong. I want to diversify and you are exactly the right person to help me. We'd make a good team, we'll complement each other. It will be brilliant!' As her voice increased in volume, Earl crept in to find out what was happening. He lay in the doorway with his ears pinned back.

'I'm very happy where I am, thank you.'

'Really? I can't believe that. Who is that woman you work with?'

'Brenda?'

'Yes, she's so out of date in her approach to forensics.'

'Yes. Exactly. Which is why we've got the wool for you to examine.' Perhaps he could divert the discussion by keeping the conversation on the subject of forensics.

'And I like to think that we understand each other.' She stared at him, holding eye contact for just that bit too long. 'It would be such fun.' She put her glass down and walked over to him. He could see down her cleavage as she leaned down towards him. 'Don't you think it would be fun?' Her hair was tickling his bare arms as her hands gently brushed his leg.

She fell towards him, laughing. 'You always did play hard to get, Phil.'

Chapter 8

Even the start of the weekend was rubbish and that was her fault, Mills decided. Phil had had his hair cut again and this time it wasn't just short, it was really, really short. It was a shock. It wasn't that she didn't like it. It just took a while to get used to. But he went very quiet after she had asked what on earth he had done to it.

'I tried to call you back last night.' Mills was lounging in a deckchair while Phil was fiddling about with the barbeque.

'When was that?'

'About ten.'

He turned his back and muttered something.

'What?'

'I was out... had to go out.'

There was something about his reply that stopped her from probing further. If he didn't want to tell her... she thought.

'I found out something about the postcard,' she called.

She looked round but he'd gone inside, so she sank back in the chair and sipped her beer. It wasn't until they had eaten that she told him her discovery.

'...so I scanned it into my computer and blew it up until I could see quite clearly that it's a sheep, a perfect little sheep. Isn't that amazing!'

'So what is this postcard? Where did it come from?'

Obviously he hadn't been listening. It had taken him ages to cook the sausages and they were still quite pink inside. She'd not remarked on them because he seemed unusually quiet, as if something was bothering him.

'It doesn't matter.'

'Yes it does. Tell me again.'

This time she included her visit to Tim O'Neill and how she'd spotted the original of the postcard in his house. 'That's why it's really strange to see the sheep on the card.'

'A tiny doodle,' he remarked.

'I suppose.'

The evening drifted on with only Mills breaking the silence to ask about Phil's week. He seemed reluctant to discuss it, which only reinforced her conviction that he had accepted Claudia's invitation to lunch.

Next morning Mills woke to the sound of activity in the kitchen below. Pulling on some shorts and a top she wandered downstairs, savouring the coldness of the stone on her bare feet.

'I'm making pancakes,' Phil shouted to make himself heard above the electric mixer.

'Can I help?'

'No. There's time for a quick shower if you want.'

She obediently went through the kitchen to the tiny bathroom, ruffling Earl's hair as she went. By the time she returned, wrapped in a towel, Phil was pouring batter into a sizzling pan. He grabbed her as she walked past and gave her a long kiss. Mills smiled and went upstairs feeling reassured.

They ate the pancakes in the garden, surrounded by lemons, syrup, sugar and chocolate.

'This is nice,' Mills said.

'I thought I should make an effort.'

'Why?'

'No reason... except, well... you come over here every weekend and all we do is hang out. I thought we should *do* things, you know...'

Was this a guilty conscience, thought Mills. Was it like buying flowers? She wiped the sauce from her mouth. Or chocolates?

'And we're going to a gig tonight,' he added.

'A gig? Where?' It was hot; she had planned to lounge in the garden, sleep in the sun.

'It's not far. It's the Grassington Festival this week. I got tickets for the Proclaimers.'

'Wow!'

'I hope you like them?'

'Of course. That's really cool.'

'I thought we could go down for the day, as it's near your quarry. It's why I got up so early. That's if you want.'

'It's really sweet of you.'

'The venue doesn't open until half six so we've got the whole day.'

She considered the options. She wanted to visit the moor where she thought she'd seen a sow kiln but she was worried that Phil would be sceptical of her find. But it would be useful to take more pictures to show Nige.

'I would like to go up to Mastiles Lane again,' she admitted hesitantly.

'OK.' He paused for a while. 'We could hire bikes in Kettlewell and cycle up there,' he suggested with a grin. 'That's if you're up for it.'

'Sounds like fun,' she said, 'although I haven't been on a bike for years. Is it far?'

Studying the map outside the garage in Kettlewell, Phil suggested they take the bikes to Kilnsey and then up onto the moor to Mastiles Gate. That way, he said, they could judge whether they were fit enough to do the complete circuit via Malham. Although Mills found she could stay upright quite easily, it took time to master the numerous gears. Phil rode beside her, reminding her to change up or down as they progressed towards Kilnsey. When they took the tarmac road behind the pub, Phil pointed out the Old Hall, the seventeenth century farm of the Cistercian monks of Fountains Abbey and for a while Mills was distracted by its history. However soon she was concentrating on pushing her bike up much of the rough track which was Mastiles Lane.

When the route began to flatten out, Mills recognised the terrain she had wandered over alone on her previous visit. She dismounted and pointed across the fields to where she had parked the minibus earlier in the week. Now there were a couple of cars by the gate. Leaving the bikes behind a wall, they took the rucksack that held their purchases from the baker's. Mills threw herself down on the nearest grassy bank while Phil produced cans of beer, sausage rolls, pork pies and parkin. Flapping at the insects, they chattered with their mouths full until the food was finished, then they opened more beer and relaxed in the sun. Finally Mills impatiently insisted that she show Phil the place where she believed she had identified a sow kiln.

'So what are you going to do about it... if it *is* one of these kilns?' Phil asked, after admitting that it looked interesting.

She had been thinking hard about it. 'There's no point making a fuss about it until I'm sure, is there? I thought I'd get Nige to do a survey for me, to see if there's anything under the turf. He can test the resistivity and use the ground penetrating radar on it. He said he would.'

'Well, if you want a hand...'

'That's nice but it won't take much doing. Just getting permission from the owner and transporting Nige over here with the instruments.'

Phil waited patiently while she took more photographs, insisting that he take one of her standing next to the depression in the ground that was so important to her. Finally she reluctantly agreed that it was time they moved on and they retraced their steps back to the bikes.

'Are you happy to keep to the green lanes?' Phil asked as he packed the map away. 'We can take the track back down to Hawkswick if you like. Otherwise we can carry on to Malham and back along the road but it'll take a bit longer.'

Mills was hot and tired. The shorter way sounded attractive so she followed Phil along the lane until he turned down a fork to the right. The going was not too bad until they turned right up a grassy track, where she found herself pushing the bike uphill once more. Her face felt salty when she licked her lips.

'I thought you said this was the easier route!' she shouted to Phil, who had also admitted defeat.

'Not much further,' he called back.

At last they reached the summit and Mills began to descend very gingerly on the rocky parts of the track. Gradually the route improved until she began to enjoy travelling at speed downhill and was quite disappointed when they met the road beside a caravan site and crossed the bridge into Hawkswick. The tarmac road was easy and they had plenty of time, so they stopped beside the river, dabbling their feet in the cold water.

'You know, this has been a really nice day,' said Mills, looking up at Phil.

'Good. I wanted you to enjoy it.'

'Any special reason?'

'No. I just wanted you to have a good time. Although I think you should have used that sun cream I offered you.'

She touched her cheeks. 'Are they very red?'

'A bit.'

She washed her face in the river, splashing Phil as she did so. They rode slowly back to Kettlewell allowing their hair and clothes to dry in the heat of the afternoon.

'We have exactly two hours before we need to be in Grassington,' Phil announced when they had returned the bikes. 'I suggest we find a pub somewhere. Any ideas?'

'No.'

'In that case, I suggest we go to Linton. "The Fountaine Inn" is nice and we can sit outside, although in your case...'

The pub was busy but there was plenty of room overlooking the green, where children were playing in the shallow water and running across the little bridge over the stream.

'What's that old building?' Mills asked Phil when he returned with their beer.

'Fountaine Hospital. Almshouses for the poor.'

'Are they still lived in?'

'I believe so.'

'Somewhere for you in your old age, Phil!'

He grinned. The age gap between them was only a few years but occasionally Mills liked to tease him about it.

They found a table inside when the food was ready, spending longer than usual over their meal. There was no to hurry since they had plenty of time before they had to make their way to the venue. By the time they reached the field where the Proclaimers were performing, a large number of people had gathered. Consequently they were some distance from the stage but it was a friendly crowd and the time passed quickly. Mills was looking around, noting the wide age range in the audience when she spotted a face she recognised at the edge of the crowd. Her immediate reaction was to tell Phil, to suggest that they go over, but he had been so very sceptical about her interest in Tim O'Neill and his wife's disappearance. She remained silent, watching Tim as he turned to talk to a woman beside him. Mills was unable to see the woman's face but eventually he moved aside, revealing yet another familiar figure. It took her a while to grasp who it was, but as Tim put his arm round her, Mills realised that she was his sister-in-law, April.

'Are you OK?' Phil asked.

'I'm fine. This is great, isn't it?' She kept an eye on Tim and April throughout the evening, but it didn't prevent her from enjoying the music. The couple looked like an item, which left Mills wondering how long they had been together. The way April had spoken, she had assumed they were hardly in touch. But the woman had appeared with Tim's postcard with remarkable rapidity after their chat.

As the field emptied, Phil led the way out towards the road, almost passing Tim and April as they wandered slowly along the edge of the crowd. Mills kept her head down, hoping they wouldn't see her.

Phil squeezed her arm. 'Are you feeling all right? You're very quiet tonight.'

'No, I'm fine. Bit tired after all that sun.'

'As long as you're not getting sunstroke.'

The ride back through the dales was almost magical with the moonlight creating shadows across the hills. An owl flew slowly across a field to a barn; rabbits scampered along the side of the road, sometimes for hundreds of yards before darting under a wall or gate.

By the time Phil had sorted out Earl and settled him down for the night, Mills was hardly awake.

'Thanks for a lovely day, Phil.' She yawned loudly as she turned over to sleep.

'That's all right. I hope it's one of many to come,' he said, switching off the light.

It was after ten when Mills woke to find the cottage empty. It was not unusual for Phil to go for an early morning run with Earl so she took a mug of tea back to bed and lay pondering why Tim's relationship with April had been such a shock to her. It hadn't been mentioned when April visited her at the university, but why should it be? It was more important to decipher why Georgina had drawn a tiny sheep on the postcard. She definitely needed to see Tim again...

Her contemplation was interrupted by the sound of the kitchen door opening. She waited for the urgent barking that marked the preparation of Earl's breakfast. But there was silence except for footsteps downstairs. Mills pushed back the covers slowly, placing one foot on the floor.

'Hi! I let myself in. Are you still in bed you lazy boy!' It was a woman's voice. 'I thought we should continue where we left off last time I was here!'

Mills pulled her foot back under the duvet as a blonde head peered round the door.

'Phil?'

'No.'

'Where's Phil?'

Mills, who was speechless, could only stare at Claudia, who sidled through the doorway, stood her ground and stared back. She was wearing a sundress made of some sort of voile that was so thin it was almost transparent in the sunlight.

'Where is he?' she demanded again.

'He's out. Can I help you?' Mills asked, sitting bolt upright in bed. It sounded weird then and when she looked back on the encounter, she could have laughed out loud had it not been so shocking.

'I came to see Phil. He said to come by any time.'

'So you've seen him since the wedding?'

'Oh, that's where I saw you. Were you with Phil? Yes, we've met a few times since. I can understand if he hasn't mentioned it to you.'

Mills could feel her heart beating faster. 'So what do you want?' She hoped she sounded cool, in control.

'I came to see him. I think he'll be pleased to see me. He usually is... very pleased.'

'Are you and he... ?

'What do you think, darling?' She turned. 'This is awkward, I'll wait in the car.' She disappeared as quickly as she had arrived.

'Hey, wait!' She threw back the duvet but by the time she reached the top of the stairs, the kitchen door was being slammed. Her legs were shaking as she pulled on her clothes, shoving things into the rucksack, picking up bits and pieces from the bathroom.

Mills was fighting back tears when she left the cottage so she avoided any further confrontation. But once she was well down the lane, she turned to see Claudia leave her car to make her way down the path and into the house. Phil would be coming back across the fields so she kept to the road, walking towards Reeth without thinking what to do next. Or did she remain on the road because she hoped Phil would appear? After ten minutes, a quarter of an hour, she slowed down, almost stopping in the hope she would hear the engine of the bike behind her. But it was silent except for occasional bird song.

Despite the slow progress she was finally in Reeth with no plan of how to get back home. She didn't even know if there were buses on a Sunday. She wasn't hungry despite missing breakfast but she decided that a coffee would help her see things more rationally. By the second cup she was not only rational but angry. Angry with Claudia, yes, but furious with Phil for messing her about and annoyed with herself for having been such a fool.

There was a notice pinned up in the café listing local amenities, including a taxi service. Calmly she decided to travel back to the nearest railway station. But when she turned on her phone there was a message to call Jake about travelling back that evening. She rang him, with a sigh – it was going to be embarrassing to admit her situation, so she resolved to tell him that Phil would take her back.

'Hi, Millie!' His voice, the name he used, she just wanted to cry again.

'Hi.'

'I need to check what you want to do this evening. I can pick you up at the usual time, or come later if you want.'

'No.'

'Usual time then?'

'I... I...'

'Are you all right, Millie?'

She swallowed hard. 'Yes. I just wanted to say... that I don't need a lift this evening.'

'Oh.' He sounded disappointed.

'I'm going to do some work on my site in Wharfedale this afternoon.' Why did she say that?

'Oh, right.' A long pause when neither spoke. 'How are you getting down there?'

She tried to sound calm. 'I'm not sure yet. I don't know exactly. Phil's... he's sort of busy.'

'Forensics, eh! Well, I can take you. It would be a chance to have a look at the site, you know, for Nige.'

'No...'

'Yes, it'll be fun. I'm not doing anything. I can be there in less than half an hour.'

'Not at the cottage, Jake. I'm in Reeth. I'll be on the green.'

She stayed in the café until Jake was due, even though it was getting busy and they clearly needed her table. She didn't want to see Phil now, even if he did come looking for her. He'd cheated on her, it was over and it was probably her own fault, although she didn't know why.

When she spotted Jake's car pass the window, she quickly grabbed her rucksack, paid the bill and ran up the hill after him. It was comforting to see a familiar face and quite like old times as they set off through the dale. Mills let Jake chatter on about his weekend, his young brother's escapades and what was happening on his parent's farm. She was content to sit quietly contemplating what had happened earlier in the day until they reached Threshfield. She gave him directions up the lane past the caravan site to where they could park close to Mastiles Lane. She showed him the depression which she was sure was an early kiln and he grinned.

'What?' she demanded.

'Nothing. I'm sure we can establish whether it's a kiln or a dewpond,' he said as they marched back down to the car.

'It'll be good for Nige to get back into the geophysics,' Jake said as they drove back to the main road. 'And what about the group that excavated the sow kiln you told me about at Kilnsey? Can they help?'

'I've had a response from the local archaeological group. In fact...' She reached for her rucksack. 'I've got the number of a member who said I could ring her if I wanted more information. Do you think it would be rude to contact her on a Sunday?'

'Could be a good day. At least she might be at home.'

A woman called Sarah answered and immediately expressed interest, offering to send copies of reports and photographs to Mills straight away.

'And she said to get in touch any time by e-mail. Wasn't that nice?' Mills said, as, without a word, she deleted three messages from Phil asking her to call him.

'So I guess you want to get back to see what she's sent you?' Jake asked.

'Could we? What about your stuff?'

'No problem, I brought my things. I sort of guessed you might not want to go back to Arkengarthdale.'

He knew! Mills hoped he didn't notice her redden.

*

Nina and Nige were surprised to see them back so soon but eked out their Sunday roast, supplemented by some vegetables sent by Jake's father and an upside-down cake baked by his mother. Jake described to Nige what he had seen on Malham Moor and they were soon deep in conversation about radar, signals and electrical gadgets. Nina fed Rosie with mashed up chicken dinner while she asked Mills about her weekend, and then told her that Phil had rung several times to see if she had got back safely.

As soon as the meal was over, Jake and Nige settled down to watch football.

'It's really important,' pleaded Nige when Nina objected. 'England are playing Germany.'

Mills went to her room on the pretext of looking for the e-mails from Sarah, sat on her bed and cried. After fifteen minutes of feeling sorry for herself, she washed her face, switched on her laptop and threw herself into work, as she always did in such circumstances. She pushed the door closed to reduce the increasing level of noise coming from downstairs – the football, it seemed, was becoming more exciting. Sarah had sent a vast amount of information: several documents on the Kilnsey sow kiln plus reports of the survey carried out on the Langcliffe quarry. Photographs in that report had been supplemented by a number that she had taken herself – in total over twenty files. Mills was finally interrupted by a call from below. Jake was leaving.

'Thanks, Jake. For the lift... and everything,' she called from the landing.

He appeared at the bottom of the stairs. 'That's OK. It's what friends are for.'

She could tell by his voice that England had lost.

Back in her room, there was an e-mail message from her father to call. She turned on her phone and deleted further messages from Phil.

'Dad?'

'Yes. Fiona wants to speak to you.' He put the phone down with a crash and Mills waited for a few seconds.

'Millie? It's Fiona.'

'Yes, Fiona?'

'Just to confirm arrangements for next Friday. I've booked...'

Mills let her chatter on, making a note of the train times.

'... so it will be just us girls that evening... then lunch with your dad...'

Finally the arrangements were complete, Fiona said goodbye and handed her back to her father.

'Hi, Dad. How are you?'

'Bearing up, considering.'

'What's the matter?'

'Just the wedding. I'll be glad when it's all over.'

Mills could hear Fiona chastising him in the background.

'I'm sure you'll love every minute, Dad,' she lied. 'I know I will.'

'You fraudster!' he replied. 'Anyway, see you next week.'

Mills went back to the reports but she was exhausted, finding she was looking at the pages but not absorbing the information. So she turned to the photographs of the quarry. There were shots of derelict buildings, rocky outcrops and views from above the workings. Most were looking into the quarry but some were across the caravans, and over into Grassington Wood. A few had figures in, some were part of the investigation but one or two looked like holiday makers out for a stroll from the caravan site.

One picture was taken along the side of the quarry with the escarpment in the background but what caught her eye was the tiny figure of a dog running free in the distance. It looked like a small terrier, very dark and difficult to determine at such a distance. Zooming in helped a little but eventually the picture went out of focus and pixellated. Mills moved the cursor around the photograph and spotted other figures, bigger but camouflaged by the trees. There was a man and a woman. The man had his head turned, as if he was calling the dog, but the woman was looking towards the camera. They were a couple because they were holding hands but she seemed to be hanging back. As Mills zoomed out they were reduced to insignificant figures in the background again.

Something made Mills zoom back in to stare at the woman again. It was difficult to make out her expression but the way her hair framed her face struck a chord. She repeatedly zoomed in and out, even using a magnifying glass to look closer, but the face went out of focus and blurred. There was nothing familiar about the man, but the woman...

Mills went to bed but lay with the lamp on, going over the scene with Claudia, imagining how it might have played out differently – with her remaining in the cottage with Phil, not Claudia. But it was not in her nature to feel sorry for herself for long. Instead of replying to Phil's numerous calls, she deleted them and switched off the light. She turned over and thought about the photograph of the mysterious couple walking their dog at Langcliffe quarry. She was not going to be able to enlarge the faces without losing definition unless Sarah had a better picture than the one she had received.

Mills was up again at dawn. She was woken by the front door closing and the sound of a car door slamming. She walked quietly over to the window to see Nina driving slowly up the road. It was unusual but not unknown for her to be called out early so Mills went back to bed with her laptop to take another look at the photographs, expecting Rosie to be awake soon enough. It was easier to see in daylight and, at the highest magnification possible without blurring the features, she could see the thick red hair framing the woman's pale face. She took a photograph out of her drawer and compared it to the screen. It seemed incredible but the woman at Langcliffe quarry was the double of the girl in the wedding photograph. She checked again the date at the bottom of the screen. It looked like Georgina O'Neill but if it was, it had been taken after she had disappeared.

Chapter 9

'Can I get you a coffee? You look as if you need it.'

Phil bumped into Brenda as she sailed through the office door. He dumped his bag, followed her to the kitchen and stood watching her make the coffee.

'There, get that down you. You look terrible.'

'Thanks Brenda.'

'Looks like you've been overdoing it young man.'

He carried his mug back to his desk, avoiding any further conversation while he read his e-mails, dealing with the easy ones, leaving messages that required any effort.

'Well, I had a lovely weekend thank you.' Brenda was beaming across the room at him. 'Do you want to know why?'

Phil thought, I expect you'll tell me anyway, and remained seated with his back to her.

'Well, on Friday I did a complete re-examination of the dust from the Persian rug. And guess what I found?' She waited but when there was no response she continued, 'I found animal hair. At first I wasn't sure but then I knew it was definitely a dog hair.'

'One hair?' He turned round to face her.

'So far. But one can be enough.'

'Can you tell what breed it is?'

'Not yet but it is possible using DNA. In fact I'm sending it over to your girlfriend this afternoon.'

'Girlfriend?'

'The fragrant Claudia.'

'Look, there's nothing...'

'Really? Is that so? That's not what I've heard.'

He studied her expression. 'What have you heard, Brenda?'

'Only what she tells me, Phil. Only what she tells me.'

Her phone rang and he turned back to hunch over his keyboard, waiting until Brenda left the room so he could call Claudia's laboratory.

'Hold on, let me find a pen. Give me the details slowly.' Brenda's tone had changed immediately to one that was capable and efficient. 'Where? What time? Where are you now?'

Phil listened, anticipating an explanation at the end of the call. He was not disappointed.

'There was an attempted murder over in Richmond last night,' she said as she began collecting her things together. 'The girl is in hospital but they've got the scene taped off. I'm going over now. Sounds like she's in a bad way.' She was making for the door. 'He was disturbed while he was beating her to death. They may save her life but still it's touch and go apparently.' She was about to leave when she stepped back. 'The envelope on the desk... if you could...' and she was gone.

Phil went over to inspect the brown envelope addressed to Bishop Laboratories. He reached for the phone and dialled the number.

Mills was waiting when Rosie woke at six-thirty, keeping her happily occupied until Nige was up, so they could have breakfast together. It was already warm in the little yard at the back of the house so she let Rosie play outside, reading to her when the toddler became bored playing on her own.

By seven fifteen all three were seated at the table eating cereal.

'Where was Nina off to so early this morning?' Mills finally asked.

'She was on call. They needed a woman officer present.'

'Why was that?'

'Don't know. Perhaps they've got a woman in custody. It'll be something like that.' He was busy buttering toast for his daughter. 'She'll be back later.'

When Jake arrived to take her into work, he and Nige continued their conversation about the trip to Malham Moor. They debated what they needed to do to survey the area and soon they were in deep discussion about the pros and cons of using ground penetrating radar and resistivity measurements.

'Will you be all right if we get off, Nige?' she asked eventually. 'I've got a lecture to give in half an hour.'

In the car Jake asked if she had any support to help with the survey they had been discussing.

'No. Nothing. Will it cost much?'

'Not a lot. It's only our time and the hire of the equipment really. Time isn't the issue but if you've not got any funds for equipment I can cover the hire charge for you.'

'And how will *you* find the money?'

'They gave me a grant for the exchange fellowship in the USA. It covers a year over there plus my first year back here. I don't need it all, there's too much to be honest.'

She was stuck for words. 'Of course I'll include your name on any reports,' she offered.

He laughed. 'No problem. It'll be fun.'

Mills felt relief. There was no reason why they shouldn't work together whenever they liked, now that Phil was... now there was no Phil anymore.

'Anyway,' he continued, 'it's a rehabilitation exercise for Nige. Did you see how animated he was this morning?'

Nina had been seated outside intensive care since six, waiting to hear whether she could speak to the victim. The girl had been in theatre for several hours overnight and it was unlikely she would ever regain consciousness but her boss, Mitch, wanted her to stay there, just in case. The corridor was familiar to her, she recognised some of the staff as they changed shift and the staff nurse greeted her like a long lost friend, asking how Nige was progressing. She nodded sympathetically when Nina explained that his physical recovery was complete but mentally...

Finally she received a call from Mitch to say they had a provisional identification of the girl. They were bringing her mother down for confirmation. As Nina waited she thought about how she would feel if she heard that Rosie had been attacked and was in hospital fighting for her life. You're a police officer, she told herself, and it's not professional to have such thoughts. But when Hazel arrived with the mother, Nina could imagine exactly what the poor woman was going through.

Fortunately the staff nurse was there to explain the girl's injuries, which were extensive. She had a cracked skull and there was pressure on her brain that they were trying to relieve. Fortunately the attacker was disturbed by a member of the public and so an ambulance arrived within minutes, otherwise she would have died at the scene.

The woman stood looking down at her daughter's limp body. Nina watched a single tear run down her face unchecked.

'Yes, that's our Kelly,' was all she said.

'I'm sorry, Mrs Lewis. It must be a shock for you.'

'I were so worried when she weren't home,' she said slowly. 'She's never later than she says. That's why I rang the police.'

Nina left the nursing staff to explain Kelly's medical condition. She'll want to be with her daughter now, thought Nina. Although she really needed to find out as much as she could about Kelly immediately.

Hazel went off, returning with two cheese baguettes. 'Sorry, it's all they had downstairs. D'you want one?'

'Yes, thanks. I'm starving. So what's new?'

'Mitch interviewed the guy who disturbed the attack. Nice man. He was on the main road into town, on his bike. He heard a commotion and thought it was kids messing about in the supermarket car park. Fortunately being a good citizen he went up to tick them off and saw the man leaving the scene. He didn't get a good look because he was more concerned for the victim. He rang for the ambulance and tried to reduce the bleeding until they arrived.'

'Did the SOCOs find anything?'

'They've got forensics at the scene but they won't report until tomorrow at the earliest. Apparently they found some hair in Kelly's hand so they're looking at that.'

'Is it just her mother... I mean, is there a father?' asked Nina.

'No. It must be hard. She seems to be coping but it must be awful...'

'I daren't think about it. Imagine if...'

They sat side by side staring at the wall opposite, eating their breakfast in silence.

Finally, when she had finished, Hazel told Nina that Mitch had left them to handle the preliminary interview with Mrs Lewis, telling them to find out as much as possible about the girl: who her friends were, where she went, what she did and what a fifteen year old was doing out so late on her own... and before a school day.

The three women sat awkwardly in the staff nurse's office. Hazel offered Mrs Lewis tea or coffee but she was fine, thank you. Nina could see that she was holding it together... just, so she trod carefully, keeping the tone matter of fact and unemotional.

'Thank you for helping us, Mrs Lewis. We want to get as clear a picture of Kelly as we can – so we can do the best job possible to find the assailant.'

She nodded. Nina was unsure whether it meant she understood or agreed with their aims. She continued. 'So what sort of girl is Kelly? What does she like to do? Who are her friends?'

The woman didn't answer at first. Then she cleared her throat. Her voice had an unnaturally high pitch, charged with emotion. 'I've been thinking about that, ever since your mate said that's what you wanted. I don't rightly know. She goes to school. She's got mates there. She goes into town with them, shopping and nights out like. But I can't say as that I know her friends right well, or exactly where she goes or what she does.'

Nina made a few notes, waiting for Mrs Lewis to continue.

'You must think that's not being a good mother but I've got three kids and she's the oldest. The others take so much time that I let her get on with things like. She's always home by the time she says. Her friends that come round seem nice enough.'

'Does she have a boyfriend?' Hazel asked.

'Depends what you call boyfriend. They go round in a crowd these days, girls and lads. I don't think there's a boyfriend like *you* mean – not a special lad.'

'So do you know who she was with last night?'

'No. I've been trying to think. She said she were going to the pictures. Usually they'll be a crowd of them. I thought she were with her mates.'

'Could you give us a list of her friends... the ones you know?' asked Nina.

'Aye.' She took the notepad and scribbled five names. 'They're her friends from school. Girls in her class.'

Nina noted down the school and Kelly's class number.

'So to summarise, Mrs Lewis,' Hazel began, 'you think that Kelly went to the cinema in Richmond and was on her way home when she was attacked?'

'I suppose so but I can't understand why she weren't with her mates.'

'Does Kelly have a computer?' asked Hazel.

'Aye, of course.'

'Do you think she may have people she meets on the internet?'

Nina felt her friend should have been more sensitive. She watched the woman's face as it changed from puzzlement to real concern. 'Do you think she met someone in a chat room?'

'We don't know, do we?' Hazel was keeping matter-of-fact. 'We have to look at every possibility. We'll need to look at her computer though.'

When they had finished, Hazel accompanied Mrs Lewis to the ward to sit with her daughter and Nina rang Mitch to tell him that she had the names of Kelly's friends.

'You need to talk to them as soon as possible. Someone must have seen her last night,' Mitch said, 'They might be able to throw some light on whether Kelly knew the man.'

When Hazel returned they sat in the corridor drinking coffee.

'...so I'm going straight to the school. Will you be here all day?' asked Nina

'Mitch told me to get statements from the other witnesses. There were a few lads outside the pub across the road that saw the man run off. I guess they'll be at work – I'll arrange to see them this evening.'

'So you get the short straw.'

'Don't worry, girl, I think you've got the worst job. Teenage girls? Rather you than me any day.'

Nina drove directly from the hospital to the school and watched from the gates as pupils moved around the building, crawling like ants along corridors to their classrooms. Eventually, when the activity had subsided, she walked across the playground and entered the school in search of the administrator. They ushered her into the library, bringing her a coffee while they searched out the girls on her list.

All five arrived together, muted and polite until she began to ask them about Kelly. They immediately began bombarding her with questions, expressing concern and disbelief at what had happened to their friend. Eventually Nina was able to establish that two of the girls had been with Kelly that evening and she decided to let the others go reluctantly back to their classroom.

'And you are?'

'Josie, Josie Smart.'

Josie was a tall, thin girl with bleached blonde hair hanging down in her eyes. Her gaunt look was accentuated by the use of smoky eye shadow and black mascara.

'Melissa Carpenter,' replied the other girl, who was plumper, with short dark hair that looked naturally curly.

'And you were with Kelly last night?'

'Yes,' they answered in unison.

'We met at the cinema,' said Melissa.

'And was it just you three?'

'Yes just us,' replied Josie.

'So what did you see?' Nina asked, poised to note down the film on her pad.

'Oh, we didn't go in. Kelly couldn't afford it.'

'So what did you do?'

'We walked up into town and wandered about a bit, didn't we Mel?'

'Yes. We ended up in 'Spoons, until it was time to go home.'

'She means Wetherspoons,' explained Josie. 'It's the pub called "The Ralph Fitz Randal". Bit of a mouthful.'

'What time was that?'

'About ten. The last bus is just after ten-thirty. So we had to go.'

'And what did Kelly do?'

Josie shrugged. 'Waited for her bus I s'pose.'

'Where exactly did you leave her?'

Melissa suddenly burst into tears. 'In the square,' she sobbed. 'We shouldn't have left her, should we?'

Josie put her arm round her friend but said nothing to reassure her. Nina could sense that the girl was close to tears herself.

She took a deep breath. 'I need to know if she had any special friends, boyfriends? Anyone she might have been meeting in Richmond?'

They both shook their heads.

'Is it possible she met any of your friends after you left her?'

They shrugged and shook their heads again.

'Will we be able to visit her?' Melissa asked, through her sobs.

'Perhaps later. She's still very poorly. I'll need you both to make a formal statement but we'll arrange that with your parents obviously. And, if there's anything you think of just call me. OK?'

They both smiled weakly and nodded.

Nina reported to Mitch Turner as soon as she got back to Newby Wiske. Attempted rape was always taken seriously but the threat to the girl's life meant it was potentially a murder investigation and she could feel the atmosphere throughout the building. Hazel was back in the office busy on the phone. Kelly was apparently stable but they were keeping her sedated until at least the following day.

'There's no point in sitting there if she's unconscious,' said Hazel, between calls.

The lecture had not gone particularly well, Mills felt. There were a number of empty seats, always a problem on a Monday morning, and the subject was not one she was particularly comfortable with. The students had little interest in statistical analysis, so everyone was relieved when it was time to vacate the lecture theatre. There was already a group of students gathering at the door in anticipation of the next lecture, which Jake would be taking. Mills fought her way through the crowd, along the corridor to the lift.

She carried a coffee from the cafeteria up to the office, aware she had just fifty minutes before Jake would be back at his desk.

There was no answer but she left a message and eventually April rang back. Mills was curious about her relationship with Tim O'Neill but needed an excuse to see if she would admit it.

'Oh hi, April. I just wanted to catch up. Thank you for bringing me the postcard. I rang to see if there was anything else you wanted to tell me. I mean, that might have occurred to you, like after we last spoke.'

Mills was grateful her blushes were invisible to April.

There was a brief silence, then, 'I'm glad you rang actually because Mum reminded me about Enrico. I'd forgotten all about him.'

'Enrico?'

'He was Spanish. Georgie went out with him for a while. It was ages before she met Tim. I said to Mum, she must have been seventeen when he was around. Anyway, Mum thought I should tell you about him, because of his behaviour.'

'Behaviour?'

'He was much older than her – in his twenties. Rather posh. He got very jealous. And when she went to university she finished with him.'

'What happened?'

'Well, nothing really. He wrote letters, kept ringing. He used to visit Mum, to see if she could persuade Georgie to go back to him. She was quite upset at the time. He could be quite... assertive.'

'Did he threaten her, or Georgina?'

'I don't think so. Just rather pushy. Anyway, Mum thought I should tell you.'

'Yes, thank you. Do you know where he is now?'

'I've got the address where he was at the time.'

Mills made a note of Enrico's full name and address. It was only when she had put the phone down that she realised she had not asked April about her relationship with Tim.

Next she wanted to use the large magnifying camera in the teaching laboratory. Practicals always took place in the afternoon so she hoped she would be unobserved. Taking the postcard, she walked self-consciously down the corridor, unlocking the door of the undergraduate teaching room. Switching the instrument on, she placed the postcard underneath with the picture facing up. It took her a while to locate the tiny sheep in the centre of view but when she found it she was amazed at the magnification. The tiny dot almost filled the screen but now it had taken on a weird perspective. It no longer resembled a sheep or cow; it was square, almost headless, like a Mackenzie Thorpe sheep, flat with two black legs and a square eye. She pressed a button, waited for the copy to appear, then turned off the power.

'I've taken the liberty of booking the equipment for Wednesday. I looked at the lecture schedule and your name didn't appear.' Jake was back in the office when she returned.

'No, that's fine but don't forget it will depend on Nina's shifts,' she replied, quickly stuffing the paperwork into her desk drawer.

'We can chat with Nige and Nina tonight to plan the campaign. It may take several days.'

'I've got to go to London on Friday.'

'That's all right. You don't have to be there.'

Mills hesitated and Jake laughed.

'Your face. It's a picture! Don't worry, we won't do anything without you in control. You're the boss on this one.'

'You are kidding! All leave is cancelled and I'll probably be on call when I'm not on shift.'

Nina had come home to find Nige and Rosie tired but happy, having spent the day in the park with a picnic. That was fine but she had the meal to prepare plus the ironing, otherwise she would have nothing to wear the next day.

Jake and Mills were looking sheepish, while Nige sat with a sulky expression. She had to smile.

'What?' asked Nige.

'Nothing love. Jake, would you help me in the kitchen? Nige, I need you to iron my blouse for tomorrow... and Rosie's dungarees.'

'I'll give her an early bath if you like,' offered Mills.

'Thanks. That's what I call teamwork,' Nina called as she followed Jake into the kitchen.

'So there's no chance of taking Nige away on Wednesday?' Jake asked as he chopped onions.

'I can't see how. Who is going to look after Rosie if I'm at work?'

Jake scraped the onions off the board into the frying pan. 'I suppose she could come with us,' he said, without turning round.

Nina didn't respond immediately. She was protective of her daughter but knew that Nige needed something practical to do to get him kick-started. He'd been so much better over the past few weeks now that Jake was keeping him involved in university life.

'Mills will make sure she's all right,' he continued. 'Rosie's got her own seat in the car and we can take her food. She'll like a day out. Look how much she enjoyed the picnic today.'

'I'll think about it, Jake...'

'Great!'

'...but I'm not making any promises, mind.'

Just forty minutes later Rosie was in her pyjamas, the ironing was done and Nina was serving supper. Any discussion of Wednesday was avoided after Jake had quietly informed the others that Nina was considering allowing Rosie to accompany them.

'So, Mills, you're off on Friday then?' Nina asked.

'Yes, I'm taking the train in the afternoon.'

'Where are going?' asked Nige.

'Back home to see my Dad,' Mills replied, although of course it wasn't home. She'd be going to Fiona's flat in Canary Wharf.

'She's going to try on her bridesmaid's dress.' Nina was smiling.

'What's so funny about it?' Nige asked.

'It's not funny, love. It just seems odd to think of Mills in a fancy purple dress, that's all.'

'You'll have to bring us a photo,' Jake said. 'When's the wedding?'

'July the twenty-fourth. Dad insisted it was after the World Cup had finished.'

'It'll be a big occasion, I guess. Presumably Fiona will want the works?' Nina was clearing the table.

'Oh yes. A pretty big affair. They're holding it in a hotel near her parent's place. Apparently it's massive.'

'Mills, can you help me get Rosie into bed?' Nina wanted to ask Mills whether it was a good idea to let her daughter go with them to Wharfedale. When they were alone she expressed her concerns.

'If you're not sure, we'll not go, Nina. We'll find another time.'

Nina could tell she was disappointed. 'Will you promise to keep an eye on her?'

'Of course. The boys will be doing all the work, so I can look after her full-time.'

'OK then.'

They crept out of the nursery and stood whispering on the landing.

'Nina, can I ask you something? It's about the missing woman, Georgina O'Neill.'

'Mills...'

'It's just that I've got a photo taken after she disappeared that looks like her. What should I do?'

'What photo?'

Mills fetched the photograph of the quarry from her bedroom and pointed to the woman in the background. 'It looks just like her,' she insisted.

'Seriously?' Nina examined the tiny figure. 'I'm sorry, but it could be anyone, Mills. Anyone at all. I'd get laughed out of the force if I showed them this. I'm sorry.'

Chapter 10

Brenda was pondering over the wording of her report when Phil came into the office, taking a seat at his desk without a word. She shrugged and carried on typing her final conclusions in the form of a list. The fibres from the rug are high in copper, consistent with wool from the region. This leads to the conclusion that it is a Heriz rug. Unfortunately this type of rug is quite common but no two designs are identical, so there is potential to find the buyer if the source is located. Dust found on the rug led to no obvious leads except for the dog hair which is being tested for DNA, which could provide information on the breed. Wonderful, Brenda thought, so all we need now is a thorough search of all houses and flats in the country for Persian rugs and a particular breed of dog.

She picked up the phone. 'Just ringing your girlfriend, Phil. Any messages?'

She heard a grunt but he didn't turn round.

'Can I speak to Claudia please? It's Brenda. She's got some DNA results for me, I hope.'

There was silence. No fancy music, just what sounded like a photocopier rattling in the background.

'Brenda, lovely to speak to you. How can I help you?'

'I wondered if you've got anything for me on the dog hair yet?'

'Really sorry about the wait. My people have been a bit stumped by the identification and we've had to pass it over to a private consultant. It's not a regular breed, that's for sure.'

'How long before we get an answer?'

'Can't be more than a day or two, I would imagine. They're very good.'

'Oh well, hopefully if it's a rare breed...'

'Exactly, Brenda. And while you're on the phone. We've been working on the other hair sample.'

'Other hair sample?'

'The one from the attack in Richmond.'

'Gosh, that's fast work. I didn't expect anything back so soon.'

'No, don't get me wrong, we haven't got any final results yet. It's just that the first set of results was, well, confusing. I just thought I'd let you know, so you're warned. I'm trying to get them done ASAP. I'll call you tomorrow.'

'Thanks, Claudia, that's really helpful. I'll speak to you about both sets of results again tomorrow.'

Brenda dialled Newby Wiske.

'Mitch?'

'No I'm sorry, he'll be back at ten. Can I help?'

'Can you give him a message, please? Tell him I'm sorry but the DNA on the hair has been delayed. I'll call tomorrow.'

'Certainly.' Nina put down the phone and scribbled a note. She was trying to compile a description of Kelly's attacker before the team meeting and had several reports in front of her, some of which conflicted. The man on the bike that had interrupted the attack was sure that the man was stocky with thin hair. The lads from the pub had obviously discussed their ideas and come up with a uniform view: he was medium height and build, with short hair. No-one had a good view of his face but they did agree that he was wearing a round necked sweater and denim jeans.

Someone thought he was wearing trainers. There wasn't a lot to go on.

Hazel arrived back from the hospital to report that Kelly remained unconscious and her mother was still with her.

'That poor woman.'

'I know, I asked if she would come in to see Mitch today but she wasn't happy leaving her daughter.'

Nina returned to her report until ten when Mitch arrived for the team conference. Hazel told them about her interviews with the lads from the pub and Nina showed them the description she had compiled.

'What about the school friends, Nina?' Mitch asked. 'We need something to start working on. So far we've got nowt.'

Nina picked up the statements. The girls had looked pale when they came in with their parents to give formal accounts of the evening. They repeated what they had told her the day before, but she was prepared with a few more questions.

'Kelly was in town with two friends, Melissa and Josie. They wandered about, ending up in Wetherspoons. They left her in the town centre when they got their bus to Catterick at thirty-six minutes past ten. She was going in the other direction towards Skeeby.'

'What time was Kelly's bus?'

'At twenty-four minutes past ten, but it hadn't come in by the time their bus left.'

'Well she didn't get on it.' Mitch paced up and down the office in his usual manner. He turned suddenly. 'See what you can get from the CCTV. There must be plenty of footage from the middle of town.'

'Let's hope the forensics on the hair gives us something.' Hazel stood up. 'Is that it, Guv? Only I need to get on with the paperwork.'

Nina was reminded of the message from Brenda and told Mitch that the forensics had been delayed.

'Damn. We need that DNA now – otherwise I can't see this case going anywhere.'

Despite careful planning, Wednesday morning began in chaos. As soon as Jake arrived, Rosie stopped eating her breakfast ignoring all Nina's attempts at persuasion. Eventually she allowed her daughter out of her sight, only if she was accompanied by a piece of toast. The plan was for them to use Nige's car but by the time they had transferred all the equipment that Jake had brought, there was no space in the back for Rosie's baby seat.

'It's no good,' Nina said, irritably, 'you'll just have to take both cars.'

'Is that all right?' Mills asked Jake quietly when they were alone.

'No problem, but you'd better go with Nige to show him the way.'

They left in convoy with Jake in the lead. Nige followed with Mills beside him and Rosie strapped in the back, playing with her toast.

It was too early to tell what the weather had in store; there was a mist over the hills that gradually disappeared as they entered the dales. The roads were clear once they reached Ripon and, as usual, Mills felt the tension leaving the muscles in her neck. She sensed that Nige's mood was affected in the same way: he had switched on the local radio station and was whistling along to the music.

Jake was waiting for them when they parked by the gate to the moor. Rosie was emerging from sleep slowly, rubbing her cheek where a red patch was slowly fading. She was lifted gently from the car by her dad, who loaded her expertly into a carrier that he hauled onto his back. The three of them struggled with the heavy equipment, making slow progress to the field Mills had targeted.

'First things first, Mills,' began Jake. 'You *have* got written permission for this from the owner, I presume.'

Mills didn't answer at first. She could feel the colour rising in her face. 'Oh crap.'

Nige started laughing. 'What has Auntie Millie forgotten, Rosie? What a silly auntie you've got!' He tickled his daughter until she was giggling with him.

'I'm sorry. I didn't think... Aargh...' she groaned.

'Not to worry. There's a farm down there.' Jake pointed towards Bordley. 'I'll go down and see if they can help.'

'I'll come with you,' Mills offered.

'No, it'll be quicker if I run.' He set off down the field at breakneck speed.

'I feel so stupid...'

But Nige interrupted her. 'Not to worry. It's not like you do this sort of investigative work often. We're always having to get permission forms completed. We can start setting up the instruments.'

'But what if he...'

'What? Doesn't get permission? Of course he will. Jake will sort it out, he always does. Brilliant is Jake, isn't he Rosie?' He picked up the toddler, swinging her round until she squealed with delight. Then he handed her over to Mills while he began unpacking the radar equipment.

Half an hour later, Jake returned waving a piece of paper. 'No problem provided we don't plan to do any digging without speaking to him first. I didn't have a form so I wrote out the wording and he signed it. I told him we'd let him know the outcome.'

Mills left them setting up the instruments, taking Rosie for a little walk round the field. There was something relaxing about moving at a toddler's pace; stopping frequently to stare at a flower or pick up a stone, turning it over, keeping it clutched in a hand or tossing it away for something more interesting. On their return journey, by the gate into the next field, they spotted a brown object, not a small boulder but a hedgehog lying in the sunshine. At first Mills thought it must be dead but there was a faint rhythmical movement that suggested it was fast asleep, quite vulnerable as it lay uncurled in the long grass. She held Rosie's hand as she explained what it was, told her about the prickles, wishing she could remember the story of Mrs Tiggywinkle.

Nige was in his element, shouting instructions to Jake, cracking jokes and smiling broadly most of the time. 'Try another run,' he called to Jake as his friend paced across the field and back. Then they were huddled over the laptop discussing the quality of the signal.

'Righto,' Nige said finally, standing up and stretching his legs. 'We'll start at the top and work down systematically. That way we won't be making any assumptions about the area. OK?'

'Whatever you say, Nige!' Jake winked at Mills. She smiled and nodded, picking Rosie up and carrying her over to the shade of the wall. It was getting hot and, although Rosie was smothered in sunscreen, Mills had received strict instructions from

Nina to keep the child out of the sun. She sat making a daisy chain watching her friends gradually progress across the field. When they reached half-way she suggested lunch. Rosie had a marmite sandwich followed by a banana while the rest of them ate the thick cheese rolls Mills had prepared, washed down with cans of beer that Jake had thoughtfully provided. She settled Rosie on a blanket, watching her until she fell into a sound sleep.

'Nige, d'you think she'll be all right here for a while? I'd like to pop down to the quarry for a quick look round. I'll only be about half an hour.'

'No problem. She'll be asleep for at least an hour; she always is after lunch.' He handed her the car keys.

She wanted to look at the place where the photograph had been taken with Georgina a tiny speck in the background. She thought she knew where it was, to the east of the quarry itself, on the path circumnavigating the huge scar that rose above the long drop to the workings below. She left the car, walking quickly across the field through the gate past the quarry entrance. The path curved left past the seat where she and Phil had sat overlooking the caravan site. She pushed on uphill until she was in the exact spot. Pulling out the folded page she smoothed the creases and held the picture up to compare, scrutinising each feature in turn. Georgina would have been in the distance. The little group must have been walking down the hill, heading towards the road between Kilnsey and Grassington... but where had they come from?

Aware that she had to be quick, after a few moments reflection she ran back to the car. At first she couldn't see Nige or Jake as she walked into the field but once she had reached the brow of the hill she spotted them huddled in the corner by the gate. She could hear Rosie crying. Nige was rocking her gently, talking quietly to her.

Mills ran over, nearly falling on the rough ground.

'What's happened, what's the matter?'

'It was the nasty hedgehog, wasn't it?' Nige said in the baby voice he used with his daughter.

'She found a hedgehog, look.' Jake pointed out the closely curled ball that the hedgehog had become.

'Oh, we saw it this morning,' Mills admitted, 'I showed it to her.'

'It must have made an impression,' said Nige. 'We looked up and she was over here playing with it.'

'Oh, no. Is she covered with fleas?' Mills examined the girl's arms and legs.

'No, she's fine,' said Nige, 'She's not hurt. She's just cross she can't carry on playing.'

He carried her back to the shade, where they sat until Rosie had calmed down. Mills apologised for neglecting his daughter.

'Don't worry, no harm done. Just don't tell Nina, please.'

Mills sat with Rosie for the rest of the afternoon, watching the boys make gradual progress across the field. They had passed the depression that most interested Mills without any comment but, as they explained to her, they wouldn't know the results of the measurements until they processed the data.

'How long will that take?' she had asked.

'A day or two,' Nige had said. 'You have to be patient.'

*

'Nina!' Hazel had greeted her in the hallway at Newby Wiske. 'We're to organise a reconstruction. Mitch has had the go-ahead to run it on Sunday.'

'Why? Oh no, has she died?'

'No, no change, but they want to jog people's memories, so they're re-enacting Kelly's movements at the exact time they happened last Sunday.'

They spent the morning liaising with the manager of the pub and the bus company staff to ensure that as far as possible the same people would be available to take part in the reconstruction. Josie and Melissa were contacted via the school to ensure they would be available and a third friend, Tanya, had been identified, who had not been with them at the time but looked similar to Kelly, in that she was slim, quite tall and had straight blonde hair.

The CCTV recordings arrived at lunch time. Hazel took the market square and Nina studied the footage outside "The Ralph Fitz Randal". They sat side by side in the tiny room that was set up for the purpose, watching in silence, speeding up, slowing down and rewinding until Hazel announced she had reached the point when the girls arrived to get their buses. Nina fast forwarded until she reached the same time frame and then backed up until she spotted the group leaving the pub.

'There they are, just coming out. Ten twenty-eight.'

'In the square at ten thirty, no thirty one,' Hazel added.

Nina was puzzled. 'That means Kelly's bus would have already gone. It was due at ten twenty-four. Can you go back and look for it?'

There was silence then, 'Damn, I can't see the numbers.'

'Don't worry for now. We've got confirmation of them leaving "The Ralph Fitz Randal" and getting to the square.' Nina, who had half an eye on the film as it ran on, spotted a familiar figure again. 'Hang on... There she is again. She's back at the pub at ten forty. What have you got?'

Hazel's speech was unnaturally slow as she concentrated on the action in front of her. 'She's standing looking lost, the bus with the others on has left. She's gone over to someone... now she's heading back in the direction of King Street.'

'What time?'

'Ten thirty-eight.'

'So she goes back down to the pub and inside.' It was Nina's turn to pause while she waited for the next sighting. 'Here she is... on her own... no, hang on... a man's joined her.'

'Where did *he* come from?'

'Inside.'

'Can you see his face, Nina?'

'No.'

'Damn.'

'He's going to cross the road... she's following him!'

'Time?'

'Ten forty-five. It must be him, Hazel. He came out of the "The Ralph Fitz Randal". He must have been in there all the time.'

'Doesn't mean he's the attacker unless he's identified as the man running away.' Hazel was already on the phone to Mitch.

'Do we have CCTV from that area?' he asked.

'Unfortunately not. Guv, we've got the girl placed back at the "The Ralph Fitz Randal"after her friends have left. She's with a man... going off with him...' A pause. 'Yes, yes, we're onto it, straight away.' She turned to Nina. 'We're to get it all written up, then push on with the reconstruction. It's even more important now. We must get that man back in the pub on Sunday evening. The latest from the hospital is not looking good.'

'Brenda, good morning!'

'Claudia, how nice to hear from you.' There was no mistaking Claudia's telephone voice. 'Do you have something for me at last?'

'Yes. The dog hair. We've managed to identify the breed. It's a mudi.'

'A moody what?'

'Mudi.' She spelled it out. 'It's a sort of Hungarian hound. I'll fax you the details.'

'Great, thanks.' Brenda scribbled on her notepad.

'Now.' Her tone had become serious. 'There's something else. Something I should warn you about...'

It was unlike Brenda to act in an impulsive manner but when she heard what Claudia had to say... the conversation became so bizarre... well, she'd slammed the phone down in the end. It was so ridiculous she was sure it could be sorted out over a cup of coffee. 'Could you repeat that last sentence?' she had asked initially. *I have a match for the hair at the attack in Richmond on Sunday night. It belongs to Phil Freedman.* 'Our Phil Freedman?' she had asked.

It was clearly a mistake, a cock-up over samples, contamination or some other strange phenomenon. Her first instinct was to sort it out before it blew out of all proportion, which was why she was travelling at sixty miles an hour across country to see the woman face to face. She had to reach Bishop

Laboratories before Claudia did something stupid. Her plan had been to discuss the methodology used, discover where the error had occurred, to laugh about it over a cup of coffee and return to base with the matter sorted. That was not how it happened.

'I'm sorry Brenda. I really don't think I should discuss the matter with you. It's nothing personal but he is your colleague. It wouldn't be appropriate.'

'So what *do* you plan to do, Claudia?'

'I have put the matter in the hands of the police officers dealing with the case. I'm finalising the report now, ready to fax off to them this afternoon.'

'You know this must be an error, contaminated evidence. Surely you can see that?'

'I've checked and double-checked. You know it upsets me as much as it does you. He's a good friend. It's very difficult.'

'Then at least let me help you find the reason that you've got this match. Where is the hair sample?'

'Sorry, it's too late. It's up to the police to decide what to do with it now.'

Chapter 11

Brenda was not rolling over and giving up on her colleague, so when she was politely shown the door by Claudia Bishop she sat in the car using her analytical skills to evaluate the situation in a logical fashion. If the match on the hair was flawed it would be shown up by other more compelling evidence, such as the witnesses' descriptions of the assailant or a strong alibi. Of course, in situations where there are no reliable witnesses or alibis, the forensic evidence is the only tool. Brenda knew this only too well and was worried. She straightened herself up in her seat, started the engine to set off for Newby Wiske.

'I wanted a word with Inspector Turner but apparently he's not available?'

The woman who had barged into the office looked as if she had just come from her allotment. She was wearing baggy beige shorts and a man's polo shirt in an unflattering shade of maroon. She looked about fifty but Nina thought she could be younger or maybe even older.

'I'm sorry. He won't be back until after lunch. Is it something *I* can help you with?'

'And you are?'

'DS Featherstone, Nina Featherstone.' The woman was brusque but Nina liked dealing with people who were straightforward, no beating about the bush. She offered her hand to the woman, who shook it vigorously.

'We've spoken on the phone a few times. I'm Brenda... from forensics.'

'Hi, it's nice to meet you at last.'

'Hmm.'

'Is it about the attack in Richmond? He'll be back later if you want to...'

Brenda sank down on a desk. 'Could I have a coffee? I came without having one and it's been a horrible morning so far.'

Nina left her alone while she went off to the canteen. By the time she returned, Brenda was standing by her desk, peering down at her report.

'Here you are! That will help, although it's from our cafeteria so it's nothing special.' She threw down the individual cartons of milk and packets of sugar on top of her papers.

Brenda hauled herself back onto the desk without any embarrassment. 'I'll have it black thanks.'

Nina sipped her coffee in silence for a few moments and then tried again. 'So, was there something about the attack that you wanted to discuss?'

The woman peered at her over her glasses until Nina felt uncomfortable.

'How familiar are you with the case?'

Now the woman was beginning to annoy her. 'Very. I'm organising a reconstruction... as you saw from my notes.' She indicated the papers on her desk.

The woman appeared to have sensed her irritation because she smiled apologetically as she asked her next question.

'So you don't have much to go on at the moment?'

'We've got CCTV.'

'Great, is there a good view of the attacker?'

'Unfortunately not. Not enough to identify him.'

'Witnesses?'

'Yes, some lads saw him run off but it was quite dark and...'

'Can I speak to you in confidence, Nina?'

She nodded, unable to imagine what the woman might want. Even when Nina went over it in her head, it was difficult to assimilate. It all started very oddly because the first thing Brenda had asked was, did she know Phil Freedman? And she didn't know Phil because she didn't know his name was Freedman, why should she? So it began all wrong. The woman spent ages telling her about this colleague called Phil Freedman who shared her office and how the hair that was taken from Kelly's hand was a perfect match for this man's DNA.

'Gosh,' was all she had said, thinking how she would feel if this had happened to a colleague of hers, like Hazel, or Mitch.

Brenda had continued to describe how she'd rushed across to visit the laboratory where the work had been done. She even described in detail her conversation with the woman in charge, and how humiliating it had been, dressed as she was in such a casual way, since she had not expected to leave the office that day.

Nina expressed surprise, sympathy, amazement and concern in turn as seemed appropriate, but all the while she was wondering if perhaps this had more significance than at first she had understood. What if this man *was* the Phil that Mills was going out with? She decided it was best to avoid mentioning it to Brenda or Mitch at this stage. It would be such a huge coincidence...

'...so the best thing would be to let Mitch know that I have serious concerns over the evidence at this stage. I suggest the hair sample is re-analysed by an independent laboratory as soon as possible.' Brenda was staring at her. 'Do you agree, Nina?'

'Yes, of course. I'll let DI Turner know as soon as he comes in.'

'Thank you. It really is *very* important that this is cleared up quickly, otherwise who knows where it will go.' She slid off the desk, smoothing her shorts down as she made for the door.

When Hazel arrived, Nina related what had happened, this time including the fact that she thought she knew the man. It didn't take Hazel long to find a photograph of Phil Freedman on the internet. It was an in-house magazine shot of an office outing taken three years ago.

'Yes that's Phil,' said Nina.

'Does he still have the ponytail?' asked Hazel.

Nina thought for a moment. 'No, he was best man at a wedding a few weeks ago.' She'd seen the photographs. 'He has it short now.'

When Hazel rang Mitch, he said he would be in straight away. It was, in fact, an hour later when he arrived but clearly he was taking the matter very seriously. Nina had persuaded Hazel not to mention that she knew Phil while the error was being sorted out. It was obviously a mistake which would be resolved as soon as the new laboratory had done the test.

So it was Hazel who volunteered to collect the hair sample from Bishop Laboratories after a number of phone calls made by Mitch behind closed doors. He rang through, asking Hazel to come to his office. She returned to inform Nina that he had located a forensics company in the south of England to carry out the work. 'Thanks a lot, Nina. Now I've got a five hundred mile round trip to look forward to!'

'Sorry.'

'Oh, please don't be. You've got to get any records on Phil Freedman in police files and extend the search out as far as necessary. I don't think you'll be home early tonight.'

Normally Nina enjoyed investigating the background of suspects and, although she felt faintly uncomfortable making enquiries about her friend's boyfriend, she was confident that it would turn out to be a wild goose chase. Routine searches through the national police records drew a blank so she moved on to trace him through his previous addresses, which proved more complicated than she had expected. It was straightforward up to three years ago but there were gaps when he was out of the country over the previous four years. Prior to that, he was based at Durham University for most of the time. She made herself a mug of tea and settled down to contact the Durham police to continue her fruitless search.

She was so engrossed in the details that she was startled when Mitch appeared by her desk.

'Got anything?'

'Quite a lot, actually.' She was reading the last section of the report to be sure she had the facts straight. Then she looked up. 'There was a suspicious death ten years ago. His girlfriend... well, his fiancée really. She died under rather strange circumstances.'

'Let's see.' Mitch grabbed the report, wandering over to Hazel's desk as he read it, seating himself in the swivel chair and swinging gently as he turned the pages.

Nina sat very still until he had finished.

'Interesting. Good work, Nina.' He looked at his watch. 'You get off home, it's after six. I'll make a call and get this Freedman brought in for a chat tomorrow morning.'

*

Phil had been puzzled by Brenda's suggestion that they go for a drink. It would have been less of a surprise if it had not been three o'clock in the afternoon. True, they finished early on a Friday, but Brenda was always the first to leave the building, exclaiming she was off to an evening class or some other pre-planned engagement.

'No, not today, Phil. I want to have a confidential chat if you don't mind.'

Their local was a few minutes away. As they walked in silence, Phil tried to imagine what Brenda could possibly want. It was either that she was going for promotion or she was contemplating early retirement. She insisted on buying the drinks and seemed disappointed he was sticking to diet coke.

'Well I'm having something stronger,' she muttered as she went off to the bar. He wandered into the deserted beer garden.

'So, are you getting married or emigrating?' Phil joked when she returned.

She took a sip of her scotch, then another, the ice clinking each time she tilted the glass. When she put it down she was not smiling.

'I spoke to Claudia Bishop this morning.'

Phil made a conscious effort to appear calm. 'And?'

'You know I was looking at the attack in Richmond?'

He nodded.

'It's about the DNA on a hair sample found in the girl's hand.' She waited, as if expecting him to speak. When he didn't reply, she leaned forward, looking at him intently. 'This is in complete confidence, OK?'

This time he nodded his assent. 'The match on the DNA... it's you.'

'What d'you mean, me?'

'I mean the hair matches your DNA. It would appear to be *your* hair.'

Phil tried to make sense of what Brenda was telling him. 'So... presumably... there's been a mistake?'

'Yes, that's what one would assume. I went to see your friend, over at the laboratory, asked her to find where it had gone wrong but she wouldn't listen. What is wrong with her? I thought you were mates?'

'It's a bit complicated but she must realise that it's a contamination problem.'

'If it is, it must have happened at her laboratory. You haven't been near the crime scene!'

'But you have. Is it possible that you transferred it?'

Brenda snorted. 'I can't see a stray hair from you being carried by me to a scene miles away and then confused with a hair found grasped in the poor girl's hand, can you?'

Phil could see that it was improbable. 'So what will happen now?'

'I've been thinking about that. If she's sent the results direct to Newby Wiske, they'll have to act on it before long. I spoke to a DS over there. I suggested to her that they would need an independent analysis done in another laboratory.'

'What did she say?'

'She agreed but it won't be up to her, will it? Meanwhile I imagine they'll be inspecting your credentials, so to speak. You'll need some legal advice. Do you belong to a union?'

Phil shook his head. It had lapsed while he was abroad.

'It's all right, I'll find someone if it's necessary,' Brenda said.

It was a lot to take in and he was still not sure whether Brenda was panicking over nothing.

'I'm going back to the office now, Phil,' Brenda was draining her glass. 'I need to keep the boss informed of what's up. I suggest you get onto a solicitor right now.'

Phil thanked her, remaining seated for some time after she had left. It then occurred to him that Claudia might have been trying to contact him herself. He jumped up and rushed back to find the office empty. There were no e-mails, no voicemail messages. He turned off his computer and went home to wait for a call.

Nina was relieved to find that Mills was busy upstairs packing when she finally got home, since she had still not decided whether to say anything to her. She didn't know whether Phil had been informed about the match with his own DNA, so she would have to be careful not to say too much. After supper, when Nige was washing up and Mills was helping her put Rosie to bed, Nina decided to mention it casually.

'So, are you ready for the weekend?'

'Just about.'

'Phil will miss you.'

'I doubt it.'

'Millie! Of course he will. Have you spoken to him recently? I mean... is he OK?'

'I expect so. He's busy. We haven't spoken recently.'

Nina was not stupid; she could tell things were not right. Clearly Mills knew something.

'Look, I'm sure it will be all right. It will get sorted out in time.'

Her friend looked taken aback. 'You know?'

'Yes of course. But...'

'Listen. I want nothing to do with him, ever again. Ever.' She stood up. 'I've got to finish packing,' she said walking to her bedroom and closing the door firmly behind her.

The rest of the evening was so strained that even Nige picked up that something wasn't right.

'I'm sorry, love,' Nina said as she climbed into bed. 'I don't want to discuss it right now. It's about work.'

In the morning the usual rush prevented any sensible discussion, so Nina simply wished Mills a good weekend and left for work.

Mills felt a certain sense of relief as she boarded the train that morning. Nina had clearly guessed that she and Phil were no longer together, and it was kind of her friend to be concerned, but at present she just wanted to forget all about it. It was time to take stock, to decide what to do next. Nige and Nina were back on an even keel now, with Jake's help, so she could leave them to enjoy a normal existence again with baby Rosie. She would miss them but part of her felt it was the right moment to move on. However, she also needed to consider what she was going to do in future regarding her career. At present she had no permanent job but she was really enjoying her work on the lime kilns, especially with Jake's help. By the time the train drew into King's Cross she had no answers and decided to forget about it all until she returned to Yorkshire.

Fiona had wanted to meet her at the station but Mills insisted that she was perfectly capable of finding the flat in Canary Wharf without her help. She took the Northern line as instructed as far as Bank, then the Docklands Light Railway to Blackwall. Fiona's flat was a modern block overlooking the West India Quays and across the river, just as she had described, was the Millenium Dome. Mills had visited the Dome with the school. She remembered that her friend Michelle had been sick on the coach and Sophie was given detention for swearing at girls from another school.

The apartment block was much grander than she had expected, even in Docklands. There were signs to the pool, to the gymnasium, even to a restaurant. She was instructed to take a lift to the eighteenth floor and was greeted by Fiona the moment the doors opened. Her future stepmother was obviously delighted to show off her luxury lifestyle, pointing out the views across London, walking her round the very stylish three-bedroom flat.

'Put your things in here and make yourself comfortable. I'll get tea. Come through when you're ready, Mills. Hugh told me you like to be called Mills. Very unusual. Very cool. It suits you.' She smiled before disappearing with a clatter of heels across the wood laminate floor.

Mills dumped her rucksack on the bed, looked round the room and walked towards the window, steadying herself as she peered down at the river, wondering if she would feel safe sleeping so far above the ground. She considered the risk of fire and high winds but quickly dismissed all thoughts as being too difficult to entertain.

Fiona was in the galley kitchen which was half open to the living room.

'What do you think?' she asked Mills.

'It's lovely.'

'A bit different from Yorkshire, eh?'

'Yes, very.'

'But I think your father will enjoy living here, don't you?'

'He's moving in here?' Her immediate thought was of the house in Purley. 'Is he selling "Heatherside"?'

She must have sounded shocked because Fiona swung round, still holding the kettle. She looked concerned. 'Didn't he tell you? I told him to tell you before you came down. He put it on the market last week. He was supposed to let you know.'

'Don't worry.' The poor woman looked so anxious that Mills felt genuinely sorry for her. 'It would be silly to keep both places on after you're married.'

'Quite. That's what I thought. I've been telling him for ages but he only recently decided to do the sensible thing.'

Sensible yes, but very final. They had lived there as a family ever since Mills was born. It was where she grew up. In particular it was where all the memories of her mother had been made.

'I'd like to visit "Heatherside" again before it's sold.'

'That's exactly what I said to Hugh. I suggest we go down on Sunday. He hasn't spent much time there in the past few months and the garden will need tidying if the estate agent is taking people round.'

They drank tea, chatting politely. Fiona asked about work and Mills explained what she was doing at the university.

'It all sounds so interesting. I wish I'd done something like that.'

Mills still didn't know what Fiona did. She simply said she was in property management but Mills didn't understand what that entailed. She assumed Fiona was an administrator but had never asked her directly. Now it seemed too late to question her. It must pay well, she thought, to have a place like this.

'I expect property management is very interesting?' She wished she sounded more convincing.

'It can be.'

'Is it mainly looking after places like this?' she asked naively.

Fiona laughed. 'Heavens, no! Although that's how I began – with a company doing that sort of work. No, I work for a company specialising in property as an investment. We find properties abroad to invest in for pensions, that sort of thing.'

'Oh,' Mills said. Now she knew how Fiona could afford such a nice apartment.

That evening they were to meet her father for dinner in town. Fiona, who had booked a favourite restaurant for eight-thirty, spent the next couple of hours washing and drying her hair, applying make-up and deciding what to wear, shouting to Mills from her bedroom every time she had to make a decision.

'Do you think it will be warm enough to wear a sleeveless top? Are you wearing a dress or trousers?' Then she appeared at the living room door. 'Is this lipstick too pink, do you think? I bought it yesterday but I think it's too pale.'

Mills answered every question with a non-committal reply. 'What do *you* think? Does Dad like it? I am sure it's fine.'

Thirty minutes before they were due to leave, Mills took a quick shower, combed her hair and, pulling on a cotton dress and sandals, presented herself for the inevitable inspection.

'Mills, you look lovely. You are so lucky to have such a perfect figure. You look so natural.'

Even Fiona's toenails matched her lipstick, which she had changed to a very bright red.

They took the lift down to street level, walking the short distance to the Light Railway and finally the Central line. It was quieter on the tube than it had been when Mills arrived, but more people boarded the train as they drew closer to Tottenham Court Road. A familiar figure was waiting for them at the barrier.

'Hi there, Fi! Millie!' her father called. 'You're late.'

'It's Mills now, darling,' Fiona reminded him as she gave him a peck on the cheek.

Mills hugged her father then followed him as he set off at a pace towards the restaurant.

The atmosphere was uncomfortable. Her father, who was irritable at having been kept waiting, complained at every opportunity. The table was too close to the kitchens, the room was too cold, the wine not cold enough. Fiona was trying too hard to make the evening a success and Mills was aware that she was not helping. She was not used to dining in such an expensive restaurant and was horrified by the prices. Her father would never have brought her mother to a place like this. She pondered over the menu until Fiona asked if she would like her to make a suggestion. She described the dishes that she had enjoyed, which allowed Mills to select one of them, gratefully. Fellow diners were noisy, raising their voices to be heard above the background music, so there was little conversation amongst them that evening.

They travelled back to Canary Wharf by taxi. It was late, so Mills excused herself saying she was tired after her journey from Yorkshire. She climbed into bed, pleased to be relieved of the need to maintain polite conversation any longer.

To her surprise, Mills felt a sense of relief when they set off for the dressmakers, leaving her father at the apartment. It was hot on the tube but she enjoyed travelling across London to Clerkenwell – it was a long while since she had spent time in the city, which had been familiar territory as a teenager.

The two hour fitting was tedious. She sat on a hard chair while Fiona fussed and fumed over her dress. It was a massive white ball of netting and silk, which admittedly was lovely but she was not satisfied until they had changed almost every aspect of it. Then it was her turn. Mills stood feeling foolish while three women held the purple dress for her to step into, fussing round with pins until they were happy.

'It's lovely, Mills!' Fiona declared and the ladies agreed.

She looked at the full length mirror where a girl stared back at her defiantly. She had to agree that the effect was startling – her hair clashing in a strangely stylish way with the purple satin. She had never had the confidence to wear a strapless dress before, but this fitted so well it felt great as she swished the voluminous skirt from side to side.

Finally they were allowed to leave with the promise that the dresses would be ready for the final fitting in a fortnight; just one week before the big day on the twenty-fourth. Fiona was in excitable mood, insisting they lunched at a "lovely little Italian" she knew in Islington.

'We can walk, it's just round the corner,' she said with a smile.

The restaurant was cool and dark, almost empty. Mills accepted a cold glass of juice gratefully while they perused the menu. Fiona chose a salad, having decided she needed to lose a few pounds before the big day, while Mills selected a pasta dish. They sat comfortably together discussing wedding plans with none of the awkward atmosphere Mills had experienced on the previous night.

'Is Dad getting nervous?' Mills asked, thinking it could be the cause of his brusqueness.

'I think so, Mills. Not the ceremony but just the whole thing, you know?'

'Leaving "Heatherside" – it's a big move, you know,' Mills suggested, playing with her cutlery.

'You're right.' Fiona looked across at her, with her head on one side. 'Mills, I do know what it means to him... and to you... to leave Purley. I do know. That's why I suggested we went down to the house tomorrow. He wasn't sure it was a good idea but I insisted. Did I do the right thing?'

Mills hoped that her smile reassured Fiona. Just at that moment she was incapable of replying because of the lump in her throat.

'So,' began Fiona when they had finished eating and she was waiting for the bill, 'what would you like to do now? It seems a waste to be in town and not do something.'

'What sort of thing were you thinking of?'

'Shopping?'

'Sure,' replied Mills, thinking she had no money to spend but was happy to watch Fiona if that's what she wanted to do. 'Can we go to Camden?'

'Definitely.'

When they got back to the apartment, Fiona was laden with bags from a range of high street shops. And so was Mills. Fiona had insisted on treating her to the jeans she had admired and when Mills told her she had nothing to wear at the evening do after the wedding, Fiona persuaded her to buy a short silk dress in vivid oranges and reds. 'The colours so suit you!' she had exclaimed. 'I'm sure your father would want you to have it.'

Mills collapsed on the sofa and drank tea while Fiona described their day to her father.

'It sounds ghastly,' was his response.

'No it wasn't, darling,' Fiona called across from the kitchen, 'it was fun, wasn't it Mills?'

'Yes it was.' And she meant it.

There was hardly time to recover before Fiona ushered them off to the West End. She proudly announced that she had managed to "pull some strings" and got them into the musical "Chicago".

'I thought "Dirty Dancing" and Hugh said we would be going without him if I booked that!' she confided in the interval.

When Mills finally got to bed late that night, she was so wide awake she couldn't sleep despite her exhaustion. She reached for her phone, turning it on for the first time that day. There was a message from Nina. The text was so beautifully written, it could only have come from her: *Did you know Phil has been questioned about the attack?* She turned it off and lay looking out at the lights of London eighteen floors below, wondering what the message meant.

Chapter 12

The clock on Brenda's mantelpiece indicated it was past lunch time. She wasn't hungry, and hadn't been since she received the message from Phil that he was going into Newby Wiske for questioning early that morning. The woman who was the cause of the problem, Claudia Bishop, was clearly carrying on business as usual even on a Saturday because she had just sent a report on the dog hair found on the Heriz carpet. It had definitely been identified as belonging to a Hungarian mudi, such an unusual breed that Brenda was sure she would be able to find the owner. And that's what she was doing now, trawling the internet for the names of breeders in the UK. The website of the British Mudi Club was unsophisticated with a simple list of breeders; just five names distributed across the country. Brenda began at the top of the list and dialled the number of the president.

'I was interested in owning a mudi but know so little about them...' she began. Soon she was having a very amicable discussion with a man who was clearly besotted with the breed. She learned that the club had only thirty members. She carefully steered the conversation round to where the dogs were bred in the UK, and by the time she put the phone down she had contact details for the other four breeders.

She sat staring out at her small back garden, deciding what to do next. There was no guarantee that the hair came from a breeder's dog but there were clearly very few mudis around the country. If *she* had one, she would definitely want to be a member of the British Mudi Club. It was like owning a classic car. She dialled the next number on the list, beginning the conversation as before, but this time introducing the concern that the dog might shed hair. She was assured it was not a problem. Might it not leave hairs over her nice oriental carpets, she pressed. It had never been raised as an issue before, she was informed rather curtly.

There was no answer from the third name on her list so she tried the last one. The woman was pleasant, answering all her questions patiently and offering advice over raising a mudi puppy.

'Are you far away?' the woman asked. 'I'm in Macclesfield, is that near you?'

'Not far at all,' lied Brenda.

'Well, why don't you pop over and see my mudis? I've got no pups at the present but there will be some in September.'

'That would be lovely,' Brenda cooed as she grabbed a pen to note down the address. 'Are you around tomorrow?'

She walked out to the garden seat and was soon joined by her tabby cat.

'I think I got rather carried away, Meg,' she said, stroking the cat's chin gently.

When the phone rang a few minutes later, she shot inside, her heart racing. She had instructed Phil to call when the questioning was over.

'Phil? How are you? Are you back home?'

'Yes, Brenda, I'm home.' He sounded weary.

'Are you alone?'

'Yes.'

'Do you want to talk about it?'

'I dunno.'

'I could come over... I could bring a bottle of malt.'

'I haven't eaten all day.'

'Nor have I. I'll bring a curry if you want.'

There was a big sigh. 'You sure?'

'Yes, in fact I insist.'

'OK. See you later then.'

They were colleagues, not friends. The age difference meant they didn't have a great deal in common but although she was senior in years, they were at the same level and had shared an office for long enough to tolerate each other's moods. From where she was standing, his problem was work related and he deserved support from a colleague. Besides, she enjoyed the drive across to Arkengarthdale, and it was nice to have company on a Saturday evening instead of watching the telly on her own.

She had to wait for her local curry house to open before she could set off, so it was past seven by the time she reached Phil's cottage. He looked pale and drawn so she poured generous measures of whisky while the food was heating up; carefully letting Phil relax before asking him how it had gone.

'Pretty awful.'

'What did they say? Did they seriously think...'

He took a deep breath and let it out slowly. 'They questioned me about my record.'

'Your record?'

'Yes, my record. I have a police record, so they went all over that again.'

'You don't have to...'

'It's all right, I don't mind... you've got a right... It was a long time ago... when I was at university. There was a girl, Rachel.' He took a sip of whisky, then another, draining the glass. Brenda topped it up. 'She was beautiful, clever, totally out of my league. Her mother was a concert pianist, her father something in the diplomatic corps. She was an accomplished viola player. She shared a flat with two girls on my course, Claudia and another one, can't remember...' He took another sip of whisky. 'We met through Claudia – a party at the flat. Rachel had just finished a relationship, I was in the right place at the right time. For me it was like love at first sight. We were together as much as possible and by the end of term I was pretty much living at the flat.' He sat staring at his glass.

'So what happened?'

'What happened? What happened?' His voice was growing softer so Brenda had to strain to make out what he was saying. 'She died. That's what happened. One morning they tried to wake her and she was dead.'

'How?'

'Suffocation. That's what they found. She'd been suffocated... in bed.'

'Was it an accident?'

There was a long pause. '*I* don't know. I wasn't there. The police... The police...' He was struggling to control his voice. 'The police said *I* killed her... but I didn't.'

'So what happened then?'

'What happened then? Nothing. They had no proof.'

'Did they try to find anyone else?'

'No.'

Brenda chose her words carefully. 'It's unusual for someone to suffocate accidentally.'

'Yes.'

'Did you ever wonder... ?'

'I wasn't in much of a state to wonder, Brenda. I stopped studying for nearly a year.'

'And what about Claudia?'

'What d'you mean?'

'She must have been very upset. Losing a friend like that.'

'She tried to help... always there if I needed to talk but in the end it was smothering. I couldn't move without her being in my face. I got out for a while, moved away.'

'Did you see her after that?'

'No, not until the wedding. The groom, he was a mate from uni. There were loads of classmates there.'

Brenda retrieved the dried out curry from the oven but neither of them was very hungry. They finished the bottle between them and Brenda crashed out in the spare room, warning Phil that she had to see a woman about a dog the next day and would be setting off early.

Brenda was happy to keep to the motorways as directed by her sat nav. Although the roads were quiet, as she had expected on a Sunday morning, it was midday before she reached the kennels. She was on a wide road lined with large detached houses. They had names but not numbers and when the sat nav informed her that she'd "reached her destination" she was beside a pair of large wrought iron gates bearing the name of the house with "home of the mudis" printed underneath. She left the engine running, pressed the entry phone and waited for a response. Eventually there was a hissing noise, followed by the creaking of the gates opening. She assumed she was expected to drive up to the large modern house, where a smiling woman stood at the door to greet her. Presumably she was the owner, May.

Brenda could hear barking as she followed her into the house. Soon she was trapped in the hallway surrounded by three large, friendly black dogs.

'Now then, girls. Settle down!' May ushered the animals through the large sitting room and out into the garden, closing the French doors behind them. They remained, noses pressed against the glass, eager to continue their acquaintance with the new arrival. Brenda did her best to play the enthusiastic dog lover despite the hangover headache that had gradually worsened during the drive. She gratefully accepted tea and nibbled the sandwich that was pressed on her.

When the dogs had calmed down and were lounging on the patio, May allowed one of them back in the room and showed her the various points about the breed. Brenda stroked its soft curly hair, remarking on the dog's gentle disposition, and began the strategy she had rehearsed on the way down. She asked May how she had come to be breeding mudis, waited patiently for her to finish then introduced the fact that her own obsession was with Persian carpets. May listened with a fixed smile.

Brenda had to try another approach. 'They are such rare dogs. I imagine their owners are the sort that might own carpets themselves,' she mumbled.

May looked puzzled.

'I mean, they must be rather special. They would appreciate the art in oriental rugs.' She was embarrassed by her lack of articulation.

May smiled. 'Possibly. Mainly they are just keen on the dogs. And they are becoming more popular. We have a number of club members now.'

'Could I join, even though I don't have a mudi... yet?' Brenda asked.

'Of course. We have events for anyone who is interested in the breed, even if they aren't an owner as such. Although most people are.' She looked thoughtful.

'I would like to meet the other members. Is there a list?'

May shook her head.

'It's so nice to share interests, isn't it?' Brenda took a breath. 'As you know, I have an interest in Persian carpets. I don't suppose any of your members share *that* with me?' She knew it sounded a little bizarre but if it worked...

May paused. 'No I don't believe so but it's possible. The dogs are the main interest of the members,' she repeated.

'Of course.' Brenda made an effort to pet the dog that was lying at her feet, apparently asleep. It jumped up when she touched it and she had to prevent herself from crying out. She bravely patted its head as it nuzzled her lap in what she felt was a rather threatening way.

'She obviously likes you,' May said with a polite smile.

Brenda stayed as long as she felt was necessary, then made her excuses. But before she left she expressed her continuing interest in a puppy and May promised to keep in touch.

'Stupid, stupid old bat!' Brenda shouted, thumping the steering wheel as she swung out of gates. 'What were you thinking of?' she asked herself. 'The poor woman must have thought you were completely mad.'

*

Mills looked at the shop windows as they crawled through the busy London streets while Fiona and Dad argued about the route. She was thinking about the message from Nina having re-read it several times. Since it wasn't clear whether Phil had been attacked or witnessed an attack, she wanted to ask her friend about it, although in reality it was none of her business anymore. Now it would be Claudia who would be running to his side if he was hurt. She sighed and turned back to the window. Shoppers were dressed in shorts and T-shirts but inside the car it was cold. Dad liked the air conditioning on high.

They made slow progress through Streatham and then Croydon, which was far more familiar to Mills. Finally she spotted the IKEA chimney and they were moving down the Purley Way towards home. She thought of it as home although she hadn't lived there since she was eighteen. The familiar wide roads were lined with large suburban houses, many unrecognisable since they had been extended and modernised but "Heatherside" hadn't changed. Mills was shocked by the peeling paintwork and the weeds growing up through the gravel drive.

'God, Hugh, it needs sorting out before the viewings,' Fiona remarked as they waited for him to unlock the front door.

Suddenly Mills was fourteen again, coming back from church parade in her guide uniform, the smell of Sunday lunch filling the house. Her mother would be in the kitchen, Dad in the garden. She went straight up to her old room, walking over to the window with the view of the back garden. It looked neglected, like the rest of the house. There were cobwebs on the glass, dust on the window sill and a fusty smell from the curtains. It was a house that had not been lived in properly for years. Perhaps it was for the best if it was sold, particularly if it could be occupied by a young family again.

Downstairs Fiona was making a start on the kitchen. She was standing in front of a cupboard regarding the contents.

'What shall we do with all this?' she asked.

Mills looked at the jars and bottles. 'Dump them,' she said. 'Get rid of everything.'

She had to go into the garden to hide her tears. It was stupid but she felt as if she was saying goodbye to everything that had happened in that house. There were happy memories recorded in photograph albums which could be kept and she hoped that there would be enough space for Dad to keep some mementos of their days as a family. She joined him at the end of the garden where he was trying to start an old petrol lawn mower. There was a time when he had seemed most comfortable pottering round the garden, tidying or mending. Now he looked out of place in his silk shirt and chinos.

'Here, let me.' She took hold of the string and yanked it until the engine burst into life then died. She repeated it a few times and soon it was running rather hesitantly, but it was working. He tried to take the mower from her but she resisted, walking the length of the lawn and back just as she had done as a teenager. It was her job when she was old enough. Mum would do the edges while Dad tackled the hedges, a major job all season. Mills grinned at him as he watched her, waving her arm to indicate that he should find something else to do. It was almost therapeutic to be marching behind the machine as it ploughed relentlessly up and down the garden. By the time the lawn was looking respectable again, the compost bin was overflowing with grass. She trimmed the edges with a pair of rusty shears she'd found in the shed, replacing them carefully on the hook to the left of the door, standing for a moment to breathe in the musty, hot air mixed with turpentine and potting compost. These were the smells of childhood summers she didn't want to forget.

She had planned to return to Yorkshire that evening but they spent so long at the house, she was persuaded to stay in town overnight and return in the morning.

'It will be so much easier tomorrow,' explained Fiona, 'without the engineering works messing up the timetable.'

There was a cool breeze and most of the visitors had returned to their B&Bs and holiday cottages for the evening when Nina parked in Richmond. Just a few people, determined to make the most of their holiday, were sitting outside the pubs across the road. Nina hoped they included the lads who'd seen the attacker running away. She had spent much of the week publicising the reconstruction to everyone involved, including the regular Sunday evening customers at "The Ralph Fitz Randal". She had spoken with the school friends and Tanya, the girl who had volunteered to stand in for Kelly. They were all to gather inside the pub by ten o'clock. The bus company had been most co-operative, ensuring the same driver was on duty that night. Several colleagues were already inside "The Ralph Fitz Randal" with DI Turner, noting the names and addresses of the customers as they arrived. Nina wondered whether they would be required to provide DNA samples, despite a match already being made.

Hazel came over, pulling her gently to one side. 'Kelly Lewis died this morning,' she informed her quietly.

'Do her friends know?' Nina asked.

'Oh yes, can't you tell?'

The atmosphere was tense and it was noticeable that very little alcohol was being consumed.

Eventually the place filled with regulars, providing a low hum of conversation which built gradually until the mood lightened a little. Silence fell when, just before ten, Hazel called for everyone to listen carefully. She explained that they were going to follow precisely the movements taken by Kelly, Josie and Melissa. They would walk up to the market square together at exactly ten-thirty, by which time the ten twenty-four bus would have already left. Josie and Melissa would leave on the ten thirty-six and Tanya would walk back down to the pub. The girls looked nervously at one another.

'Could the rest of you carry on doing whatever you did last week? Please try to remember when you went home and go at the same time. We'll be by the door to record the time against your name,' Hazel added.

Nina led the girls outside, where it was drizzling with rain. Two of her male colleagues followed a few paces behind. They walked in silence up towards the market square, observed by a few youngsters sheltering in shop doorways. Nina could see tears running down Josie's face as she grabbed Melissa's hand. When they reached their bus she told them to go home, just as they would normally. She knew their parents were waiting anxiously at the other end but she nodded to a young DC to accompany them anyway. Two pale faces peered out from the back window as the bus left the square.

It was eerily quiet as they waited a minute or two to simulate the moments when Kelly realised that she had missed the bus. The CCTV had shown her talking to someone but there was no-one around now. Nina looked at her watch and waited until it was ten thirty-eight.

'OK, Tanya. We'll go back down now. We can walk quickly.'

The girl strode off as if pleased to be moving and they were soon at the pub where Tanya was ushered back inside by a uniformed officer. Nina waved at the young man on the bicycle who was waiting outside for the moment when he would recreate running to the girl's rescue. Nina went in to see what was happening during the five minutes or so before Kelly left with the man who was to attack her.

Hazel and her colleagues were moving from table to table asking if anyone remembered the girl coming back in alone but people were shaking their heads and muttering apologies. It was already ten forty-five when the young DC called Ian reminded them that it was time to leave. He would represent the unknown man who accompanied Kelly. The entire room watched as they left, Nina hurriedly following to observe as they crossed the road. The two uniformed officers who had been stationed on either side of the road since ten o'clock were stopping any vehicles in case they had been passing a week ago. The man was still waiting at the kerbside with his bike.

As agreed, Nina walked down the road to "The Fleece" where there were three of the lads who had been there last week. Meanwhile Ian accompanied Tanya to the supermarket car park, running out and down the street past them a few minutes later. Nina questioned the boys again but they could not remember anything else about the evening. The DC walked slowly back to join her and she suggested they went into the bar in case some regulars had sheltered from the rain. It was as lively inside as it had been quiet in "The Ralph Fitz Randal" and it took some time to get round all the customers. Most had not been in on the previous Sunday evening and those that had been there recollected nothing significant.

They returned to "The Ralph Fitz Randal" without anything to offer. Hazel confirmed that after Tanya's parents had come to take her home, everyone else had decided to call it a day and the place was virtually empty. Nina and Hazel agreed that the evening had been a complete waste of time.

Chapter 13

Brenda was in work very early on Monday, determined to finish her report on the dog hair so that she could draw a line under the findings and forget about her ridiculous attempt to establish a link between the dog and the rug. She was unsurprised that Phil was not at his desk at nine, but by ten o'clock she was concerned. He was not answering his phone and their boss was looking for him although she didn't say why. When she came looking for him on the third occasion that morning, Brenda could contain herself no longer.

'Is it the police?' she asked. 'Do they want to talk to him again?'

'I can't say, Brenda. You know that.'

'Shall I try to reach him? It's nearly lunch time. I could pop over.'

'There's no need,' she said, but Brenda could see she was grateful.

'Is there a message?'

'Just get him to ring me. It's really important.'

Brenda heaved herself out of her chair and hurried down to the car park. She was becoming anxious about her colleague and drove with less caution than nomal, nearly colliding with a lorry as she pulled out onto the main road. The traffic was heavier than usual and she cursed as she waited at the pedestrian crossing outside the library. It took longer than expected to make the journey but she was rewarded by the sight of Phil's motorbike outside the cottage.

She hammered on the door without success, peering in through the tiny window into the kitchen.

The dog was staring at her with a puzzled expression, slowly stretching and stepping elegantly out of its basket towards her. She banged on the door again, convinced Phil was inside, calling his name through the letter box with a few choice expletives for good measure. Finally there was a noise above, a window was opened and a head appeared.

'Is that you?' Phil asked rubbing his eyes.

'Who d'you think it is? Let me in, you muppet!'

There was a long wait until the door was finally opened. Phil stood there in boxers and a T-shirt.

'You needn't have got dressed up for me, sunshine.'

'Come in. I'll make some tea.' He was clutching his head.

Brenda sat quietly until her colleague had boiled a kettle.

'You look like crap,' she said.

'I feel like it.'

'Have a bad day? My head was suffering a bit yesterday.'

'Hmm. I didn't really get up yesterday except in the evening.'

'Did you eat?'

'Not really.'

'Drinking?'

'Yep.'

'Well take your tea, have a shower and get dressed. Your boss wants a word with you.' She went over to the teapot, pouring two mugs of tea, adding milk to both.

'I can't leave Earl.'

'Then ring her. It's urgent.'

He grabbed the mug and the phone, disappearing upstairs. She could hear the shower running while she chatted to the lurcher.

'Have you ever met a mudi, young man? Very rare breed they are, all black and curly.' She ruffled his head and he backed away. 'Suit yourself. I don't really like *you* either.'

'Have you rung her?' Brenda asked when Phil ran back downstairs, this time dressed in jeans and clean white T shirt.

'Yes. Can I come back in with you? Earl will have to go next door.'

In the car, Brenda asked Phil outright what the boss had wanted.

'She's got the report on the new DNA test.'

'And?'

'The result's the same. The DNA on the hair is a perfect match with mine.'

Brenda slowed the car.

'In that case it *must* be your hair. We just need to work out how it got into the girl's hand.'

'There's to be an investigation. That's why she wants to see me.'

Brenda had no experience of the situation. It was practically unheard of, except where the technician handling the sample had contaminated it through lack of proper measures. She was so busy considering possible explanations that she nearly missed the lights, screeching to a halt in front of a nervous pedestrian.

'Steady on, Brenda. It's me that's supposed to be anxious, not you.'

'There's nothing for you to worry about, sunshine. This sort of thing happens all the time.'

'Yes, I'm used to your driving.'

'I mean contamination of evidence. Risk of the business, isn't it? I have no doubt at all that it will be sorted out in no time.'

Despite her assurances, Brenda waited impatiently in the office while Phil had his interview with his superiors. When he returned she could tell by his demeanour that things had not gone well.

'So?' she enquired.

He leaned on his desk.

'There's to be an urgent enquiry. Until then I'm on gardening leave.'

'What?'

'It means I'm suspended on full pay.'

'I know that. But why? You've done nothing wrong!'

'Brenda, she made it quite clear that at the moment I'm very lucky that I've not been arrested for attacking that girl. There's a course of action that has to be followed and she's following it.'

'And what happens then?'

'Either the matter will be sorted or I'm on a charge for attempted murder.'

It was almost mid-day when Mills finally said goodbye to Fiona at the station. Her father had popped his head round the door while she was still in bed but Fiona had taken the morning off to look after her.

'You really shouldn't have,' said Mills. 'I could have seen myself out.'

'No. Certainly not. I want to see you off. I want to make sure that you get to the station and find the right train.'

Mills thought she was more likely to manage than Fiona was, but she smiled and thanked her again for a lovely weekend.

'Now don't forget. You must come down on the Friday before the wedding. I need you at my hen night.'

With that image in her head, Mills found a seat and settled down for the journey, wondering if it was *her* job as maid of honour to organise the hen night for Fiona. Surely not.

The rocking motion of the train, combined with the warm, airless atmosphere soon sent her into a sleep disturbed only when her head flopped suddenly onto the window. She bought a drink to wake her up but soon she was dropping off again, so it was with relief she was finally able to step off the train into a cool breeze.

She'd not been looking forward to seeing Nina when she came in, knowing she'd behaved badly to her and feeling guilty about it. But her friend was her usual generous self and soon they were sitting outside drinking tea, exchanging pleasantries until Mills could build up the courage to ask outright about Phil.

Her friend was begging her to describe the bridesmaid dress and her weekend with her father... and Fiona.

But first Mills wanted to know what the text message had meant. 'So how was Phil attacked?' she asked.

Nina sighed audibly. 'It's more complicated than that. Didn't he tell you?'

'No, Nina. We don't talk anymore. You know it's over.'

'What? I'm sorry. No, I didn't know that.' She paused, as if letting the news sink in. 'But you said you knew. You said it would all blow over soon. I'm sure that was what you said.'

'Phil and I. Us. It would settle down, we'd... I'd move on.'

'Oh dear. Well I suppose it doesn't matter then.' Nina stood up. 'I guess it's for the best in the circumstances.'

'Circumstances? What circumstances? Nina, tell me what's happening.'

Her friend was as reticent to discuss this case as she was any other that she was working on, but this time Mills was able to persuade her to relate the events of the weekend. Including the interview with Phil on Saturday, carried out by Nina's colleague Hazel with her boss Mitch Turner.

'It was routine,' she said. 'They have to get a statement. It will help identify where any contamination of evidence occurred.'

'And they think he might have tried to kill the girl?' The words sounded bizarre when expressed aloud.

'Of course not, Mills. It's just routine. They have to examine every possibility and it's routine... in certain situations.'

'What d'you mean?'

'Nothing, I shouldn't have told you this much really. Don't mention I spoke to you about it, will you?'

'No. As you say, it's not really my business... anymore.'

Nina changed the subject but she couldn't stop thinking about Phil Freedman. He was a nice guy and it was a shame that he and Mills had split up. But she would have been trying to help if they had still been a couple. There might be something she could do even now and perhaps, when it was all over, they might eventually get together again. On the other hand, if Phil was the girl's attacker, Mills was far better off without him.

As soon as Nina was back on duty, she located Hazel.

'Has Phil been arrested?' she asked.

Hazel raised her eyebrows. 'I thought you promised to keep out of it?'

'Well, apparently Mills isn't seeing him anymore so there isn't any reason...'

'Hang on a minute, not so fast. We agreed didn't we? I haven't mentioned that you know him to anyone but you must keep your distance. A deal?'

Nina shrugged. She'd already had an idea and as soon as Hazel left she made a call.

'Brenda? Can we have an "off the record" chat?'

Two hours later they were sitting in a small coffee shop in Northallerton, waiting for their lattes to arrive.

'Thanks for coming all the way over, Brenda.'

'No problem. I was on my way to Bishop Laboratories this afternoon anyway.'

'On business?'

'Not exactly. To be honest, Nina, I wanted to have another go at Claudia.'

'Claudia?'

'Claudia Bishop. She runs the lab that did the DNA test first time round – the one that connected Phil with the hair.'

There was a pause while the coffees arrived.

'She was very off-hand with me when I went over last time. Wouldn't discuss it, just sent the information off to you lot. I didn't expect her to hide evidence but *I* would have had a good look at where it might have gone wrong. Wouldn't you?'

Nina sipped her coffee, playing for time. 'It's difficult...'

'Oh come on, Nina. If it was one of your people, wouldn't there have been some sort of internal look-see before handing it over to the complaints authorities.'

Nina smiled across at her, hoping to calm her down. Brenda was definitely an emotional woman when it came to protecting her colleagues. 'The reason I wanted to talk to you Brenda was because I agree with you that it's most likely some sort of mix-up. I thought you might know how it could have happened? Don't these laboratories have safeguards in place?'

'Of course. But I don't know how good Bishop Laboratories are at that sort of thing. Naturally if there's contamination from one of the technicians it would be assumed to be an unfortunate accident but Phil had nothing to do with case – he wasn't involved in collecting the evidence or assessing it. The hair hadn't been through our site so it could only have come from Claudia's laboratory.'

'And he wasn't even working there!'

'Ah... well... no, but he had *been* there. I know he went over there a week or so ago to pick up some results for a case he was working on because he took some samples over for me.'

'Is that all?'

Brenda was stirring her coffee slowly. 'No, it isn't actually. I think their relationship might have been more than just a professional one.'

That would explain why he had split up with Mills, thought Nina. 'You mean he was seeing her?'

'I don't know. He told me they were at university together. Anyway, I think they've both worked at the forensic labs at Wetherby in the past.'

Now was Nina's chance to broach the subject; the reason she had wanted an informal chat. 'Look, did Phil ever talk about his university days?'

'What do you mean?' Brenda was looking at her defensively.

'About his friends.'

'Who did you mean exactly?'

So she did know something. It was time to be open with her. 'We know what happened to his girlfriend, Brenda.' The woman seemed unwilling to be drawn. 'I'm only trying to help him, Brenda. But with his past it makes it more... well... difficult...'

'He told me all about it. It must have been a terrible experience.'

'Did he tell you that he was under suspicion for a while?'

'Yes.'

'So you can see why the situation could be serious for him.'

'Yes. That's why I'm going to see Claudia.'

'So what are you going to say to her?'

'I'm not sure. I want her to acknowledge that it's a cock-up at her laboratory and the sooner the better.' Brenda seemed to relax. She leaned back in her chair and grinned. 'Unless your lot find the true culprit, somehow I have to con her into admitting that Phil is an innocent victim of a horrible mistake. Any suggestions?'

'Obviously we are doing everything to find out who did do it.'

'Any leads?'

'No.'

'And how is the girl?'

'It's not good news. She died on Sunday.'

'So it *is* a murder charge,' she muttered. 'Is Phil going to be arrested?'

'I don't know. I presume they are deciding now. This is in confidence, yes?'

'Nina, I know he didn't do it. Can I call you when I've seen Claudia Bishop?'

'Of course,' Nina said as she rose to leave.

'Just one thought,' Brenda continued. 'If you've got a copy of the chain of custody, does that mean you have all the other documents for the analysis at Bishop Laboratories?'

'I suppose so.'

'Then could I ask you for a favour?'

Mills was in her office at the university, mentally listing five good reasons why she was not going to get stressed about Phil's problem. Firstly, they were no longer in a relationship. Two: they weren't even friends. Three: there was nothing she could do anyway; four: his work would sort it out and five, well there didn't need to be a five. No, five: she was going to get on with *her* life.

Now that Jake would be teaching until the end of the afternoon, there was something she wanted to look at which was in her desk drawer. She pulled out the large magnification of the postcard and laid it carefully on the desk, smoothing out the creases.

It was the first opportunity she'd had to examine the creature properly. It was indeed a strange representation if it was a sheep or cow but perhaps on such a small scale it had been difficult to provide much detail. The shape was quite square, even the eyes were square. Surely it was easier to draw circles than squares on a small scale. She experimented on the back of the paper, taking her efforts along to be expanded and printed to see the effect. To be honest, she thought, it doesn't make a lot of difference. So she spent several minutes reproducing the strange beast over and over again at different scales until she was pleased with the result. Then, since she didn't know what else to do she put the papers back in her desk.

In the drawer lay the original postcard. She drew it out cautiously, turning it over to reveal the message on the back and spent the rest of the afternoon staring at it. *I'd like to start fresh with the help of my guardian angel. I'm moving to a new address. "Look after yourself." XXXX.* The longer she studied it, the stranger it seemed. Before going home she rang April, leaving a message asking her to call when it was convenient.

Nina stood over the fax machine, feeding it with papers from the folder containing evidence provided by Bishop Laboratories. Claudia had not been helpful and Brenda had rung at three to break the news. As agreed, Nina then spoke to Hazel, suggesting that the scientific information be passed to an expert for evaluation. Hazel had not been fooled but she couldn't see why it would harm if the originals remained in the office. Even so, Nina felt jittery as she kept a watchful eye on the door in case the boss appeared while she was in the middle of faxing. It wasn't until she had returned the file to its box that she was able to relax sufficiently to realise that it was time to call it a day.

It was normally the case that once she was at home with Rosie and Nige, Nina was able to leave work behind and relax. But this evening she was reminded of Phil Freedman's situation every time she looked at Mills. Jake had come round with a curry so he and Nige could get together to discuss the work they had been doing for Mills. She watched quietly with Rosie falling asleep on her lap while the three archaeologists discussed their findings.

'So there is definitely *something* there?' Mills was asking.

'That's right.' Nige was virtually back to normal now, Nina thought. He was taking a class later in the week, talking excitedly about returning part-time initially but aiming to be full-time in a few months when the academic year started again.

Nina could tell that Mills was excited by the boys' findings – she was gesticulating wildly, as she tended to do when warming to her subject.

'I should go back to the National Park to let them know at once!' she exclaimed and Jake snorted.

'Perhaps wait until tomorrow!' he said, laughing good-naturedly.

Nina wondered idly whether Jake knew that Mills had split up with Phil. Should she tell him, she thought – they made such a nice pair. But it was not sensible to interfere and she rebuked herself for meddling.

The three friends were still talking shop when Rosie was in bed and Nina had tiptoed quietly back downstairs.

'I suggest I do one last visit to get a set of photographs to put in the document,' Mills was saying. 'If you can write up the geophysics for me, I will put all our names on the report and acknowledge Jake's funding of course. Hopefully the National Park will feel it's worth supporting a full survey.'

Brenda took a break from reading to make herself another coffee. It was silent in the corridors and the fluorescent light in the kitchen flickered for several minutes before it settled into an unfriendly glare. The clock was at eleven twenty-two and Brenda acknowledged that she should have gone home hours ago. There seemed little point now – there was a sofa in the rest room and it wasn't too uncomfortable in the past. She'd spent four hours on the papers but found nothing to raise alarms. SOCO had discovered three hairs caught in Kelly's fingernails when she was seen at the hospital. They were immediately bagged and sent off to Bishop Laboratories. The chain of custody confirmed that the evidence bag was received by Claudia Bishop, who then took one of the hairs for analysis. It was divided into three sections of similar length: two were placed together in a separate labelled bag and the third was given to a named technician for DNA analysis.

Details of the analysis followed, including a full report from the laboratory on the findings. Interestingly, because the match was someone in forensic services, Claudia had included a detailed statement explaining why cross-contamination could be ruled out, since Dr Freedman was not employed by Bishop Laboratories. There was not, Brenda noted, any mention of the fact that Phil was a friend of hers who had visited the laboratory recently.

She knew that when Claudia was asked for a sample to repeat the analysis at the other laboratory she would have sent one of the two remaining pieces of the same hair, or perhaps both. So the original hair must have been Phil's. The question was whether it was really found in Kelly's hand. If it was, how did it get there? If it wasn't, who switched it for the original hair – and why?

Chapter 14

Brenda woke when the cleaning woman arrived. Her main concern was to get some paracetamol and a coffee but she had to wait for the feeling to return to her left leg before she could even stand.

'Hard night?' the woman asked, as she vacuumed round her.

Brenda nodded as she buttoned up her jeans and made for the kitchen in bare feet. The coffee helped, followed by a splash of cold water on her face. She pulled a comb through her hair, surveying herself in the mirror. 'I'm sorry, love,' she told her reflection. 'We'll find some lipstick later. Just let me sit down for a minute.'

The boss called a meeting for ten, where she explained that Phil was on leave for the time being while there was an investigation into a contamination problem at the laboratory in Harrogate. Everyone treated it as routine but when Brenda stayed behind to ask what was happening, it was clear that the situation was becoming more serious.

'I've had a message from senior management. They are very concerned. The police are treating it as more than suspicious. They are already talking to the CPS.'

'That's nonsense! They can't really believe Phil's involved personally in any of this?'

'Brenda, please sit down. You know I don't think there's any substance in this but it doesn't help if you go off the deep end when we are discussing it. I have asked you before...'

'I know, I'm sorry. It's just so ridiculous.' She was about to say that she'd seen the paperwork from

Bishop Laboratories but managed to stop herself from getting into more trouble. 'If there's anything I can do...?'

'As a matter of fact there is, Brenda. You're a friend of Phil's. Keep an eye on him. Make sure he's... well...OK. Yes?'

'Yes, of course. But what can I tell him?'

'Nothing. At the present time there is nothing to tell.'

'But what are they doing? The police. What's happening?'

'That I can't say. I guess they'll weigh up the evidence they have and the CPS will decide whether to go ahead.'

'You mean they could actually charge him?' Brenda was standing again but this time she didn't care. 'If they do that... if they do that... I'll hand in my resignation!' She didn't wait to hear her boss's response because the door was slamming behind her.

Phil was looking down at Reeth from Fremington Edge. It was a walk he always went back to when he needed to sort things out. The weather had been dry so the path was not too muddy underfoot. Earl was running backwards and forwards along the track in front of him, occasionally disturbing a grouse but not creating a nuisance. He had met a couple of walkers travelling in the opposite direction who gave him a strange look but otherwise he had the entire moor to himself.

He couldn't decide whether it was being off work in the week that made him feel so disoriented or the lack of proper food or sleep. The last hot meal he'd had was the curry that Brenda brought round the other night. He scratched his head, rubbing the greasiness of his hair from his hand on the back of his jeans.

'Time for lunch, Earl!' he called. The dog came running to share the picnic he'd put in his pocket.

He divided up the bread but refused to give Earl any cheddar.

'You know what it does to your guts!' He picked the mould off the edge of the cheese before popping it into his own mouth.

The can from his pocket showered him with beer as he opened it but he managed to save at least half. He wiped his mouth, surprised by the prickliness of his chin. It was a great day for walking, he decided, calling the dog and turning back towards home.

The views down into Arkengarthdale were just perfect and his mood was positively buoyant until he reached the cottage. Brenda's car was parked outside.

'Where *have* you been, Phil?'

'Out walking. What d'you want?'

'Aren't you going to invite me in?'

He didn't want to. He wanted to go inside and sleep until it was dark then drink himself into oblivion. But she hadn't moved.

'At least give a me cup of tea before I go.' She was smiling, trying to please him. Trying to keep him happy. He nodded and she followed him into the cottage.

While he made the tea she kept wandering about, peering at his stuff.

'Stop it. Keep still won't you?'

That stopped her. She sat down then stood up quickly, removing Earl's rubber rabbit from the chair before settling herself down again. He watched her examine the mug, wiping round the rim then sipping from the wrong side. She thought he hadn't noticed but he had. How long would he have to stand looking at her before she told him why she had come?

'So, Phil, how are you?'

'Fine.'

She was looking round his kitchen, fixing her eyes on the pile of dirty clothes in the corner. Now she was looking at the dishes in the sink.

'You can wash up if you want to.'

'Phil. I just wanted to say that I'm here if you need to talk.'

'Why would I need to talk, Brenda?' He deliberately emphasised her name. Their relationship was not what he would call friendship. She was just a work colleague who usually moaned at him for being too noisy or untidy. He disliked this new apparent camaraderie.

'OK, I'll cut to the chase.' Brenda was standing up. 'The boss says there is a chance you may be arrested if the CPS feels that the police have enough plausible evidence. You of all people should know the drill.'

She stood staring at him expectantly with her hands on her hips. He was tired. It was all too much to deal with before a drink.

'Thanks Brenda, I'll bear it in mind.'

She stood with her head on one side. 'You always were an awkward bugger Philip Freedman!' She almost spat out the words before storming out of the cottage.

He could hear her car revving noisily as he opened the whisky bottle.

April was surprised to hear from Mills again. She had agreed that she could come over, provided it was before the boys were home from school. They would want to know who she was and then Dave would find out. He'd made it plain he didn't want it all raked up again. It was already ten past two and she was looking out anxiously. If she left it much longer, it would be too late. Finally, at two-thirty, an old minibus appeared, with "The University of North Yorkshire" painted on the side. She almost ran to the door.

'I'm so sorry I'm late.' The girl's face was pink and shiny with sweat.

'Come in, it's cool indoors. I'll get you a cold drink.'

April indicated for her to sit in the lounge while she hurried to the kitchen. When she returned with the squash, Mills was sitting with something in her hand. She recognised her sister's postcard.

'Georgie's card?' she asked as she handed her the glass.

'I've been trying to work out what it means.'

'What it means?'

The girl read the message aloud. She had a southern accent so it didn't sound like her sister at all. 'Can I read it?' April asked.

Mills handed it over and she read it quietly to herself.

'D'you see what I mean?' Mills asked. 'It sounds really odd, don't you think?'

'It doesn't sound like her. But I don't suppose it would, would it? I mean I wouldn't write the same way I speak, would you?'

'But it doesn't make sense either. Don't you see? Who is her "guardian angel", for example?'

'I don't rightly know.'

'What about "I'd like to start fresh" – that's an odd way of speaking, don't you think?'

'I suppose,' April said, unsure what Mills was driving at. 'What do *you* think?'

And then the girl told her to look at the picture on the front. She had recognised the drawing as soon as Tim had shown her the original hanging in their house. She told Mills.

'And what about this?' she asked, pointing at a speck in the middle of the picture.

April strained to see but it was just a tiny speck. Then, almost triumphantly, Mills produced a sheet of paper with a shape in the middle.

'What's that?' she asked.

'It's the dot, magnified. It's a sheep or a cow.'

April couldn't tell what it was but if she thought it was an animal, she supposed it was.

'Does it mean anything to you?' Mills asked.

April shook her head, 'No, nothing.'

'Well I think she was trying to tell Tim something in this card. I think she was hiding some sort of sign.'

'A sign?'

'Yes.'

'What sort of sign?'

'That's what I don't know. I never met her, I don't know what she would do or say. I thought you might know what she was trying to tell us.'

April tried to grasp what was being asked of her. This girl, Mills, she's clever, she thought. She's an archaeologist, at a university. If she can't understand the message, why would I?

'I thought you might be able to give me a better picture of your sister – what she was like, what she liked doing?'

April tried to think. It was difficult. She had been so quiet. That's why it was odd that she had run off with someone.

'For example,' Mills continued. 'Did she like sport, what were her hobbies?'

'She was younger than me. She was a very private person. She enjoyed reading, her art. She wasn't one for parties. We didn't really go around together when we were growing up. She tended to stay at home.'

Mills was writing in a notebook. 'So she stayed at home, reading.'

'Sometimes.'

'Sport?'

'She didn't really like sport. She preferred board games like scrabble.'

'Word games, eh?'

'Yes and puzzles like word searches.'

'Crosswords?'

'Yes, definitely crosswords. She even did those cryptic ones – you ask Tim. They could sit for hours working away at those. It drove my Dave mad.' April wished she hadn't mentioned Dave. It made him sound insensitive.

'Your sister and Tim seemed to have been an ideal couple.' Mills was looking at her now.

'They were. They were well suited. We all said that as soon as they started courting.'

'Do you know if Tim has met anyone else?' Mills asked, still staring at her.

'No, not that I know of.'

'Only I thought I saw him with someone at the festival in Grassington the other week.'

April could feel her cheeks colouring. She hesitated, trying to decide what to say. Had she recognised her? Did she know it had been her with Tim? What had she seen?

There was a ring on the bell which signalled the boys were home. Relieved she jumped up, telling

Mills that it must be her children. Once they were through the door all possibility of a quiet chat was at an end. To her relief, Mills took the hint and left soon afterwards.

'Was that the lady we saw at Nana's?' they asked when she'd gone.

'No, love.'

'Were that her van outside? It says it's from the university.'

'No, love. It was just someone doing market research.'

As far as Mills was concerned, the visit to April Webb had raised more questions than answers. She had not exactly lied about being with Tim at Grassington but she hadn't admitted it, and she was almost obstructive when it came to describing her sister's interests. She would call Tim O'Neill when she got back to see if he could be more help. Meanwhile she tried to recall what she *had* gleaned from the visit, apart from the fact that April was hiding her relationship with Tim, whatever that was.

As soon as she had returned the minibus, she made her way back to Priory Road to find Nige. He was busy on his computer so she went upstairs and printed the wording from the postcard onto a clean sheet of paper.

'Have you finished the crossword already?' she asked when she went downstairs.

'No. Don't have time for crosswords anymore, Millie. I've got work to do now. I'm finishing off the geophysics report on your site. Did you get the photographs done over in Wharfedale today?' he asked without looking up.

'Yes.' Mills smiled. It was wonderful to see him so engaged with his university work again. But it was his proficiency in solving crosswords that interested her. 'Nige?'

'Yep.' He was still staring at the screen.

'I need help with a puzzle.'

'What sort of puzzle?' Still he was tapping the keyboard.

'I'm not sure. It's certainly puzzling.'

'An enigma?' Now he was looking at her.

'Certainly cryptic.'

Now she had his full attention she handed him the page. 'What d'you make of that?'

He spent several minutes examining it, then handed the card back.

'It certainly has the format of a traditional cryptic clue,' he said. 'At least the first sentence does. Is it from a crossword?'

'Could it be?'

'I guess so.'

'So what could it mean?'

He took the paper again and sat in silence for a while. 'It's difficult to know where to start,' he said slowly. 'Usually there'll be one part which is the clue to the word we're looking for and then another part which has the meaning. It's hard unless you know which is which. For example, is the answer a guardian angel? If so, we need another word which means the same thing.' He turned to the keyboard and typed in the words "guardian angel". 'You see: protector, keeper, custodian. Now, does the first bit lead us to any of those words?' He paused for a long time. Just as Mills was about to speak he continued. 'No, it doesn't.'

'So nothing jumps out at you?'

'No, sorry. But leave it with me. Sometimes I wake up suddenly with the answer. It might come later. All you really need is a thesaurus.'

Mills grinned, about to make a joke about a dinosaur, but Nige was a step ahead. 'You know what I mean. On the internet.'

'OK.' Mills went back upstairs, where she made a list of words meaning the same as guardian angel, guardian and angel. They included *protector, defender, champion, supporter, guard, sentinel, keeper, custodian, warden, seraph, archangel and cherub. Rescuer* was an interesting one when used in the same sentence as "help" but since she had no idea how cryptic crosswords worked it seemed rather pointless. She stared at the rest of the message as it appeared on her computer monitor. "I'm moving to a new address" was an odd statement in view of the fact that she didn't give the address. Was that the clue, perhaps? If she could solve the first sentence would it lead her to the new address? Her eyes moved down to the "Look after yourself". That was a puzzle. It was a phrase her father would use, or her grandmother. She wouldn't use it; would Georgina? April Webb had talked about her sister and Tim "courting" which was not a phrase she would have used either. She clicked on it: *take care of yourself, fend for yourself, support yourself, maintain yourself, go your own way, manage on your own.* It wasn't helpful.

She checked her watch. There was just time to ring Tim O'Neill before she would need to start supper. He answered almost immediately and didn't seem surprised that she was contacting him.

'April told me you'd been to see her,' he said. 'She said you were asking about Georgie's interests. Is there something particular you want to know?'

Mills realised that he probably found it strange when she had already approached *him* for the information.

'Yes, I wanted to ask about her hobbies, things she did when she was younger; before she met you.'

'And did it help?'

'I think it might have done. For example, I think she liked puzzles, word games, that sort of thing.'

There was a pause at the other end. 'Yes, yes she did, actually.'

'Crosswords?'

'Yes crosswords but also numbers: soduko, kakuro...'

'The sort of crosswords with cryptic clues?'

'Definitely. I don't know how she did it. I couldn't make head nor tail of some of the clues.'

'Thanks, that's helpful.'

'Why, have you found something?'

'I'm just trying to get some background. By the way, Tim, did you enjoy the Proclaimers gig at Grassington?'

She waited for his answer.

'How did you know...?'

'I was there. It was great wasn't it?'

'Er, yes. It was.'

'Did I see April with you?' She hoped her question sounded casual.

'Yes, as a matter of fact you did. I was let down by my friend. I asked if she'd like to go.'

'That's nice.'

'Yes, but if you don't mind... it's just... Dave, my brother-in-law, he didn't know she was coming with *me*. I'd appreciate it if you didn't mention it to anyone.'

'I understand,' said Mills. At least I suppose I do, she thought, as she turned off her phone.

She could hear Nina in the kitchen but there was something she wanted to do before going back downstairs. She turned on her laptop, waiting impatiently for it to open her pictures file. She found the shot of the girl with red hair, zooming in until she could see the blurred image of her face. If it was her, she was in Threshfield days after she disappeared. And if she *was* trying to send a message on the postcard it meant she wasn't there voluntarily and she was seeking Tim's help. Mills couldn't let it go without trying to do something. She took everything downstairs with her, including the laptop, determined to confront Nina with what she had found.

To her surprise the kitchen was empty. She could hear music in the yard and stepping outside she found Jake and Nina, glasses in hand, watching Nige light the barbeque. Rosie was slumped in her push-chair sleeping soundly.

'Mills! What are you drinking?' Jake indicated the line of bottles and cans arranged along the wall.

'What's this?' she asked. 'Someone's birthday?'

Jake ignored her, pouring a glass of wine and handing it to her. 'Right. Stop a minute Nige.' He indicated to his friend to take his glass. 'A toast. Here's to Nigel Featherstone – back as full time lecturer at the University of North Yorkshire!'

Mills went to congratulate him but Nige held up his hand. 'Wait!' he instructed. 'And to Jake! Jake's been a thoroughly good mate through all... through all...' He took a swig from his glass to hide his embarrassment.

Nina took his hand. 'I'd like to thank you both,' she said looking at Mills and Jake. 'You've been truly good friends.'

There was an awkward silence until Jake began topping up their glasses.

'So, you're back full time now?' Mills asked Nige.

'Yep. I'm taking the first year introductory science module on physics and the second year geomorphology course.'

'That's great,' said Mills.

Nina disappeared into the kitchen, returning with bread and salad. It was not the time to discuss Georgina O'Neill.

But later, when they had all had too much to drink and were indoors drinking coffee, she decided to show them the photo and the card – something she would not have done if she was sober.

They passed the postcard round, peering at the sketch on the front and laughing at the message on the back. It wasn't right, she knew, but at least Nina was looking at it now. Then she showed them the photograph, magnifying it until they too could see the red-headed girl.

'Where d'you say this was taken?' Jake asked, studying the paper.

'It's near Threshfield. That's what's so odd. It's by the quarry that we pass on the way to Malham Moor.'

'The quarry we passed when we went to your site? By the caravan site on the left?' Nige asked as Jake handed the picture to him.

'Sort of,' replied Mills. 'The caravan site is on the left but there's another site to the right of the quarry... a bigger one.'

Nina gave it a cursory glance, handing it back to Mills. 'It still may not be her,' was all she said.

Undeterred, Mills revealed the magnified addition to the sketch – her sheep or cow. Everyone laughed in turn at the suggestion it was a sheep.

Nige was turning the paper round, studying it from every angle. Finally he said, 'You know it looks like a caravan to me.'

Mills stared at it dumbfounded. Of course it was. Once the suggestion had been made, there was nothing else it could be. It was a small white caravan with two square windows and a pair of black wheels.

Chapter 15

Nina just had to get out for some fresh air during the ten minutes she allowed herself for lunch. The atmosphere was humid and there were grey clouds in the distance. She always had a bad head when it was stormy.

The news had come through first thing that Phil Freedman was going to be brought in for questioning again. She took her mobile out of her bag to call Mills – it was only right to let her know. There was a text message from Brenda Yardley, asking her when it was convenient to talk. Could they have a confidential chat?

'I'm on my lunch break,' she told Brenda when she got through. 'What did you want to know?'

It was Phil. He'd "scarpered", as Brenda put it. She was in no doubt because he'd left his dog with a neighbour, saying he might be gone for several days. Nina suggested that he was having a bit of a holiday but Brenda gave a snort and said, 'Yeah, right' in a sarcastic way.

'They'll be searching for him,' Nina persisted. 'He's wanted for questioning.'

'I'll question him when I see him.' Brenda sounded angry. 'I tried to help him and he threw it back in my face. I've a good mind to give up on him.'

'Please don't.' Nina couldn't understand why she felt so strongly about him. 'Do you know where he might have gone?'

'No offence but I wouldn't tell you if I did.'

Nina thought for a second. 'I know what you are saying but it will only look bad if they can't find him.' She paused to think. 'If you do know anything, you can depend on me not to be unhelpful, if you see what I mean?'

'I know. And you *have* helped already. The papers you sent? I'm sure there must be something funny going on at Bishop's. I'd like to take a look but that might need your assistance.'

'If I can help...'

'I'll let you know. Got to go. Thanks.'

Nina sat for a minute uncertain whether to ring Mills to warn her. Eventually she replaced the phone in her bag, walking slowly back to the office where the news of Freedman's disappearance had already reached Mitch. The immediate response was to issue a warrant for his arrest.

Nina e-mailed the news to Brenda who responded almost immediately on what was apparently an entirely different matter: *I have to visit Bishop Laboratories to discuss the results of the analysis of a hair from a rather unusual breed of dog. In view of the sensitive nature of the relationship between our own laboratory and Bishop's my boss has recommended that I am accompanied by a police officer. Are you free?* Nina replied, querying why a police presence should be necessary. Brenda responded with a friendly text telling her not to ask too many questions. Mitch was so preoccupied with his police search that he hardly acknowledged her request, waving an arm and shouting 'Whatever!' at her, so she jumped in the car and headed for Harrogate.

The rain started almost as soon as she set off – a few heavy drops at first, then the downpour, drumming heavily on the roof. The road was clear but she kept to a speed where the wipers could cope with the amount of water landing on the windscreen. When she reached the laboratory she was unsure whether to wait but Brenda's familiar figure appeared from the entrance, waving at her to come in.

Nina asked for a briefing as they climbed the stairs but the door at the top flew open and Brenda was introducing her to Claudia Bishop, owner of the laboratory, explaining that she was accompanied by a police officer because of the sensitive nature of the Phil Freedman case. The contrast with Brenda's appearance was startling: the tall blonde woman was dressed in a red floral sundress with cap sleeves and matching red patent shoes. The body language between them indicated that Brenda's dislike of Claudia Bishop was reciprocated.

'I'm delighted to meet you...'

'Sergeant, I'm Detective Sergeant Featherstone, Dr Bishop.'

Brenda shot her a glance. Yes, she had done her homework, although Claudia looked a lot older than the photograph on the website. Nina let Brenda take the lead, since she had little idea why they were there. Claudia led them into her office, offering tea which Nina accepted gratefully as she sank into the sofa. Brenda remained standing, refusing to have any refreshments.

'I found the results on the dog hair very interesting,' Brenda began, when Claudia had re-appeared with Nina's tea. 'It appears to be a very rare breed. I wondered whether I could see where the analysis is done? Just for my own interest, of course.'

Claudia glanced at Nina, clearly suspecting that there was more to the question than met the eye.

'Would you like to come as well?' she asked Nina.

Behind her, Brenda was shaking her head.

'No, I'll stay here if that's all right.'

'And if you show me the lab I can chat to your technicians while you speak to the Sergeant,' added Brenda.

Nina had no idea what was expected of her, so she drank her tea while she waited for Claudia to return. They were making polite conversation for a while until Claudia suddenly said. 'I'm sure you're not here to pass the afternoon. Did you want to question me about Phil Freedman?'

Nina was flustered. 'Not officially, no.'

'Unofficially then, I see.'

'Actually it's rather difficult...'

'Oh I understand. I expect he's been making all sorts of claims about our relationship.' She was smiling.

'Your relationship?'

'It wasn't how it looked of course. He was always a bit of a fantasist.'

'You knew him at university, I believe?'

'Yes, we go back a long way. I shared a flat with Rachel.'

'Ah.'

'You know what happened to Rachel? Awful. We couldn't believe it.'

Nina didn't have to ask questions; the woman didn't stop talking.

'Phil was... very possessive. I think Rachel found it difficult to deal with, if you know what I mean?'

Nina didn't know what she meant but if she remained silent she was sure that Claudia would tell her.

'He was always around. Wouldn't leave her alone. It was stifling her. She liked her freedom.'

'So you think she killed herself?'

'Oh no! She wouldn't do that. I just think... No, I mustn't say any more.'

Nina knew exactly what the woman was trying to say, or rather not say.

'And then you met up again here?' Nina asked brightly, trying to change the mood a little.

Claudia straightened her back and smoothed her dress. 'I started the company after I left Wetherby. It didn't suit me there, being told what to do all the time. I decided I would have my own business by the time I was thirty and here I am.' She beamed.

'And you analysed samples for Phil and Brenda?'

'Yes. I don't usually get involved with older cases but they come along.' Her smile was synthetic. 'To tell the truth, it's not so interesting but it pays the bills. I prefer current investigations, like the attack in Richmond.'

'It must have been a surprise to get a match with Philip Freedman's hair though.'

She put her head on one side. 'To be honest I found it shocking. At first I wondered if it was a mistake, of course. But then I began to think about Rachel and in a strange way it began to make sense.'

'Can you explain that?'

She shifted on her chair, leaning forward confidingly. 'I suddenly realised what he was capable of.' Without warning she jumped up. 'I wonder how they're getting on in the lab?' she said, heading for the door and leaving Nina feeling uneasy.

Finally the downpour had stopped and, outside in the car park, the air felt fresher. Brenda turned to Nina excitedly. 'Listen, I spoke to the technician who carried out the DNA test. I asked him very specifically about something that was worrying me about the hair. He was the person who cut it into the three pieces. He confirmed that the three pieces were each about two centimetres long, which means the original hair was six centimetres – over two inches long!' She used her two index fingers to indicate the length.

'Yes?'

'Have you seen Phil's hair recently?'

'I know he had it cut for the wedding. Is it longer than six centimetres?'

'No, no, no! He had it cut even shorter after that. It's really short. Much shorter than two inches.'

'But the tests proved it belongs to him, even the second laboratory showed that.'

'I know. It doesn't make sense but it means that something is not right. Did *you* find out anything?'

Nina was irritated that Brenda expected her to have been snooping in her absence. 'No, not really.'

The woman eyed her suspiciously. 'You didn't have a little chat with Claudia?'

'We spoke, yes.'

'I see. It's all right for me to share my findings with you but...'

'It's not that. If there was something I would tell you but she only spoke about the university days.'

'The dead fiancée?'

'Rachel, yes.'

'That is another reason why it doesn't look good for Phil, isn't it?'

'Yes. If you know where he is...'

'I don't. I really don't... and I wish I did.'

Perhaps Nina wanted to believe her.

Mills couldn't get the puzzle of the message on the postcard out of her head. She spent most of the morning trying to make sense of it. The drawing of the caravan was even more distracting. She decided to revisit the school where Georgina taught as soon as possible. But now it was time to teach the second year preservation class and she had prepared nothing.

When she finally emerged from the lecture theatre, Jake was waiting for her. He insisted that they have a meeting with Nige to discuss the proposal for the National Park.

'But it's not ready yet,' she protested.

'Exactly,' Jake responded, 'you need to get down to it. What have you been doing?'

'It's been difficult...'

He steered her to the cafeteria, where Nige was already tucking into a Cornish pasty. Jake insisted on getting Mills a sandwich while she kept Nige company.

'What's the rush?' she asked him.

'It's Jake,' said Nige. 'He's rung the National Park office and the guy we need to see is going on holiday next week. He thinks we might miss the boat if we don't speak to him tomorrow. He wants to make it a success for you.'

'Does he?' She wasn't sure she wanted him to be interfering in her plans.

'After all, he did put his grant money into it, didn't he?'

'Yes. Where's Rosie?' she asked to change the subject.

He grinned guiltily. 'In the nursery.'

'What here?'

'Yes.'

'Does Nina know?'

'Not exactly. I thought I'd see if they'd take her and when I went in to ask they said she could give it a try.'

'What? You mean you brought her *here*?'

'What else could I do? Nina's working all day and Jake said it was vital to come in. I thought she would be OK with us but Jake suggested trying the nursery and they seemed happy to give it a try for an hour.'

'So are you going to register her?'

'If Nina agrees. It seems the best plan if I'm coming back full-time.'

Jake arrived with a tray and handed Mills an egg mayonnaise sandwich. 'It's all they had left in brown bread. And one cappuccino, no chocolate.'

The next hour was spent discussing how best to finish off their approach to the National Park. Mills had to admit that Jake was focussed when it came to the application. She supposed it was the experience he had gained in the States. She and Nige obediently acquiesced to his suggestions, as he divided the report into three sections.

'If you finish the geophysics, Nige, I'll write an introductory part and cover the finances. Have you got the section on the background to the sow kiln, Mills?'

'Nearly.'

'We'll need a programme with a timescale,' he warned.

'So you're doing that as well?' Mills knew she sounded irritated.

'Won't you want to do that?' Jake asked.

'I can do, if you're sure you don't mind,' she replied sarcastically.

Nige, clearly embarrassed, looked at his watch. 'I should be getting back to the nursery. Rosie didn't seem very happy when I dropped her off.' He picked up his rucksack and left hurriedly.

'I'm sorry, Mills, if you think I'm taking over but you don't seem to be progressing things and we've got to see this guy before he goes away. He's agreed to see us at short notice tomorrow.'

'Tomorrow?'

'Is that a problem?'

'No, it's fine,' she sighed. 'I'll get started on it right away.'

Back in the office, with Jake at the other desk, she started on her section of the report, making several attempts to write an introduction to the sow kiln. She could hear Jake tapping away on his keyboard while she was deleting almost all of her first draft. Somehow she could not concentrate on the task in hand when there was the recent revelation that the tiny drawing on Georgina's postcard was not a sheep but a caravan.

She waited until Jake had gone off to lecture to the second years before calling Tim O'Neill. He was at work, sounding formal when he answered the phone, but he relaxed when he realised who she was.

'How are you?' he asked. 'Have you found anything?'

Mills explained that she had discovered a tiny drawing of a caravan on the postcard and asked him whether there was any significance attached to it.

'A caravan?' There was a pause. 'The only caravan we've stayed in is the one that my brother-in-law's parents own on the coast at Filey. We went there once before we were married but it rained and we never went back.'

'Is it still there?' asked Mills.

'Oh yes. April and Dave take the kids. They go quite often... and Dave's parents.'

'Can you remember the name of the site, Tim?'

'Not off-hand. I can find out, if you like?'

'It could be useful.'

'Righto. Anything I can do – just let me know.' He sounded almost enthusiastic and, once again, Mills felt guilty for raising his hopes.

'It's probably nothing but...' she began.

'I understand. But anything is better than doing nothing.'

She put the phone down and tried to concentrate on the report. She printed out a map of the area, intent on making a connection between the limestone quarry and her sow kiln on Malham Moor. She was disturbed by a telephone call from April. Tim had rung her to ask about the caravan at Filey. She gave Mills the name of the site where her in-laws still had a small caravan. Yes, they often went there. Yes, Georgie had stayed there several times before she was married but not much since. She and Tim probably wouldn't even remember how to get there.

Mills had a thought. 'You live quite near Leeds, don't you April?'

'Not far.'

'Would you do me a favour? I wanted to visit the school where Georgina taught. Do you know it?'

'Yes. I've been to concerts there. What do you want?'

'I just needed to talk to her friend. She's called Penny Meadows.'

'I think I've met her.'

'Great. I just wanted to ask her about this Jaguar. The caretaker saw a green Jaguar outside the school. He says the man picked her up on the day she disappeared.'

'The police didn't say anything.'

'Well it seems he didn't mention it.'

'So you want me to find out about this green Jaguar?'

'Pretty much. Or if she knew of any man in a Jaguar.'

'OK. I could probably go tomorrow.'

'And I'm looking for a connection with the quarry near Threshfield.'

Mills replaced the receiver and went back to the map. As her finger traced the area around the quarry she could see, in her mind's eye, the tiny figure of Georgina in the photograph of the track beside the quarry. A tiny figure and a tiny caravan. And then she remembered the day that she and Phil had walked along the same track, sitting on the bench overlooking the caravan site. Her thoughts were disturbed by Nige arriving with Rosie, to offer her a lift home. He declared that his daughter had been fine in the nursery, although her red-rimmed eyes were evidence to the contrary.

'Nige, you know I asked you about that cryptic message?' she asked as they sat in traffic.

'Yes but it's complicated without some clue as to what the solution is.'

'You said. So I was thinking that you might want to put Threshfield into the equation.'

'Threshfield?'

Mills spelt it for him.

'OK. I'll see what I can do. But I've got to work on the report tonight. Jake wants all the text by the end of the evening.'

'Does he?'

'Yes. He told me to say that you can e-mail it to him up to eleven o'clock but no later.'

'So when are we seeing this man and where?'

'Bainbridge. We've got a meeting at three tomorrow. Jake's putting together some sort of PowerPoint presentation.'

Mills sighed. He was taking over her project – and the most galling thing was that he was right to do so because she really had not been concentrating on her own work. Was it because she no longer had a strong desire to remain in the Dales now that Phil was gone?

She went up to her room as soon as she had finished eating, to get down to her report. She forced herself to concentrate, making good progress once she was engrossed in the origins of the sow kiln. She had made a sketch of how the kiln must have looked when it was being used, overlaying it on the photograph of the area as it appeared now. Nige would provide the technical part of the geophysical data but she described how the measurements were translated into the diagram she had sketched out.

Her mobile rang and she checked the number; it was not one she recognised. Curious, she answered, almost dropping it with the shock of hearing Phil's voice.

'Mills, are you there? Mills? I've got to see you, please!'

'I can't.'

'Why not?'

'I'm... I'm...'

'Tomorrow, please? Just for a few minutes. I want to explain...'

'I can't tomorrow. I've got a meeting.'

'Not just for a quick chat? I can meet you nearby.'

'I have a meeting. It's important. The National Park. I can't not go. I'm sorry.'

She dropped the phone, dabbing her eyes with a tissue. She wasn't sure why she was crying. She didn't want to see him. She sobbed quietly for a while, feeling angry and upset, and then went to the bathroom to wash her face. She had important things to do.

Three hours later she e-mailed her completed report to Jake with a feeling of satisfaction. She had shown him she was perfectly capable of managing the project herself. He replied immediately to say that he would pull the entire document together and print four copies ready for the next day. She sent a reply thanking him for his help, which she really meant this time.

The atmosphere was subdued in the car on the way to Bainbridge. The boys had clearly made an effort to dress up for the occasion, Mills noted approvingly. She regretted wearing her thick black trousers but they were the only smart ones she owned. She opened the window and leaned over to feel the cool air. Jake was asking Nige to go over the geophysical evidence for the kiln so he would be able to explain it properly at the meeting. They had agreed that they would each cover their areas of expertise so she was expected to speak knowledgeably about the development of kilns over the centuries. She had been up half the night preparing herself. She closed her eyes, enjoying the breeze on her face. She was thinking about her presentation but must have dropped off because when she opened her eyes again she could see dry stone walls and sheep on the fells. Before long they were approaching Bainbridge, a familiar feeling of trepidation gripping her stomach in anticipation of the meeting ahead.

They waited until three before being ushered into a hot, stuffy meeting room where four members of the

National Park Historic Environment Team were seated. After the introductions, Jake connected up his laptop while everyone sat in silent anticipation. Mills could tell how he was nervous when he began to introduce the project, but soon he was describing the work in his usual enthusiastic style. Nige was in his element, blinding everyone with the science as he described his favourite subject, geophysical investigation. Finally it was her turn. Her knees felt wobbly as she rose to walk round to the computer. She began by explaining how lime kilns developed from sow kilns through to the more common lime kilns with their recognisable chimneys dotted around the dales even now. Then she described the sow kiln in more detail, mentioning in particular the one identified in Kilnsey by the Yorkshire Dales Landscape Research Trust. Throughout her talk she watched her audience nervously and by the time she was seated again the sweat was running down her back.

As it turned out, she needn't have worried. The people from the National Park were patient and responsive, asking questions that they were able to answer and showing real interest in their findings. To her surprise, Mills found them most receptive to the idea of relating the sow kiln with the limestone quarry close by. There were plans for developing the quarry once it was closed, which included a number of tentative proposals, including a visitor's centre or even an archaeological facility. The sow kiln could possibly be a focus for a development of that kind.

'We'd like to give you the opportunity to explore your proposal more fully,' the head of the section said, leaning back in his chair. 'Obviously we can't give any promises that it will come to anything but it is worth investigating.'

'What do you suggest?' asked Jake.

'Perhaps a bigger piece of work to excavate the site further. If it seems viable we could apply for lottery funding to do a full study.'

Mills was disappointed but as soon as they were outside Jake punched the air. 'Yes!'

'But they've given us nothing!' said Mills.

'Of course they have,' said Nige. 'If we can present them with a bit more information I reckon they'll go ahead.'

Mills stared down the lane while Jake searched for his car keys. In the distance was a familiar figure leaning against the wall, next to his motorbike.

'I reckon we deserve to stop down the road for a drink after that,' declared Jake, climbing into the driver's seat.

'Yeah, I'm starving.' Nige stood by the door waiting for Mills.

'I think I need some fresh air,' she said. 'I'll meet you down there in a while. I won't be long.'

Nige shrugged, climbing in the car. He and Jake sat for a minute then drove down the lane past the man with the bike.

'What are you doing here?' she asked Phil as soon as she drew level. She was alarmed at the sight of his unshaven face. His eyes were hidden by the glasses.

'I wanted... see you,' he said, the words slurring into one another. 'I knew you'd be here. I've... waiting all day.'

'What?' He wasn't making much sense. 'Where have you been? They're looking for you!'

'I know. Brenda's given me... tent. I found a spot in Wharfe... dale. There's a wood...'

'Have you been drinking?'

'No, I don't need alcohol.'

Mills could tell there was something wrong with him when he removed the sunglasses and squinted at her. There were dark circles and he seemed to be having trouble focussing.

'So what do you want?' She was looking round to see if there was anyone watching. He seemed distraught, possibly dangerous. How could she trust him?

'I wanted to know why you left. What have I done? I just want to know...' He moved forward and she stepped back, an involuntary movement that stopped him immediately. 'Why did you go when you did?'

'Do you really not know?' she asked. 'Well, I'll tell you.' She was angry now. 'I met your friend Claudia while you were out. She told me all about you two. She made it clear there was no room for me. That's why I left!'

He looked confused, rubbing his forehead vigorously. 'Claudia? But there's nothing between Claudia and me! It's a lie. Don't you see?' He went to move towards her but stopped himself. 'Surely you don't believe *her*?'

'I don't know. I really don't know what to think about any of it, Phil. Look, I'm going. They're looking for you. You should go to the police before you get into more trouble.' She was moving away as she spoke and he stayed where he was, making no attempt to follow. She had to get to the pub or they would be wondering where she was, she told herself, wiping the tears from her cheek as she ran. She heard the bike engine roar as he sped off in the opposite direction.

Chapter 16

Phil waited down the road from Bishop Laboratories until the car park was almost empty except for Claudia's sports car. It was her unmistakable voice that answered the buzzer when he pressed it.

'Who is it?'

'Delivery,' Phil mumbled.

There was a click as the door yielded to the pressure of his gloved hand. He bounded up the stairs and was waiting on the other side of the glass door when Claudia opened it. He pushed past her into the office, taking a seat beside her desk as he pulled off the gloves.

'It's you!' Claudia was clearly shaken to see him. 'What do you want?' She was moving towards the desk. He quickly placed his hand on the telephone.

'Sit down, Claudia. We need to talk.'

'Do we?' she asked shakily as she lowered herself gently into the leather chair behind her desk. 'You know the police have a warrant for your arrest?' She was looking round the room, as if searching for someone or something to assist her.

Phil waited until he had her attention. 'What have you been saying to Mills?' he asked.

'What d'you mean. Who's Mills?'

'Mills is... was my girlfriend. You lied to her. You told her...' His head ached, his hands were shaking. He pushed his right hand into his pocket, his fingers tracing the outline of the small square bottle. Not yet, he thought. Just get through this and then... 'What did you tell her?'

'Nothing. I don't know what you're talking about. I suggest you get out before the police arrive.'

He knew she was bluffing. 'I know what you said to her. You're a liar. There is nothing between us and you know it.'

'Christ, why would I want anything to do with you?' She spat out the words. 'I offered you a partnership in this company and you rejected it!' There was disgust in her face. 'You could have shared my business and you could have had me – you threw it back in my face!'

Her aggression alarmed him. He'd not seen this side of her before. Even when Rachel...

She was reaching towards the telephone but he moved quickly, pulling on the cable with his free hand so it smashed to the floor on his side of the desk. Still clutching the bottle in his pocket, he spoke to her calmly.

'Sit down Claudia. I want you to listen to me carefully. You are going to speak to Mills to explain that it was all a big misunderstanding. You are going to tell her the truth – that there is nothing between us, all right?'

She was staring at him belligerently.

'Right?' He was getting angry again.

'I don't see why I should do anything you say. The police are looking to arrest you for attempted murder. Why would anyone be interested in a relationship with you now?'

'You know that's all a mistake, Claudia. You of all people must know that.'

She looked directly at him. 'No, Phil. Actually I know that it's not. The hair clutched in that poor girl's hand was yours. I supervised the analysis myself.'

It was only then that his suspicion was aroused. Until that point it had never occurred to him what she was capable of.

'It was you, wasn't it? You're responsible for this mess, aren't you?'

'What d'you mean?'

A door banged in the distance, footsteps came along the corridor outside, then the sound of someone running downstairs and the door slamming behind them. Phil waited until it was silent again.

'I mean you set me up. The hair wasn't mine, was it?'

'Of course it was yours,' she snapped back at him. She was sitting rigidly, her hands tightly clasped on the desk.

'Oh, yes. The hair you analysed was mine. I agree. But it wasn't the hair found in the girl's hand was it? When did you switch it? Oh yes, of course, once you received it here in the lab.'

'No-one will believe you, Phil. The hair has been analysed by two independent laboratories. It is proof enough. No-one will listen to you. You're a murderer, on the run. They'll get you... and not just for her death... for Rachel's as well!'

He considered for a moment the reason for her behaviour. 'Did you do all that just because I didn't want you?' he asked, incredulously.

She didn't answer.

'But you did it. Just tell me truth, so I know.'

'What do you think, Phil? Don't you think I'm smart enough? I've had good teachers here in the lab. I've worked on cases where the offender was much cleverer than I've been.' She was smiling confidently as she pushed her chair back and stood up. 'Now, I really must be going.'

Phil couldn't find the energy to stop her; instead he followed her out into the car park. His fingers were playing with the bottle of pills and he could hardly wait to unscrew the lid. She was sitting in her car, talking into her mobile phone and he knew he had to get away as quickly as possible. It wasn't until he was alone in woodland miles from Harrogate that he was able to find the release he sought in the small square bottle.

April hadn't told Dave she was going to visit Georgina's old school, but she did ring Tim. They kept in touch quite frequently now and she enjoyed having him to chat to. She knew Dave would not have approved.

She planned her trip so she would be back in time for the boys coming home from school, which meant she would have to catch the teacher at lunch-time. It was a risky strategy but when she arrived, the noise from the playground confirmed she was lucky. The school secretary was not unfriendly, offering to seek out Miss Meadows for her. So she waited in the deserted library, wandering along the shelves and studying the notice board to pass the time. There were timetables and match fixtures, toys for sale and holiday cottages to let. A yellowing card caught her eye particularly because of the name that jumped out at her. It was an advertisement for a caravan, available for holidays in Upper Wharfedale – *at Threshfield*. She was jotting down the phone number when a young woman arrived in tennis whites. It was Penny Meadows.

April introduced herself as Georgie's sister and they chatted for a bit about the teacher's disappearance. She knew her questions sounded awkward and the woman appeared puzzled by them, even irritated.

'I don't remember a Jaguar, green or any other colour,' she replied. 'Did someone say they saw her in it?'

'I think so.'

'No, I don't think she was involved with any man. She wouldn't have told me, mind. But you can guess, can't you?'

'Can you?' April wondered how easily one would know. She had never thought of Georgie with anyone but Tim. He was such a sweet man.

She finished by asking about connections with Threshfield, but it meant nothing to Penny Meadows apparently.

'I see there's an advert for a caravan in Threshfield,' she said, indicating the card on the board.

The teacher peered at it. 'It looks rather old. I wonder if it's out of date now,' she said with a shrug.

April set off home feeling that it had been a wasted journey, until she remembered the yellowing postcard. She parked outside her sons' school with a few minutes to spare and, taking out her mobile phone, carefully entered the number.

'Allo.'

'I'm ringing about the caravan. '

'Oh, yeah.'

'Is it available for rent still?'

'Yeah.'

She thought quickly. 'May I have a look at it, as it's not so far away from me?'

'Yeah. When are you be thinking of?'

'Tomorrow? As it's the weekend?'

So it was settled. She would meet the owner at eleven thirty next morning. Excitedly she rang Tim's work number to let him know, but it went to voicemail. It would be better if he was able to come along, she thought, acknowledging that it was possibly her excuse to see him again. So she called his home number and left a detailed message explaining exactly where the caravan was and the time she was meeting the owner on the following day.

In the staff room, Penny Meadows was describing her conversation with Georgina's sister to her colleagues. Most of them had arrived in the last couple of years, so did not remember the woman who left so suddenly. They asked her to tell them about what happened, expressing surprise and concern that someone could disappear off the face of the earth like that. She realised that out of all the people in the staff room, only the Deputy Head and Archie remembered her friend.

Nina was waiting for Nige when he returned from the Dales in the afternoon. She'd received a call from the university nursery regarding her application for a place for Rosie. Despite her protestations they had assured her that they had a form in front of them asking for a place as soon as possible for three days a week.

'But I don't understand, Nige. How could you go ahead with something as important as that without discussing it first?'

Nige looked miserable. 'I thought it would be a nice surprise.'

'It was certainly a surprise, Nigel Featherstone. More of a shock, I would say.' She sighed. 'You certainly know how to surprise a person.'

They sat for an hour discussing the pros and cons but, most of all, the cost of placing their daughter in the nursery.

'...and she might not take to it. How do we know whether she'll settle?' asked Nina.

'We gave it go yesterday,' Nige replied sheepishly.

Nina was speechless. She went into the kitchen to put the kettle on while she cooled down. She knew that he would become upset if she shouted at him but, honestly...

She heard him come into the kitchen behind her.

'Changing the subject,' he said. 'I thought you said that Mills wasn't seeing Phil now?'

'She isn't.' She knew she was snapping at him but...

'Well he met her in Bainbridge this afternoon.'

'What?' Was he trying to distract her? He wouldn't know there was a warrant out for Phil Freedman. Had someone told him? 'What d'you mean, Nige?'

'He was waiting for her after we'd been to the National Park office. He'd parked his bike outside.'

'Listen, did he say anything to you?'

'No, he didn't see us. She stayed behind to talk to him. She seemed upset when she came into the pub.'

'Whatever you do, Nige, do not tell anyone. Understand? Do not tell a soul that you saw him.'

'Why?'

'Don't ask. Just forget you saw him.' She knew it sounded melodramatic but it was the only way to instil into him not to let on. Despite his acknowledged academic abilities her husband could be rather naive at times and she had found it was generally easier to keep things simple. Nige went off to sulk in the garden while Nina cooked supper.

As soon as Mills came in, she went to join him. 'I got your message, Nige. Did you find something?' she asked.

'Sort of. Look, I've got it written down here to show you.'

He produced a page of A4 covered in scribbles. At the bottom were a series of letters crossed out and re-arranged into the word "Threshfield".

'It's a bit random but not unlike the way the Times crossword works. To be honest I often can't finish it.'

'So what does all this mean?'

'Well, you asked if I could connect it to Threshfield. If I take *I'd* and *fresh* with *the* and re-arrange them, I can make Threshfield but with just one letter missing.'

'What letter is that?' Mills was trying to work it out herself.

'An *l*. Which is the first letter of *like*. D'you see? *Like to start*, that means the first letter of like – it's what they do in cryptic crosswords.'

'So *I'd like to start fresh with the* means Threshfield?'

'It could do, like if the clue was, say, *I'd like to start fresh with the – village in Wharfedale* then it would be obvious it was Threshfield.'

'Right.' Mills was impressed. That would not have meant anything to her. 'I wonder what the rest of the message means.'

'No idea.'

Mills considered it without the first part: *help of my guardian angel. I'm moving to a new address. "Look after yourself." XXXX*. Well the *help* was obvious, she supposed, but *guardian angel*? Presumably that was her husband, Tim.

'I was wondering whether *I'm moving to a new address* was another clue,' said Nige. 'You know an anagram of *I'm* and *address* but I haven't been able to work out anything sensible.

'Mills, can I have a word?'

Nina's face was set. There was no friendly smile or gentle rise of the voice at the end of the question. It was not a request to be taken lightly.

'Of course.' She followed her friend inside anxiously. 'What's the matter?'

'Sit down. We need to talk, seriously. I know you've seen Phil today. You know there is a warrant out for his arrest?'

Mills sank onto the sofa, almost relieved that someone knew. She told her friend, through her tears, about their conversation and how frightened she had been by his demeanour. 'He says there's nothing between him and Claudia but she was there, in the cottage.'

'Do you know where he is living now?'

'No,' she replied truthfully. 'You don't think he killed that girl do you?' Her tears were unstoppable now.

'To be honest I don't know what to believe. This Claudia seems an odd one. She certainly didn't seem to be very fond of Phil, the way she spoke. From what she said, she seemed convinced that he was capable of... such an act.'

Mills waited to see what would happen next, uncertain whether Nina was treating their conversation as informal or was it more serious.

'Mills, I beg you to persuade Phil to hand himself in. It's the only way this is going to be resolved. If he doesn't, I'm going to have to report that he's been seen.' She rose and went into the kitchen, leaving Mills to consider what to do next.

Brenda was pulling the curtains although it was only eight and the sun had not set.

'You're taking a big risk coming back here,' she told Phil, resuming her position in the one comfortable armchair.

Phil was perched on the tiny sofa, his long legs stretched across the rug, almost touching the fireplace. His knees were shaking visibly.

'Have you eaten?' she asked. 'I can make some beans on toast if you're hungry.'

He shook his head without speaking, so she assumed he was rejecting the offer and remained seated. Seeing that it was a physical effort for him to concentrate, she waited for him to tell her why he had taken the risk to visit her again.

'I've come because I... I've seen Claudia.'

'What? You must be insane!' she shouted, and then stopped. Let him talk, she told herself.

'She... she admitted it.'

Brenda remained silent until she could control herself no longer. 'She admitted what, Phil?' she asked trying to sound calm.

'The hair... she said the hair was not...'

'Not yours? But they analysed it!'

'She admitted it. She said no-one would believe me.'

'Oh my God! Why would she do that? Why on earth would she do that?'

'I think...' She could tell it was a huge effort for him to continue. 'I think ... that she... wants me... to be charged with... murder.'

'But there's no connection, Phil.'

'No, no. I think she wants me... to be charged... with Rachel... Rachel's murder.'

She told him to relate his meeting with Claudia word for word. It took a long time and at the end he fell back exhausted.

'Phil, are you all right? You seem... have you been taking something?'

'Just... You know...'

'Oh no. I thought you'd finished with that years ago.'

She tried to persuade him to stay, just for the night. She didn't want him driving in that state but he was adamant and dragged himself off, back to the wood in Wharfedale. She hadn't seen him like that for a long time, in fact he hadn't turned back to the drugs since he returned from the Balkans.

She lit a cigarette. Once she had followed a small tot of whisky with another, and then one more, she had thought through the whole thing. If Phil was telling the truth, it was Claudia Bishop who should be arrested. Her attempt to incriminate Phil would make sense if she was the real murderer but they knew that Kelly Lewis had been attacked by a man. So did she really frame him just to get her own back on him for not wanting to be involved with her and her business? It seemed extreme. If she was willing to see him imprisoned for goodness knows how long just for rejecting her, what else was she capable of? Would she really want to have him accused of Rachel's murder? There would be no logical explanation for that unless...

She picked up her mobile to call Nina, and then looked at her watch. It was late but this was important.

Chapter 17

Brenda slept late, as she always did on a Saturday morning, but cursed when she saw the time. She had planned to have a proper breakfast before catching the train to Oxford, but now she would only be able to grab a slice of toast before jumping in the car and speeding the short distance to the station.

Once she had found the correct compartment and settled into her seat, she took out the scrap of paper with the name and address of the man with the mudi. Yilmaz, it appeared, was a Turkish name, which made some sense if he really was in the rug trade, she thought. She had done a bit of research when she had received the call.

'It's such a coincidence,' May had said on the phone, 'I met Mr Yilmaz at a show in London last week and when he told me he imported carpets, I remembered what you said about it being a hobby of yours and I thought what fun it would be if you were to have one of his pups!'

The journey to Oxford was straightforward with no changes but it took four hours so by the time she arrived she was desperate for a cigarette. She sheltered outside the station watching the rain bounce off the pavement, wondering which of the cars belonged to Mr Yilmaz. As she stubbed out her cigarette and was wondering whether she had time for another, a man in a trench coat walked up to her and used her name.

'I knew it was you,' he said. 'Your description of your shirt was most accurate.'

He had laughed when she'd told him that she would be wearing her lime green blouse with the red and yellow flowers. They shook hands and she followed him to where he had parked a brand new Bentley. Brenda, who liked to think she knew a bit about cars, sank into the passenger seat and enthused about the interior, the exterior and the engine as they left Oxford behind. He smiled but said little until they turned from a narrow lane through wrought iron gates onto a long tarmac drive. It seemed like several minutes before the hedges on either side disappeared revealing a very large mansion.

'Wow! Is this yours?' Brenda was immediately embarrassed by her question but Mr Yilmaz seemed pleased by her outburst of admiration.

'Yes, it's all mine,' he said quietly.

He led her behind the house and unlocked the back door, quickly pushing buttons on an alarm system. She could hear dogs barking somewhere beyond the house.

'Do you live here on your own?' asked Brenda.

'No, I have a son who is still at home. He's gone shopping. Always he is shopping!' His teeth were white and straight when he smiled. 'I will make coffee. Do you like Turkish coffee or will I make it the Italian way?' he asked courteously.

He's a good looking man, Brenda thought, accepting Turkish style coffee.

She perched on a stool, studying the spacious kitchen which was probably the floor area of her house. Surely he didn't look after this all by himself?

He carried the tray through an imposing entrance hall to a grand room at the front of the house, offering her a seat on a large sofa. It was leather and cream... and very comfortable. The floors were polished wood. There were very expensive rugs strewn around the room. She knew they were expensive because it was her job to know about such things.

'So where are the dogs?' she asked.

'When we have finished coffee, we will visit kennels.'

'So your dogs live outside?'

'Not all the time. When I am out, they go in kennel but when I return, they join me indoors.'

'They must be very well behaved.' She indicated the furniture and the floor. 'Do they come in here?'

'Well, no. Actually we tend to live at the back of the house, generally, unless we have guests.' He smiled, gesturing to her to help herself to more of the sweet pastries. 'So, you are interested in having a mudi puppy? Or maybe more than one?'

She fabricated more lies, embellishing them with nieces and nephews who would be delighted if she had a dog. She had done her homework and described how she would cope with the training, the exercise, even diet.

'You sound very knowledgeable, Brenda. May I call you Brenda?'

'Of course, Mr Yilmaz.'

'Please call me Naj, everyone does. Now, if you would like to come outside...' He led her back through the kitchen into the garden which had views across fields far into the distance. Everywhere was neat and tidy, particularly the wooden kennels at the far end of the house. Two figures were bouncing up and down at the wire fence, barking furiously. Brenda felt quite nervous but knew she had to appear delighted by the large, black creatures. She steeled herself as Naj unlocked the gate, releasing them. She need not have worried. They greeted their master energetically but fell still on command until he permitted them to approach her. They did so gently, sniffing her delicately.

'She is Maisie and this one is Eleanora.'

Brenda stroked them tentatively as they followed obediently into the kitchen and lay down on the floor at their feet. She asked him numerous questions about the dogs, including how long he'd had mudis.

'I've been breeding them for just two years but I've had mudis for many years. Probably fifteen.'

But eventually she knew she would have to start asking more difficult questions if she was going to find out whether he was capable of murdering a woman, rolling her up in one of his very expensive rugs and burying her in the sand near Whitby – even if he did seem a charming man, quite incapable of such actions.

'You have such a lovely house. I wonder how you keep it so nice. You must have a lot of people working for you, like gardeners and cleaners?'

'Of course.' He smiled his winning smile. They come to help, of course. I have two cleaners and two gardeners but that's all. But I expect you have someone to help you too?'

She smiled enigmatically. As if she could afford someone to clean her house. They stood in silence for a moment while she compiled her thoughts. A door banged in the distance and Naj looked relieved.

'That must be my son,' he said, leading her back into the garden and round to the front of the house, followed by Maisie and Eleanor.

The boy who emerged from the Mercedes off-roader was tall and blond, contrasting physically to his father. He smiled politely and didn't change expression when Naj asked him to run Brenda back to the station. He promised to let her know when Maisie next had pups and helped her into the car. He stood in the drive watching them leave until they turned a corner and Brenda settled back in her seat.

She knew how to talk to teenagers. Her sister had three boys and it was simple.

'Cigarette?'

'Thanks.'

She lit two, handing him one, watching with amusement. He was an experienced smoker.

'How old are you?'

'Seventeen.'

'So you're studying?'

'Yes.'

'A levels?'

'Yes.'

'University next?'

'Yes.'

'Subject?'

'Engineering.'

The formalities over she knew she had to be direct if she was to gain any information before they reached the station.

'Did your father say he was separated from your mother?'

'I doubt it. He never talks about her.'

Brenda cringed inwardly at her gaff but she needn't have worried.

'She left when I was small,' he volunteered without a hint of emotion.

'That's a shame,' Brenda offered, embarrassed by her lack of – what did they call it? – emotional intelligence. Oh well, in for a penny...

'Did she go off with someone?'

'Dunno.'

'And she's never got in touch?'

He shook his curly blond head.

'And you've never...'

'No, I couldn't. Dad would go ballistic if he found out.'

'I suppose you had a string of nannies while you were growing up then?'

'No. I go to boarding school in the week and come home at weekends. Always have since we moved from Guisborough. We don't need anyone else.'

So the wife and mother had disappeared not, as she had imagined might be the case, an au pair or nanny. Her thanks were heartfelt when she said goodbye to Naj junior at the station. She had at least something to go on when she got back to base.

April had expected Tim to have rung her by now. She checked her mobile for the fourth time, and then turned it off.

'I'm going to pop over to see Mum,' she told Dave. He was slumped on the sofa, reading the paper.

'No football?' she asked, surprised to find the television off. It seemed as if he had watched it non-stop for a month.

'No. It's the losers tonight but they're not on until this evening.'

'The losers?' She was about to make a witty remark but decided against it. Sarcasm was lost on Dave anyway. She looked at her watch. If she left now she would be in plenty of time. She could take it easy; maybe even stop for a coffee and call Tim again.

'Can you give the boys some dinner when they get back from swimming?' she called, not waiting for a reply before she pulled the door behind her.

The traffic was worse than she expected. Perhaps it was the rain but there were queues through town. It wasn't until she was past Ilkeley that she was able to put her foot down. It was nearly eleven already, so she would only have a few minutes to take a look round the caravan site before meeting the owner.

The site was bigger than she had expected, with a large number of permanent mobile homes the size of her own house. She was impressed by them, wishing she could live in such rural surroundings all year round. The rain was barely a drizzle now and the sun was trying to come out. A few children were playing outside the caravans and a couple in anoraks were wandering along holding tennis racquets. She wasted valuable minutes finding the plot number before seeking out a suitable parking spot, wondering if she was supposed to have a permit or report her presence on site. She stopped under a tree, locking the car carefully while she looked round to see if anyone was observing her, but this part of the site was deserted.

The caravan was small compared to its neighbours. The windows are mucky, she thought, and the tyres need pumping up. But she supposed the wheels weren't important unless the caravan was going somewhere. She walked round, peering through the windows and wasn't impressed with what she could see. She waited outside for a few minutes then idly tried the door. The handle turned, the door opened outwards and she climbed inside.

The musty smell suggested it had been closed up for months and the heat was unbearable. She opened the door to go back outside but there was a man standing at the bottom of the steps. They were face to face with just centimetres between them. She was perturbed, expecting him to step back, to put some space between them. But he stood his ground so she backed into the room and the man followed her, shutting the door behind him.

'Is this your caravan?' she asked, half hoping he wasn't the owner.

'Yeah. You've come to view it?'

'Yes. I rang.'

'Yeah. Well 'ere it is. This is it.'

She was uncomfortable with the way he stared at her. She lowered her eyes but she could feel him watching her as she pretended to examine the view – although the windows were so smeared it was difficult to see out.

He opened and shut cupboard doors until he found what he was searching for and pulled out a kettle, filling it from the tap at a tiny sink. He produced a box of matches from a drawer and attempted to light the stove, cursing under his breath as the gas failed to light. 'We could brew up some tea but the gas 'as run out. Sit down, sit down,' he instructed, waving at the bench along the back of the tiny room.

She obeyed, forcing a smile despite her increasing anxiety. She had come to find out if her sister had any connection with the owner of this grubby little caravan but it was clear that she wouldn't have been in a relationship with him. She knew that she should be asking the sort of questions a prospective holiday maker would pose but the man's demeanour made her mind go blank. Shouldn't he be telling her about the site and its amenities?

'This seems like a nice location,' she remarked trying to produce a convincing smile.

The man was peering through the window, as if looking for someone. 'Yeah.' He didn't look round but continued to stare. 'Nice and quiet. You won't be disturbed.'

Maybe that was what Georgie had wanted – peace and quiet. 'That's good because I want to work here. Yes, I've got plenty of work to do and I don't want to be disturbed.'

'So what line of work are you in?' He was looking at her now, waiting for a response.

She hesitated. 'I'm a... teacher.'

'Really? Were your Mum and Dad teachers too?'

'No, why?' April replied, puzzled by the question.

'With your sister being a teacher too, like.'

'You knew Georgie?'

'Oh yeah, she was a teacher at my school.'

'*Your* school?'

'Yeah, you were there yesterday, wasn't you? That's where you got my number. Penny Meadows said.'

So that was the connection between Georgie and the caravan. It belonged to someone at the school. She felt a sense of relief. 'So did she use the caravan?' she asked innocently.

'She might 'ave done.' He grinned and she noticed how brown his teeth were. If she was going to discover the truth she would have to get past her disgust for this man from Georgie's school.

'And what do you do at the school?' she asked, as pleasantly as she could muster. 'Do you teach?'

The man guffawed. 'You don't consider I could be a teacher, do you?' She tried to protest but he ignored her. 'No, of course not, far too poorly educated to be a teacher. Well, let me tell you, I could teach those toffee-nosed teachers a thing or two.'

The bitterness in his voice frightened her and she stood up, determined to get out of the caravan. But he moved towards her. 'Sit down,' he ordered, and then smiled – a smile that was like a sneer. 'We 'aven't got to know each other properly yet.'

Nina had persuaded Mills that she needed to go shopping for the wedding.

'I have the dress and shoes,' she argued. 'What else do I need?'

Nina frowned at her and began counting on her fingers while she listed the items. 'First there's make-up.'

'Fiona's got someone coming in on the day to do all that.'

'You'd let another person do your make-up?' Nina looked shocked.

'Yes.'

'OK. So there's jewellery.'

'Nina, you know I don't wear jewellery... at least not the fiddly stuff you mean.'

'Earrings! You must wear earrings with the dress.'

'Fiona has chosen some for me – a present she said.'

'Mills Sanderson you are no fun. I thought at least I'd get a shopping trip out of this wedding.'

'I don't mind coming if you want to go out,' Mills offered.

'There's no point in going to Leeds unless it's for something special.' Nina looked thoughtful. 'Have you bought them a present?'

Mills considered. She hadn't even thought of getting her father a wedding present. She wouldn't know where to start.

'Do they have a list? They must have a list. Where is their list? Harrods?'

They both giggled.

'I suppose I should give them something... but I'm not going to buy china or bedding from some fancy store.'

'No, I'm sure they would prefer something personal. Let's go and look for something personal.' Nina was flushed with excitement.

Mills agreed, only because it was so obvious that her friend wanted to go out shopping.

Nina offered to drive them to Leeds while Nige looked after Rosie. While she was busy giving him instructions on what to give Rosie for lunch, Mills checked her mobile. There was a missed call from Tim O'Neill. She rang him immediately.

'Hi, Dr Sanderson. I wondered if you've spoken to April today?'

'Why?'

'She left me a message yesterday but I didn't pick it up until today. She's visiting a caravan in Threshfield and wanted me to go with her. I've tried her mobile but I can't get through.'

'Threshfield?'

'Yes. She said she found an advert at the school. She left me directions and everything but I didn't get the message until about half an hour ago.'

What was she to do? April was going to a caravan at Threshfield?

'Who is she seeing there?' Mills asked.

'She didn't say. The owner I suppose. Her message wasn't clear, except to give the site number and the time. She was to be there at eleven-thirty.'

Mills looked at the phone, it was nearly three o'clock. 'She could be back home now.'

'I suppose.'

'Have you tried ringing her home number?'

'No. I don't use that number. It's Dave... he...'

'OK. Look I'll call her and ring you back.' It was not long before Dave picked up. She asked for April but he told her she was out.

'Will she be back soon?'

'Don't know, love. She's visiting her Mam. She didn't say.'

Mills called Dawn but she hadn't seen her and wasn't expecting her. She rang Tim to let him know. The man seemed disappointed and anxious but Mills reassured him that it was probably a simple misunderstanding and promised to let him know if April rang her.

In the car, Nina confided that she wanted to buy Nige a Father's Day present. 'I didn't even think about it and he was so disappointed. I did get him a card from Rosie but I think she would have wanted me to buy him a special present now that he's better, don't you.'

Mills said nothing but nodded with a smile. The sales had started so it would be really busy in Leeds and Nina would spend hours choosing a gift for her husband – she just knew it.

It was three hours later when they were drinking coffee in a small Italian snack bar that Nina finally relaxed. The apron she had purchased for Nige was perfect for the barbeque but she wouldn't stop there. When she saw the Disney alarm clock, she decided he would love it. It was only after she had spent a fortune on a silk tie for him that she was satisfied.

'I think he'll look really smart for lectures in that,' she said, examining it for the third time.

'Yes, after he's been woken up by Mickey Mouse... and when he comes home he'll be able to protect it while he barbeques using his lovely apron.'

'Oh no,' Nina said seriously, 'he's not to wear the tie in the garden.'

Mills laughed and finished her muffin without speaking.

'You may laugh but what about this present for your Dad and Fiona, young lady?'

'I've got no idea.'

Nina looked at her watch. 'We've got another hour on the car park. Come on, we'll have a look in Harvey Nichols – they are bound to have something suitable.'

Mills followed Nina reluctantly to the Victoria Quarter. She had to agree that the building alone was worth visiting but once inside she was overwhelmed by the vastness of it all. Nina dragged her along to the china and glass but Mills eventually had to admit defeat.

'They have two homes, Nina. They don't need anything like that. Anyway, I don't have Fiona's taste. Let's go home. Please?'

In the end Nina, accepting that Mills was not going to buy anything, agreed they could leave.

While Nina paid for the car park, Mills checked her mobile. There was a text from Tim. *No news of April yet.*

'They say Georgie went off with someone in a Jaguar,' April had offered, hoping that at least the man might give her information of some kind before she left. That was when she thought she would be leaving the caravan unharmed.

He had laughed again. 'Yes, I told that girl about a mysterious Jaguar... and she believed me.'

'So was it not true?'

'No, not really.'

'But why lie about something as important as that?' She had been angry with him then for playing with Georgie's memory.

'Because it was *me* what picked her up.' He waited for her to react but she couldn't. She didn't know whether he was joking. 'See, you can't believe it either but she came with me. She chose to come away with me.'

April wanted to be sick. She didn't want to believe that Georgie would go off with this man voluntarily but the alternative was worse. She considered for a second.

'So where is she now?'

No answer.

Then he'd taken her mobile, locked her in and driven off to get the whisky. She had broken down, weeping uncontrollably for several minutes until she knew she had to pull herself together and tried unsuccessfully to open the windows to escape.

She was in the airless caravan for two hours before he returned. He was no longer the aimable owner but her captor and she was terrified by the certainty that he had been responsible for Georgie's disappearance. He wouldn't let her leave but he didn't say what was to happen to her. She daren't make for the door again because she couldn't bear for him to manhandle her in the way he did when she tried before. She sat rigidly on the bench seat while he stood by the window, staring out as if waiting for someone, slowly finishing off the bottle of whisky.

She hadn't asked him why he was keeping her there. She didn't want to know because she didn't want him to confirm her fears. She tried to remember what she'd heard on the radio when they were interviewing someone who'd been kidnapped in

Beirut. Make friends with your captors, they'd said. How could she bring herself to befriend him?

He looked at his watch.

'What time is it?' she asked, hoping her voice didn't reveal the terror she was experiencing.

'Plenty of light left. You should get yer 'ead down. We'll be 'ere for a long while yet.'

Now she knew that something awful had happened to her sister and although she didn't want to hear it, she needed to know before... before...

There was a tremor in her voice but she was going to make him tell her. 'So what happened to Georgie?'

When he turned to stare at her his eyes were glazed and he almost fell onto the chair beside him.

'She 'ad an accident.' He looked weary as he slumped against the wall.

'An accident?' she asked warily, anxious not to annoy him.

'Fell over the edge.'

April had to take several deep breaths before she could ask the next question. 'Fell where?'

'Into the quarry.'

She emitted an involuntary squeak then regained control. 'And... was she hurt badly?'

He shuffled his feet. 'Yeah. Badly 'urt. Very badly 'urt.' He looked pathetic sitting there. Old and pathetic, despite his tattooed arms and crew cut.

'Where is she now?' asked April calmly.

'She's at peace now.'

'Where?' she demanded more confidently.

'None of your bleeding business!'

He seemed to recollect where he was and what he was doing, standing unsteadily. She raised her arms to defend herself, cowering into the wall as he came towards her.

Chapter 18

It took Tim longer than he'd anticipated to reach Threshfield and then more time to find the caravan site, despite April's directions. He knew he was foolish to race over there but felt a compulsion to satisfy himself that she was safe. He hooted gently at the children playing football on the road as he peered at the mobile homes, trying to work out where to go. In his anxiety he found himself going back out the way he had come, turning to retrace his route until he recognised April's car parked close to a small touring caravan. He checked his watch. It had been a long visit if she was still in there.

Anxiously he approached the caravan and peered through the window. It was difficult to make out the interior but there was a faint sound from inside. He pressed his face to the Perspex to get a clearer view, quickly ducking down again to avoid being seen by a man as he moved away from the seat where April was lying.

He was confused, unsure what the scene he had witnessed meant. It would be foolhardy to rush in, even if the door was unlocked. He didn't know the man, but they obviously knew each other. He edged to the corner of the pitch, out of line of sight from any windows. Was that a cry or a laugh? He was calling Mills when there was a loud scream and he launched himself at the caravan door, rattling at the handle ineffectively. Miraculously it flew open but he soon realised why – the man was on top of him punching and kicking. Tim was defending himself with his arms, trying to gain leverage using his feet against the caravan steps. He opened his eyes to see the man coming down with his fist again, and in the background April was at the doorway buttoning up her shirt.

'It's him. He killed Georgie!'

And that's when he found the strength to take the man's wrist and twist his arm sufficiently to push him away and land on top of him. Tim had the advantage of him now and was beating his head on the ground until he went quiet. April begged him to stop and Tim hauled himself off the man, who was moaning quietly.

'Find some string or something to tie his feet,' he said, panting heavily as he pulled the limp body into the caravan, not caring that his head was bouncing on each of the three steps.

Tim could feel April shaking as they sat side by side on the bench seat. As he put his arm round her, she began to cry, quietly at first then howling loudly. He rang the police and waited.

Mills had picked up his missed call.

'What will you do?' she asked.

'Keep him here until the police arrive.'

'But what if he gets violent?'

'I've tied his feet together.' He sounded amused. 'I had to use my belt. I couldn't find anything for his hands and I don't want to leave April. She's very shaken.'

She continued to talk to him, just to keep him company and then she said she had an idea.

'Tim, I'm going to make a call. I've got a friend down there that may be able to help you. You saw him at the wedding.'

April grabbed his arm, pointing to the floor where the unconscious man lay – except now he was coming round. He struggled to undo his feet, lashing out at them where they sat. Tim put his foot on the man's legs, telling him to stay still or he'd knock him out again.

'Who are you?' he asked the man, who was rubbing his head and moaning.

'He's from the school.' April spoke at last. 'He's the caretaker. His names Archie and he abducted Georgie.' Her voice went up to a cry as she sobbed yet again.

Tim was not a violent man. He knew people saw him as gentle and caring. Georgie always did. She used to say that he wouldn't harm a fly. And yet he wanted to hurt this man in so many ways.

'He brought her here,' continued April. 'The car broke down so he offered her a lift, but he brought her *here*.' She dabbed her eyes. 'He kept her as a prisoner. He would have held her here forever if he hadn't killed her!' She cried silently into her tissue.

'It was an accident,' complained Archie.

'Accident?' demanded Tim, turning on the man prostrate under his foot.

'We was walking by the quarry when she tried to scarper. She jumped over the bleeding fence!'

Soon afterwards a man called Phil rang, asking exactly where they were. Another fifteen minutes and a motorbike roared up. April opened the door when he knocked three times as arranged, and Tim recognised the best man from his cousin's wedding. He had brought ties for the man's feet and hands, and water for April.

Tim considered himself astute. He knew that any confession made to him by the caretaker who had murdered his wife would probably not be considered reliable evidence. But if an independent person was present, particularly someone from the forensic services, that would be acceptable. So once Phil was there, he asked Archie to tell him what happened to his wife.

'I want you to tell me what you did to my wife?' he asked again.

'Nothing, I told you, it was an accident.'

'You said she fell.'

'She did. She jumped into the quarry. When I got down there, she was dead. Satisfied?'

'Where is she now, Archie?' Phil asked quietly.

'She's still there.'

'Really?' Phil paused. 'I think she would have been found by now if that was the case.'

'I didn't leave 'er lying there like that,' the man replied. 'I did the right thing by 'er.'

Tim went to get up but Phil motioned him to stay seated.

'Where is she, Archie?'

'She's in the pond. I put 'er in the pond so not nobody would disturb 'er.'

Tim watched Phil slowly rubbing his forehead. He could feel April sobbing silently next to him. And he felt suddenly exhausted. Georgie was lying under the water nearby and he couldn't feel anything. He couldn't sustain the anger... his fury had subsided to a sadness that he could now acknowledge as loss. He had lost Georgie for ever... he knew that now. Strangely it didn't make it any better that he knew for certain now she hadn't run away from him. She'd been taken away, irretrievably removed by the man lying moaning at his feet, and no amount of punching or kicking or screaming at him would change that fact. They could cry... they could descend into a deep despair but nothing would change. Georgie was gone forever.

Phil asked Tim if he wanted to leave with April; perhaps take her outside while they waited for the police. April had become quiet but continued to hang on to him tightly, her fingers pinching his arm. He shook his head. So they sat in silence until there was a siren in the distance, gradually becoming louder as the police cars entered the caravan site.

Suddenly the spell was broken. Voices and movement everywhere. Names and addresses, explanations and lies, harsh words and nearly another fight. Finally Tim was left alone with April, watching the cars disappear; just the motorbike remaining as it was left, thrown on the ground in Phil's hurry to help.

'I don't understand,' said April as she attempted to smooth her hair and tidy her clothes. 'Why did they take the man who came to help us?'

'Phil? They said he was involved in another incident. He's helping them with their enquiries, I suppose.'

The bike was heavy and Tim was struggling to get it upright, moving it behind the caravan for safety.

'You'll be wanting to get home,' he offered. 'Dave can bring you back to pick up the car tomorrow.'

She smiled gratefully. 'Thanks, Tim. I'm sorry it had to end like this.'

'End? What d'you mean?'

'That we had to find out about Georgie this way.'

'Yes, I see.'

Nina had been waiting for news since Mills had rung her in a panic. At the time she'd been able to check that a car was on its way and reassure her friend. So when Nina heard that Phil was being held downstairs, she asked Hazel whether it would be all right for her to see him.

'Not my place to provide permission, but I'd be careful you don't find yourself in trouble with Mitch.'

So she sat back down at her desk and continued filling in her timesheets, wondering if it would be out of order to let Mills know what had happened but texting her just the same. Her work was interrupted when DC Ian Walker came in waving a sheet of paper, saying that the girl behind the bar in "The Fleece" was an artist and had made a sketch of the man she had described as creepy.

'What *are* you gabbling about, young Ian?' Hazel asked.

'She works in "The Fleece" most weekends but she's been away, trekking in Nepal.'

'Lucky her,' remarked Hazel sarcastically.

'No, Sarge, lucky us,' he replied with a cheeky grin, 'because we now have a photo-fit!' He handed her a piece of paper, which Hazel displayed to Nina. It was a pencil sketch of a young man's face below a floppy fringe. He had narrow eyes and a thin mouth. Nina moved closer to scrutinise the earring hanging from his left ear.

'That's pretty distinctive,' she said.

The others looked more closely and agreed that not many lads sport an anchor hanging from their ear-lobe.

'Have you got a statement from her yet?' Hazel asked.

'Not yet but I brought her along. She's downstairs if you want to ask her anything about him.'

'Well why didn't you say, our Ian?'

The girl was in her twenties, not from the area, judging by her strong Liverpool accent.

'I was telling 'im about the bloke we 'ad in the other Sunday night. Dead creepy. Makes a pint last for three hours, sitting up at the bar the 'ole evening. Talking about weird stuff. Keeps trying to chat me up. In the end I told me boss and 'e told 'im to leave.'

'What time was that?' Nina asked.

'Couldn't be sure but about an hour before closing.'

'Half ten, eleven?'

'Yeah.'

'Was he local?'

'Wouldn't know.'

'Yorkshire accent?'

She looked around, then stared at the ceiling for a moment. 'Yeah. Local all right. He comes from Catterick right enough.'

'How d'you know that?' Hazel asked.

'Because he's in every weekend. Some of the locals know 'im.'

Hazel looked at her watch. 'Get down to "The Fleece", then into "The Ralph Fitz Randal". They'll be open. Flash the picture, find out who he is and bring him in pronto.'

Ian left the room obediently. As he did so, another DC came in with a note for Hazel. She read it, folded it carefully, offering the girl tea, and asking her to remain there until they could take a statement.

Outside Nina grabbed her arm. 'This is it, Hazel. We've got him. You see, it was nothing to do with Phil Freedman.'

'Let's wait and see, shall we?' Hazel moved swiftly away and disappeared into another room, leaving her in the corridor with a sense of alienation that troubled her. She followed, catching a glimpse of the occupant as Hazel shut the door firmly behind her. It was Phil. She went slowly back to the office. There was a voicemail from Brenda asking her to call urgently, so she let her know that Phil was in custody. The voice at the other end was excitable.

'I'm glad you rang back, Nina. I have a piece of information, well two pieces actually, that may be of great significance.'

Nina waited.

'Are you still there?'

'Yes.'

'I know a man who has a Heriz rug *and* keeps mudis.'

Nina paused, wondering what she meant.

'D'you see?'

'Sorry, I'm not with you.'

There was a sigh at the other end. 'You are aware of the body on the beach? The hair of the dog? The Persian rug?'

'Not directly.'

'Well, can you pass on the information for me? It's very important.'

'I can do that, if you send me a fax with the details.'

'All right, all right. His wife disappeared about ten years ago, the son says. What are the chances of someone having a Heriz rug, a mudi and a wife who goes off ten years ago?'

'You tell me, Brenda.'

'Pretty small by any standards, I'd say. They'll need to get DNA from the son to test for a match but I'm willing to bet on it. Or dental records, yes that's what they need... dental records.'

'Send me the report and I'll make sure it gets to the right officer.'

'Thank you, my dear. Good...'

'No, don't go yet.' She explained to Brenda her frustration that Phil was in custody although there was a real suspect who was being brought in for questioning. She promised to update Brenda as soon as she heard any news.

It was another three hours before they had tracked down the man in the sketch and brought him back to Newby Wiske. Not that he'd been avoiding the police. In fact he was sitting in "The Fleece" as large as life, harassing the barmaid. He'd been drinking, which combined with the shock of seeing the uniformed officers, caused him to panic and he attempted to make a run for it. There was quite a struggle when they caught up with him. He protested that he'd been nowhere near the pub at the time of the incident, and demanded a solicitor but he'd had so much to drink it was decided to let him sleep it off overnight.

'Spent time in Afghanistan,' declared Hazel. 'He'll probably get off with a psychiatrist's report.'

'You're getting cynical in your old age,' Nina said. 'So has Phil gone?'

'Just going to tell him.'

'Can I come?'

'If you like.'

Phil was slumped on the table. He looked up wearily when they went in, as if expecting the worst.

'You're free to go, Dr Freedman,' said Hazel, holding the door open wide for him.

He pushed himself to his feet and slouched to the door, hanging on to the handle for support.

'Do you remember me, Phil?' Nina asked, hoping she sounded friendly.

He smiled at her, stumbling into the doorway.

'Let's go down to the canteen for a cup of tea,' she suggested, offering her arm. 'It's OK, Hazel. I can manage.'

She made him have a drink with something to eat, watching him struggle to concentrate. It was obvious he was on medication of some sort, whether legal or not. He couldn't drive in that state, so she would have to think of a way of sobering him up before he left. It was after six and she should be on her way home by now. She made a decision. 'Phil, you're coming home with me.'

He protested half-heartedly but she could see he was in no state to make much fuss.

Fortunately Nige and Mills were so surprised to see Phil that nothing was said as she left him on the sofa to sleep off whatever he was on. The others followed her silently into the yard then bombarded her with questions.

'Look,' Nina said when they paused for breath, 'he's been through a lot. I know you may not be entirely happy having him here but there was nowhere else for him to go. So that's settled.'

She went indoors, standing for a moment to watch Phil lying peacefully along the sofa with his feet dangling over the end. Resisting the urge to remove his socks for washing, she called Brenda to give her news of his release. How could she refuse when the woman begged to be allowed to come to see him?

Mills woke early on Sunday morning, going over the events of the past few days. Nina had explained to her in graphic detail how they had found Georgina after searching the pond in the quarry. She'd described the horrific ordeal that April had been subjected to and admonished Mills for poking her nose in where she shouldn't. Fortunately April was safely back with her family but it had been a huge shock. They were all trying to come to terms with the news.

She'd heard the front door slam half an hour ago and when she came downstairs the house seemed deserted. She put two slices of bread in the toaster and stood waiting for them to brown.

'Good morning.'

Phil was in the doorway. She didn't turn round.

'D'you want some toast?'

'No thanks. Nina made me breakfast before they went out.'

'Out?'

'Just a walk with the baby. It was such a nice day, she said.'

How tactful, Mills thought, to leave them alone. As Nina had pointed out so forcefully, she'd asked him to help Tim and April, and by doing that it was her fault he'd been arrested. What could she say to him?

She buttered the toast, layering the marmalade thickly, spreading it around... playing for time. Finally she turned without looking at him. He moved from the doorway to let her pass, following her into the yard.

'Mills. I want to speak to you. You don't have to say anything but listen, please.'

He was sitting to one side, so she didn't have to look at him. She nodded slightly and tried to eat.

'I was arrested for a crime I didn't do. Now the right person has been caught, I have been released unconditionally. Do you understand?'

She nodded.

'I was a suspect because my hair was found on the victim. The reason why? Because Claudia Bishop framed me. She lies, Mills. She told you we were in a relationship... we're not, and we never have been. She's devious and malicious. You do believe me, don't you?'

Mills nodded again. But it didn't make it any easier. She couldn't go back to how they'd been. It had been spoiled. How could she tell him?

'Mills. I've got to tell you this because it will explain the rest. When I was at university I was engaged to a girl called Rachel. She suffocated, or she was suffocated. That's why the police were so quick to arrest me this time. I found it hard to deal with Rachel's death and I became addicted to drugs, nothing illegal but prescription drugs, and it took a long time to get back on track. That's why I went abroad. I found a change of lifestyle helped shake me out of the depression. I'm telling you all this because it's happening again and I'm going to have to take a break again. Maybe a few months. Maybe a year.'

He'd stopped talking as if he expected her to say something but what did he want her to say?

'I'm going to have a bath now,' he continued. 'I didn't want to make a noise upstairs while you were still asleep.'

After he'd gone she dried her face with her sleeves and took her plate inside, the toast untouched.

Nina was relieved to find Phil looking refreshed after his night's sleep and coherent once more as he chatted with Brenda. Mills offered to prepare the food while Nige lit the barbeque, which meant that she and Brenda could have the quiet chat she requested. It was inevitable that the day would be dominated by football once Nige had lit the charcoal, so they retired to the nursery with Rosie where no-one would disturb them.

'Any news of my Mr Yilmaz?' Brenda asked immediately.

'No, not yet. I passed the information on to DI Turner. He'll make sure it's followed up.'

Nina lifted Rosie gently from her lap and placed her in the cot.

'In that case I want to talk to you about Phil.' She fidgeted on the small chair she had lowered herself into. 'I told you he's been to see Claudia to confront her over her lies. She as good as admitted to him that she falsified the evidence by switching the hair samples.'

'Are you sure?'

'Not only that. He thinks she may have been responsible for his fiancées death.' She stared expectantly at Nina, waiting for a reaction.

Nina sighed.

'You may puff and blow but I think he's got something and I think we should pay her a visit.'

'Not again!'

'Wait, I've got a plan.'

Nina listened very reluctantly. 'All right,' she agreed when Brenda had finished. 'But I'm not happy about it.'

Downstairs Nige and Phil were seated side by side on the sofa, engrossed in the football final between Holland and Spain. Mills watched from the doorway, waiting for the sausages to brown.

'By the way,' said Nige, without taking his eyes from the screen, 'I've been thinking about that message on the postcard. The rest of the message, like. The address thing doesn't make much sense but there are a couple of references that point to the same thing.'

'What's that then, Nige?'

'The *guardian angel* and *look after yourself*. They both mean caring, sort of, don't they? *Look after yourself* – it means take care. And a *guardian angel* takes care of you. See?'

'Yes, you are so right Nige – he *was* a care taker. The man who killed Georgina O'Neill was Archie, the school caretaker.

Chapter 19

It was difficult to believe that the man sitting in the interview room was capable of murder. He was young and Nina knew that behind the tough exterior he was probably terrified. In her opinion it was probably a sexual attack under the influence of alcohol that had gone dreadfully wrong. Although Hazel was happy for her to sit in, now that Phil was not in the picture, Nina was only observing and she was happy to do just that. Her colleague had recently attended the specialist interviewer course and she was there to learn from her.

In the event the lad was anxious to make his statement, prompted by his solicitor. 'It weren't like it looked,' he pleaded. 'She were happy to go with me. I said we could go to the car park, where it were quiet like.'

Nina expected Hazel to move in, asking what his intentions had been but she sat placidly with a slight smile on her face. There was quiet for a moment, then he continued.

'She wanted it. We were just kissing and cuddling a bit, then she changed her mind, started struggling like. I don't remember much but she must've fainted. I panicked and took off... I shouldn't 'ave left her.'

'Jamie, when you met her in the pub did you offer her a lift home?'

'I might've done. I don't remember a lot about it to be honest.'

'And do you have a car?'

He looked down at his clasped hands. 'No.'

Hazel took Jamie over the night, minute by minute, extracting what he could remember of the incident until he admitted, quite voluntarily, that he thought she'd agreed to have sex with him. When Hazel suggested that he may have been mistaken, he said that he was too drunk to be sure. When she described Kelly's injuries he appeared genuinely shocked and looked to his solicitor for reassurance. And at that stage Hazel offered him a break and a cup of tea.

'I'm guessing you found the course useful?' asked Nina, as they stood beside the coffee machine.

'You noticed?'

Nina smiled.

'Yes, I did,' admitted Hazel. 'They pointed out that I have a tendency to assume guilt and they suggested I did less talking and more listening.' She drained the paper cup and threw it in the bin. 'And it seems to work.'

Nina was impressed by how quickly it had worked. They returned to the interview room, where their suspect was waiting to make a statement. It was clear that he didn't recollect all the events of the evening but he admitted that he had accompanied her across the road where there had been a struggle and he had run from the scene leaving Kelly unconscious. It would only require corroboration of the timings to prove that no-one else had approached the girl before the cyclist discovered her just after Jamie had run off.

'You'll be busy here with the paperwork for the rest of the day, won't you?' Nina asked Hazel when they were back in the office. 'Would you cover for me – I've got a bit of investigative work to do down in Harrogate.'

Hazel sighed and nodded as she dragged a large file onto the desk in front of her.

*

Claudia had her back to Phil as he took care to close the door gently without shutting it fully. But she must have sensed his presence because she turned round suddenly, startled to see him on the other side of her desk.

'Good morning, Claudia.'

'What do you want?' She looked nervous but stood her ground.

'Shall we sit down?' he asked. 'I'd like a quiet chat, if I may.'

She moved sideways to the leather seat behind the desk without taking her eyes of him and lowered herself carefully into it.

'I wanted to let you know that the owner of the hair... the real hair that is, has been arrested. I understand he has confessed, so now there will be a full investigation into how you came to find my DNA in the sample *you* took.'

She shrugged her shoulders.

'It doesn't worry you?'

'Not really. Samples get contaminated all the time. I'm sure it will blow over.'

Phil could hear footsteps coming up the stairs, quiet but perceptible. 'Not if I tell them what you told me last time I was here.'

'But you won't, will you Phil?'

'Why shouldn't I tell them that you falsified the evidence? That you tried to frame me so I was arrested for attacking someone?'

'Because even if I did, no-one will believe your story against mine.'

'Why not?'

'Because I will tell them that I can prove you killed Rachel.'

'You know I didn't.'

'Do I?'

'Yes you do. In fact I think you know who did.'

She scrutinised him without speaking as if deciding whether to go along with him. 'What do you mean?'

'I mean that I think *you* killed her. I think you suffocated her.' He was watching her closely, trying to gauge her reactions, aware how important it was to get her to admit it. 'What I don't understand is why.'

'You just don't get it, do you? You and Rachel. Always the same. Love's young dream. It made me sick!' She was looking out of the window.

'Were you jealous of her?'

'Jealous?' She seemed surprised by his question. 'Not jealous of *her*, no. Jealous of her happiness perhaps. Everything she did. Everything she touched. Just for once she'd been dumped and *she* was asking *me* for sympathy, seeking out my company. For once we were equals.' She was staring into the distance, apparently reliving the past. 'And then along you come, making it all better. And, once again, Rachel is the fairest of them all. I'm sorry, but I'd just had enough.'

'Are you saying that you suffocated her?' he repeated.

'Yes, Phil.' She stood up. 'Yes I did and you can do what you like. If you so much as mention a suspicion of this to anyone I swear I'll ensure that you're convicted of her murder yourself.' She smiled at him. 'So, goodbye.'

Phil was unsure what to do next but suddenly the door opened.

'Thank you Claudia,' Brenda said, 'I got all that loud and clear.'

Claudia's face went through a series of emotions to one of intense anger. 'I don't care what you heard, no-one will be interested in what you have to say, you stupid little woman! Just get out.'

'Oh yes they will, Claudia. I have a colleague who would like to speak to you.'

Nina was embarrassed by her dramatic appearance from behind the door but it was obviously her duty to ask Claudia to come in for questioning. The tape would not be adequate evidence if she had a good lawyer but Claudia would need a very good story to wheedle her way out of a conviction. She called for a car and waited downstairs, where she warned Phil she would need a statement from him also.

'No problem. I'm not leaving for about a month.'

'Leaving? Where are you going?'

'Abroad again. I'm thinking of going to Colombia to help with the search for the disappeared there.'

She looked at Brenda, who shrugged. When Phil had left, Nina commented that she would be losing a good colleague.

'I was thinking of leaving myself,' she admitted.

'Really? Where would you go?'

Brenda looked up at the building behind her. 'I was thinking that this laboratory might be up for sale soon. I rather like the idea of taking it over... You look surprised. I have an inheritance that was meant to be my pension which might just take care of it, if she needs a quick sale. After all, whatever happens she's not going to be in the forensics business much longer, is she?'

'I guess not.'

'Anyway, more importantly, is there any news of my Mr Yilmaz?'

'Yes. They're investigating the wife. So far there's been no indication of her living over here or abroad. There has been no activity on her bank account or credit cards since she left, and so they're checking her dental records for comparison with the body. They'll know more then.'

On the way back to Newby Wiske she tried to compile a logical explanation of why she had called for Claudia to be taken in. She knew she was on shaky ground and so was not surprised to find an urgent note waiting for her in the office asking her to see the DI immediately.

Mitch did not lose his temper readily but she could see he was furious. She was trying not to cry as she explained why she was asking for Claudia Bishop to be brought in for questioning.

'It's not even our case, Nina. It's Durham's. There's a DI coming down from Aykley Heads this afternoon. He'll be dealing with it.'

He returned to the papers on his desk and began writing. The interview was over.

She collected her bag and made her way home in despondent mood. Even Rosie's cheeky face failed to lift her spirits. If she was going to get on in the force she would have to emulate Hazel and get a thicker skin.

She carried her daughter out to where Mills was working in the yard.

'Everything all right, Mills?'

She looked up and smiled. 'Yes, fine. Thanks for asking.'

'It's been a bit difficult for you recently. I just thought...'

'No, really. I'm good. In fact, I've been working on my kiln project today and we're going over to

Wharfedale tomorrow to talk to the owner of the farm about starting the excavation.'

'We?'

'Jake's coming with me.'

'Oh, I thought perhaps...'

Mills looked at her. 'Phil? No. We're not seeing each other again until he comes back from Colombia. Except for the funeral.'

'Funeral?'

'Georgina O'Neill's funeral. Tim rang. He doesn't know when it will be yet, there's the post mortem, but he's planned it all. He wants me and Phil to be there.'

'Mills, I thought I should tell you that Claudia is being questioned about the death of Phil's girlfriend, Rachel.'

'Rachel? She was his fiancée.'

'Yes. Claudia's virtually admitted it. I think that's why she took Phil's hair and fabricated the DNA test.'

'It's been a horrible mess, Nina. I just want to get on with my work to forget about it all for a while.'

'It's only just over a week before the wedding.'

'I know. I've got to go down again this Friday for the final dress fitting.'

'Have you thought of a present yet?'

'No. I can't afford anything big anyway.'

'I'm sure they wouldn't expect it. Just something personal.'

'For the couple that have everything?'

It was such a relief for Mills to be out in the field working again, with nothing to worry about but how to approach the excavation. Initially, when they'd passed the quarry and she thought about Georgina's body lying in the pond for so many years, she wondered whether she would be able to cope with visiting the site over the summer but, as Jake said, she's not there now so it shouldn't be considered an unhappy place.

The owner of the field had been sufficiently interested in the project to provide all the necessary permissions on the spot, so Jake suggested they "cracked on". As they carried the tools up from the minibus she attempted, rather awkwardly, to thank him for supporting her in the venture.

'No problem. To be honest I'm a bit short of original proposals myself so if I can collaborate on this one it will help me as well. You did say you would include my name on any reports?'

'Of course.'

It was like the old days, the two of them working side by side, uncovering the soil beneath the turf. He had taught her much of what she knew about the practical techniques but now they worked as equals and as colleagues, nothing more, nothing less. She was sure of that now.

Mills knew that the first stages would be slow but at the end of the day they had made reasonable progress. Jake suggested a drink as they packed up, driving them to a tiny pub in Arncliffe where the beer was served from a jug and they sat on the grass outside with a view along the main village street. The conversation inevitably turned to Nige and how well he had managed his return to work.

'Has Nina forgiven him for putting Rosie in the crèche?' Jake asked with a laugh.

'Actually, better than that. She's agreed to give it a try.'

'It'll make it easier for them to manage, with them both working full time.'

Mills agreed. 'It means they don't need me anymore. I've been thinking about moving out for some time.'

'Into Phil's?'

'No.' She'd responded too sharply. 'No,' she repeated, more lightly, 'I'm not.'

'So you're looking for somewhere to stay?'

'I'd like to find somewhere over this way, for the summer at least.' She wanted a place that was hers, where she could live alone and do whatever she wanted, when she wanted.

'That'll cost a bit,' was all he said.

'I know.' And I've not got it, she thought.

Mills worked in Wharfedale for the rest of the week but on Friday she travelled down to London for the final fitting of her dress. Fiona was already standing forlornly in her wedding gown in the middle of the shop while two assistants fiddled at her back. Mills thought she could detect tears.

'It's too tight,' Fiona muttered under her breath.

Mills was amazed at how restrained she was, considering. She had seen Fiona fly into a rage over quite minor failures in a restaurant but this time there were no recriminations.

'You'd better try yours on, miss,' one of the girls said.

To her relief the dress was absolutely fine. In fact it was more than fine, it was brilliant and she told them so. This didn't seem to help Fiona who continued to bite her lip as they undid her buttons and released her laces. Eventually they agreed to make some last minute alterations that would adjust the fit. As they went to leave, Fiona called back, 'And just add a little extra in case of... any... additional...'

Once they were on the pavement she burst into tears. Mills was embarrassed, unsure whether to say anything or not.

'It's so disappointing about the dress but in some ways I don't care,' Fiona wailed.

'What's the matter?' People were looking at them from the buses going past.

'I suppose I can tell you. Yes, of course I can. Mills, you're going to have a baby brother or sister.'

She burst out laughing. Just couldn't help it.

'Isn't it wonderful?' Now Fiona was laughing too, tears still rolling down her cheeks. 'Look at me. I must be a complete mess. But I'm so glad you're pleased.'

'Of course I am,' said Mills, relieved that her reaction had been so misunderstood.

It was one thing to accept that Fiona was pregnant, quite another to take in the idea that Dad was going to be a father. The hen night was off, Fiona announced, since it would be inappropriate for a pregnant lady to be out boozing before her wedding.

'But your father is still having his golfing weekend in Marbella as planned. He has no consideration.'

So it was just the two of them for supper that evening. Fiona had opened the doors onto the balcony and they sat looking across the city as they ate pasta from the delicatessen in Canary Wharf.

'I've chilled some wine just for you, darling!' Fiona filled an enormous glass with an expensive tasting chardonnay that Mills agreed was perfect.

Fiona leaned back in her chair, her hands on her stomach.

'You know, this is the most exciting thing that's ever happened to me.'

Mills was anxious that she might burst into tears again but she was smiling benignly, looking more relaxed than she had ever seen her. Wait until the child is born, thought Mills, recalling the juggling act that Nina had to perform every day of her life.

'Will you carry on working?'

'No way!' Fiona looked shocked. 'This baby is a blessing and I intend to enjoy every minute of her existence.'

Surely it's too early to know whether it's a girl, thought Mills. But she was ignorant about those things so didn't question the statement.

'I'm so pleased you decided to stay until Sunday,' Fiona said as they were clearing the dishes. 'It gives us a chance to get to know each other and... on a more practical matter, you can tell me about your relatives that are coming to the wedding. I've not met any of them. Do you think they'll like me?'

Mills surveyed her future step-mother in her tiny gold skirt, five inch heels and bleached blonde hair. She was not what they would be expecting, that was certain. But she would be in a wedding dress, if she hadn't expanded too much by next Saturday.

'I am sure they'll love you.' Once they get to know you, she added silently.

'Oh, and before I forget, darling: Hugh said could you come down on the train with your Grandmother on Friday? She's a bit nervous of travelling across London on her own, poor dear.'

'OK.'

'And talking of transport, Hugh and I were discussing about what to do with my car.'

Mills had only ever seen Fiona driving Dad's sports car.

'We decided we need a bigger vehicle if we're having a family,' she said, placing her hand on her stomach and smiling.

Mills smiled back, wondering where this was leading.

'My mini has been in the garage ever since I moved in. It's totally impractical now. Hugh wondered if you'd like it?'

Mills stared. What did she mean: would I like it? Of course she'd like it, it was a car, wasn't it?

Fiona looked puzzled. 'You haven't got a car, have you?'

'No, no, of course not. But I...'

'Good. You would like it, wouldn't you?'

'Of course but I'm not sure I could afford...'

'Oh it's very economical and it's taxed for another five months. I'm sure the insurance wouldn't be too much.'

'But the car?'

She expressed her amusement with a shrill laugh. 'We don't want anything for the *car*, darling. That's just a present from us. That's agreed then... you can take it away when you come next week.'

Chapter 20

Mills had been reticent to get in touch with Tim after the caretaker had been arrested, feeling responsible for him discovering that his wife would never return alive. She still couldn't eradicate the thought of Georgina's body lying in the pond for so long – knowing exactly the state it would have been in after three years in the water. However, Tim sounded delighted that he was finally able to lay his wife's body to rest. In fact he had been very busy making plans for the funeral.

'There's a green burial ground near here called Tarn Moor. We went to help scatter the ashes of a friend there and we both thought it was a lovely place to be. Georgie was ambivalent about cremations so I just feel that she's had enough. We'll bury her there.'

Mills told Nina about Tim's plans, expressing surprise at how quickly the body had been released.

'The PM was turned round rapidly, because the identification was not difficult and to be honest the state of the body meant it was done as quickly as possible. Poor Tim, it must be devastating for him.'

Mills took the opportunity to ask about the caretaker and Nina was surprisingly open.

'He's the vilest man, Mills,' she said with a shudder to emphasise her revulsion. 'He has no remorse whatsoever. I watched Hazel interviewing him with Mitch. She tried to use her new tactics of letting him talk but he was simply using it to taunt her.'

'What d'you mean?'

'He said that Georgina went voluntarily with him. That they lived in the caravan for weeks quite happily.'

'And *did* she fall by accident?'

'So he says. The post mortem shows she had a smashed skull.'

'*He* could have done that.'

'Yes he could have, although it is consistent with a fall from that height apparently. Obviously the body was in a pretty bad state – the only other injuries they found were from being bound hand and foot.'

'So what will he be charged with?'

'There are a number of things, including abduction and violence towards several people. However, we have statements from Phil, Tim and April all corroborating that he admitted to holding Georgina against her will – and that she fell to her death trying to escape from him. I think he will be inside for a long time.'

The morning of the funeral was cloudy and dull. The instructions had been to dress brightly, something floral perhaps, so Mills defied the weather, pulling out a strapless sundress in pinks and yellows. She had got up early to pack in preparation for the trip to London later that day but her bed was still covered in clothes when Nina came in to say that her lift had arrived and she was off to work. She had offered her own car to Mills for the journey to the funeral in Skipton, suggesting she brought it back to her at Newby Wiske. That way she could take Mills to Northallerton station to begin her journey to London.

'Will you be seeing Phil?' Nina asked.

'Yes, I said I'd meet him beforehand for a few minutes. It'll be a rush afterwards.'

'Can you tell him that the body at Runswick Bay has been identified? The name is Yilmaz. Can you remember that?' She spelled it out for her. 'Are you listening? Look, just tell him it's the wife of the man that Brenda found who breeds dogs.'

Mills had agreed to see Phil for the last time before he went to South America. It was not a meeting she relished but she agreed that it would be grown-up to say goodbye properly before he went abroad. It seemed to be the story of her life. Was there something about her, she asked Nina jokingly, that men need to leave the country to be shot of her?

The clouds were clearing by the time Mills left the house. In the Dales, the sun was shining and it promised to be a beautiful day as she drove into the car park of the Craven Heifer and waited for Phil to arrive. She decided it was too early for a drink so they sat in the car.

'Nina says they've identified the body at Runswick Bay.'

'Yes, Brenda told me. She won't stop going on about it,' he said moodily.

Phil opened and closed the door several times, as if he was uncomfortable sitting in the car with her. Neither spoke until Mills put an end to the silence.

'Tell me about your trip,' she suggested. 'Have you organised it yet?'

At first he was hesitant, as if aware he should not sound too excited by his plans to leave. But he was obviously looking forward to the freedom he found in such a venture.

'I was approached about a month ago by a Dutch team working in Colombia. They're excavating the graves of victims of the paramilitaries out there. I know one of the guys from before. At the time I... I wanted to go but...'

She guessed what he was trying to say. 'So how long will you be out there?'

'A few months I guess but he mentioned one or two other projects they have in the pipeline.'

'That'll be interesting.'

'I know it seems like I'm running away. I suppose I am. But I'm not in a good place at the moment, Mills. I need to sort myself out... again.'

'I understand, Phil, really I do. If it were me I'd do exactly the same. Honestly.' He took her hand in his and squeezed it. She pulled it away, muttering an apology and looked at her watch. 'We'd better get to the funeral,' she said, starting the car.

'But it's only round the corner.' Phil was opening the door reluctantly. She watched him walk slowly back to his bike.

Tim ran over to greet her when she arrived. He was dressed very casually in a bright short-sleeved shirt hanging over his jeans. Behind him there was a colourful crowd gathering.

'As you can see, we make a wonderful summery picture!' he shouted. 'Georgie would have loved it.'

He waited for Phil to park his bike then ushered them to meet his wife's friends and relatives, introducing them as the people who helped him find Georgie. 'You know,' he confided, 'there was a moment when I thought we weren't going to be able to do this, with her body being...' he stopped to regain his composure. 'But,' he said with a deep breath, 'we were able to use a special wicker coffin which is still environmentally friendly and so we can give her a burial, which is what I think she would have wanted. It is greener than cremation, you know.'

Mills smiled, fighting back the urge to cry at the devotion he continued to pay his wife.

Soon it was time for the ceremony, which took place in a field with hills in the distance and sheep grazing close by. April made a very personal speech about growing up with her sister. Dave held her hand throughout and hugged her tightly at the end. Tim read a poem, transforming from the shy man Mills had encountered at their first meeting as he declared his love for his dead wife. A group of musician friends played a favourite song of hers and everyone joined in. It was an emotional but positive occasion. Mills, who had not been to a burial before, found it even more heart-wrenching than she imagined. When the flower covered coffin was lowered she tried to restrain herself but Phil must have noticed her body shaking involuntarily and put his arm round her shoulders.

Tim asked everyone to stay for a picnic but Mills was looking at her watch. She'd arranged with Gran to meet up at York station to take the train together to London. They were booked on the four-thirty to miss the worst of the rush hour when they arrived but it was already nearly one o'clock which meant she had just over two hours to deliver the car back to Nina at Newby Wiske before getting the train to York.

'I'd better go,' she said to Tim and Phil. 'I've got to get down to London for my father's wedding.'

Mills found her grandmother waiting as she arrived at York with twenty minutes to spare. She immediately began apologising for not having visited her since Christmas but Gran brushed her excuses aside.

'Nonsense dear, I'm sure you've had some exciting things to occupy yourself – and a young man I expect?'

Mills avoided the question by steering them to the platform for the London train.

'Do we have reservations, dear?' her grandmother asked when the train arrived with hardly an empty seat in sight.

'Don't worry. Dad said to book first class as a special treat. He knew it would be busy.'

He had expressed concern over Helen coming to see her son-in-law marry another woman and wanted her to have a comfortable journey.

Gran declared it an extravagance. 'That will be Fiona's influence I'm sure. I seem to remember your father being very careful with his money,' she said with a twinkle in her eye. 'Now tell me all about what you've been getting up to.' She leaned back, waiting for her news.

Mills had always had a special bond with her grandmother. Helen was, after all, her mother's mother. She had lost her mother but Gran had lost her daughter... they were bound together by each other's loss.

Mills found it easy to talk to Gran and was surprised when the guard announced that they would soon be arriving at King's Cross. Helping Helen down from the train, she was conscious of how slowly she walked now she carried a stick. Neither had brought much luggage but they struggled on the tube and Mills was glad to reach Canary Wharf.

'My, this *is* posh,' said Helen, leaning back to look at the full extent of the apartment building. Mills pointed out the signs to the pool and spa.

'We'd better be on our best behaviour, eh girl?' she giggled as Mills pressed the button for the lift.

Mills watched Fiona chattering nervously while Helen was very gracious, exclaiming how wonderful the flat was. 'But Fiona is so good looking – far too good for you, Hugh dear.'

Mills was amused to see how well-mannered her father was being, although he soon made his excuses and left to stay with his best man, not wishing to see the bride in the morning, before the ceremony. Fiona had thoughtfully prepared a meal so they could have a quiet evening in and it was not long before Helen, who was clearly tired after her journey, said she would have a bath and get into bed early.

The next morning went in a flash. Mills and Helen made coffee at regular intervals while Fiona's friends, all hair and heels, fussed around her. The arrival of the flowers caused great excitement until the hairdresser appeared then silence fell for a short while as they watched Fiona's transformation. Eventually, when it was time for Mills to get dressed, they gathered round her, fiddling with her hair, pulling at her dress and admiring her tanned legs. Fiona's father arrived looking hot and uncomfortable in his morning suit. After he was introduced to everyone, he hid with Helen in the tiny kitchen where they seemed to be getting on well. The photographer turned up with his video camera, initially requesting the bride and her father but after a while asking for the bridesmaid. He issued instructions as Mills awkwardly pretended to help Fiona put on her veil.

At mid-day a relative collected Helen and the friends disappeared en masse. Not long afterwards the buzzer announced that the car was waiting in the street below. Fiona panicked until her father called for calm, then with great dignity took his daughter's hand and led her to the door. Mills picked up the bouquets and followed them into the lift, where they stood in silence as the doors closed.

Mills hadn't expected to feel so emotional but when she followed Fiona up the aisle she was overcome by the occasion. The small church was full and, in the distance, her father was looking round at them nervously. With a lump in her throat she forced a smile as she walked quickly to catch up and take her seat in the pew next to Gran. Mills tried to stay focussed during the ceremony but Helen squeezed her hand towards the end so she must have realised how hard she was finding it. At last she was following Fiona and her father down the aisle to the sound of bells. Outside in the sunshine the guests threw confetti despite strict instructions not to do so and the photographer spent an hour arranging groups of guests.

It wasn't until they were at the hotel that Mills was able to give her father a hug. He looked so happy she couldn't be anything but pleased.

'I believe other congratulations are in order?' she said with a grin.

He looked puzzled.

'The baby?'

He blushed. 'I was going...'

'I think it's great, Dad. Fiona is obviously over the moon.'

'Yes, she is.'

'She'll make a great mother.' Now she did want to cry.

'Millie, you know I'll never forget your mother...'

'I know.' She couldn't hold the tears back any longer. Her father held her, gave her a handkerchief and waited until she had regained control. Finally she pulled herself away.

'Thanks, that's better. I feel OK now, honestly. I just need to go and check my eye make-up before we start eating.'

When the wedding photographs arrived a few weeks later, Mills took them down to Harrogate, as promised.

'We all look as though we're having a good time,' Helen said as they sorted through them.

'I think we did, didn't we Gran?'

'Yes, it's always good to move on, don't you think?'

'You're right.'

'And what about you, my dear?'

'Me?' Mills laughed. 'I'll not be settling down for a long time yet.'

'But you said you'd like somewhere to call home.'

'Yes.' Fat chance of that, she thought.

Helen offered her more cake and they spent the afternoon choosing photographs for her grandmother to keep.

As Mills prepared to leave, Helen said she had something she wanted to suggest to her granddaughter.

'I was thinking about what you said on the train. How you would like to stay in the Dales, at least for now.'

'Yes but...'

She held up a thin bony hand. 'Listen. You remember Laurel Cottage?'

The house in Swaledale, where she had spent the summer with her grandmother while she was still at school. She nodded.

'I still own it, did you know?'

'No, I didn't. I assumed it had been sold when you moved here.'

'Oh no. I had this silly idea that I might use it in the summer, but I can't cope with it on my own.'

Mills waited to hear what her grandmother wanted to say.

'I rent it out as a holiday let although it's empty at the moment because it has just been redecorated. I've been thinking... and I wondered if you would like to use it, while you're working in Wharfedale.'

Mills considered what a holiday cottage cost to rent. 'I'm not sure I could pay that sort of money.'

'Don't worry about that.'

Mills was stunned. 'If I took up your offer, I would have to pay you something, Gran.'

'Whatever you say. I'm sure we can find an arrangement to suit us both. I would really like you to take up the offer. Will you think about it?'

'Oh I'll definitely think about it...'

'Good. That's settled then.' She went over to her desk, opened the drawer and took out a bundle of keys. 'Take these with you. You can check that the decorators have left the place tidy. If you like it let me know and tell me what you can afford.'

Mills hugged her as they said their goodbyes, promising to return soon.

The route to Mossy Bank was still familiar although it was six years since she had been there. The terraced cottages were still standing in a row like sentries guarding the lane that dwindled to a rough track leading onto the fell. She was able to recognise the cottage with its newly painted front door immediately. She opened the boot of her new car: the red mini cooper which had looked quite sensible in town, but now stuck out like a sore thumb in the Dales. She had little luggage but what else would she need? The house was equipped with everything she would require. She carried her bags inside, returning to lock up the car.

'Aren't you coming out?' she called and waited.

Eventually a grey head appeared. Hesitantly the lurcher stepped down into the road and stood staring at her.

'Come on Earl. Don't you want to see your new home?'

The dog followed her reluctantly, his tail between his legs. The smell of lavender and furniture polish, so reminiscent of her grandmother, pervaded the tiny cottage. She gave him some water before unlocking the back door with a large old key.

'Welcome to Laurel Cottage,' she said as they stepped outside. 'I think we'll be just fine here, don't you?'